Evangeline's Power Trio

Sinfully Hers Book Two

by

Anna Lores

Evangeline's Power Trio

Contact Information: info@thewildrosepress.com

Cover Art by *Diana Carlile*

The Wild Rose Press, Inc.
PO Box 708
Adams Basin, NY 14410-0708

Visit us at www.thewildrosepress.com

Publishing History
First Scarlet Rose Edition, 2020
Print ISBN 978-1-5092-3063-1
Digital ISBN 978-1-5092-3064-8

Published in the United States of America

One, two, three men. Yes. Yes. Yes...

Jerry gazed into her empty house. No furniture. No lamps. He leaned forward and peered inside. "I'm jumping to conclusions, but—"

"Yes. I wasn't exaggerating last night. They literally took everything. A friend dropped off my laptop and office files this morning. Henry and Todd can have the rest. I'm not suing or wasting any more time on them."

She swallowed as she lowered her gaze. "I didn't see it coming. But I understand why it happened." Shaking her head, she seemed lost in her thoughts. "I'm not going to make the same mistakes again. I'm only dating a man who will support me, attend family functions, and love my friends. If they have a problem with my career choices, they're gone. If..." She rattled off an exhaustive list of "ifs," and he paid attention to every detail.

"...and if he doesn't like my excessively poochie belly, he's out the door."

He gazed at her torso. *You don't have a pooch. Who has destroyed your image of yourself?* "You've got curves where women should have curves. You're beautiful, Evangeline." *I want to see and touch every gorgeous inch of you. I want to get my mouth on your—*

"You're just saying that." She rolled her eyes at him and seemed defeated.

He cupped her face and bent over until they were nose-to-nose. "I have the luxury of being able to tell the truth. I look at you and my thoughts aren't innocent."

Dedication

To Randi, Danny C., Denise and Kelly

Author Acknowledgments

First and foremost, thank you for buying and reading this book. Because of you, I get to write sensual escapes from real life.

A book doesn't get written without a lot of thought and time and by trusting people to offer suggestions to make it better. Thank you to Kristi Cook and Denise L. I value your advice and suggestions. This manuscript is better because of you. Karen Riedel, thank you for talking through an idea I had for a scene and helping me bring it to life. Kelly, thank you for helping me brainstorm titles...again :) Thank you, Randi S., for helping me with some research and going above and beyond so I could get some important details right. Thank you to my family who continue to support and love me through this crazy adventure called writing. You are my heart and soul and always will be.

A special thank you to Dianne Rich, my editor at The Wild Rose Press. Thank you for your insight and bringing some extra sparkle into my world and that of my characters in *Evangeline's Power Trio*. I look forward to collaboration for many years to come. Sending hugs until next time...

Chapter One
Evangeline

With her drink held high in the air, Evangeline Zanipolo hooted and hollered with the rest of the crowd for another song. Sure, the lead singer struggled to sing in tune, but she'd had a few too many and so had everyone else in Maggie's Irish Pub. Liquor killed any haters.

The phone in her back pocket buzzed again. She took a swig of beer and checked the notification box, hoping it wasn't more of the same. She groaned. *Todd.*

—We're sorry everything came down via text, but when love hits as hard as it did with Rachel, we had to follow the call. Please text and let us know you understand.—

She gazed at her bare finger. *Four years of my life wasted. Cheaters. Cowards. You and Henry choose to come clean the day y'all are getting married to Rachel Innis. She was supposed to be a bridesmaid in MY wedding. Using all our plans. All my—*

Her phone buzzed. *Henry.* She tapped decline.

Want to see how much I give a fuck about you...Hen-ry. I'm finding a firefighter and screwing him in the bathroom. No. Not the bathroom. Germs. I'm not getting some disease in a bathroom. She took a gulp and finished her beer. *No sex in a public restroom.*

She raised her empty glass and nodded at the

bartender.

He met her gaze and smiled as he poured a shot of something on the other end of the counter.

Maybe I'll help him close up and sanitize the counter. I could have sex on a germ-free bar. She glided the pads of her fingers over the lip of the smooth wooden counter. *One hard thrust and I'd probably slip over the edge and break a bone. I do not want to spend the night in the emergency room.*

A crevice in the smooth grain halted her fingers traversing the possibilities of any kind of wild night with a stranger. Splinters and potential injuries stopped that train of thought in its tracks.

I should go to the wedding and make a scene. A huge scene. An embarrassing one that they'd never forget. I should stand up for myself. Stand up for all the women in the world who have been wronged by their fiancés, or boyfriends, or a man in the workplace who fucked them over and got a partnership over the owner's own flesh-and-blood daughter.

Her phone buzzed again. Her gaze drifted to the screen. *Nope. Not talking to you, big brother.*

A new text made her phone vibrate against the wooden counter. *At least you can figure out I'm not in the mood to chat. Not tonight.*

—*Happy birthday, Gelie! I'll see you tomorrow at Mom and Dad's.*—

She flipped back to Todd's text and started typing.

—*I'll try to make the reception.*—

Better not upset Henry too much or he might lose it and come after me. I hope he's on his meds or that reception won't need me to make a scene. Henry will do that all by himself.

She added to the text.

—Tell Henry I'm sorry I missed his call, and I'm not mad.—

Disappointed. Yes. Hurt. Yes. Why do I pick men who can't stand up and tell the truth? She hit send and swiped through to the "avoid at all costs" messages. A dozen or so birthday wishes, and she stopped at her sister-in-law's name.

—I overheard Rick and your dad arguing. Your dad sold the firm to someone without consulting anyone, not even your mom. Rick won't give me details, but said your father invited the person to your birthday dinner. And, if you haven't already, you better tell your father that Henry and Todd cleaned out your house and left. He might focus on screwing those two in ways we can't comprehend instead of making Rick crazy. YOU BETTER FIX THIS. If you hadn't run away to massage school—which YOU SUCK at—instead of standing up for yourself...—

Evangeline let out a sigh to end all sighs and stopped reading. *Dad does whatever he wants and always has. The best thing I ever did was walk away from Dad's firm. Massage wasn't the best decision, but walking away definitely was.*

She quickly replied to her sister-in-law.

—Thanks for the heads-up.—

A new message from Todd and Henry's group text came through.

—Btw, Rachel is five months pregnant.—

No wonder I haven't seen her in two months. I was such an idiot to think she was busy at work. Some work. More like busy working my men's dicks. She hasn't changed since high school. I never should have allowed that bitch back into my life. Damn you, Todd, for making me believe any hardships she encountered as an adult had changed her.

Enough was enough. She turned off her phone and slid it into her back pocket. The world might still be turning, but she wasn't rotating with it. She guzzled the beer Mr. Handsome Bartender had somehow filled without her noticing and placed it on the round coaster.

I'm going to kiss a stranger tonight. I'm going to have an unsatisfying one-night stand. I'm going to…sit here and drink until the bar closes and Todd and Henry are married to tall, blonde, and pregnant Rachel Innis. Maybe crash the reception once I'm too intoxicated to remember what I've done. Then I'll call Brice to help me get through it. Maybe have some sex therapy with him. No. I'd tell him I still love him after we had mind-blowing sex. Mr. Forever Bachelor would let me down easy. Sometimes love isn't enough.

The waitress handling the right side of the room's tables nudged between her and the recently vacated seat next to her. "The man at the table behind you to the right wants to buy you a drink and join you."

Evangeline glanced over her shoulder.

"The one with the red shirt," the server added.

A bald, squinty-eyed guy wearing loose jeans and a red business shirt too tight on his half-a-keg belly nodded and waved at her. On a more thorough inspection, she saw an old-school pencil protector in the pocket of his pressed shirt.

I didn't know they even made those anymore. Probably a recently divorced mathematics professor. "Tell him thanks, but I'm not interested."

The bartender refilled her beer. "This one is from

the guy in the suit in the booth near the kitchen on his laptop. No strings." He handed the waitress a pitcher of beer and four mugs.

Evangeline glanced over her shoulder and nodded at the sexy man with a blue-and-gray striped tie loosened at his collar and the first two buttons of his gray shirt undone. *Lawyer.*

He dipped his head to the side and smiled as if he hadn't wanted her to know he bought her a drink.

She tried to return the smile but couldn't quite get the corners of her lips to curl. Hiding the misery inside at the dreams that had been dashed by the men she loved and the woman she had trusted seemed too much for her fragile heart. She mouthed *Thank you.*

You're welcome, Angel, he mouthed back.

She stared as he lowered his chin and seemed enraptured by his laptop. *Do I know you?*

He rubbed the outside shell of his left ear and ran his hand over the back of his neck and against the ends of his wavy brown hair.

She couldn't place how she might know him, but she put him in the "nice" category, which meant he would never be interested in her. *I want nice. I want sexy and nice and kinky but no attorneys. I don't want to talk shop or why I'm not practicing full-time anymore. I need a businessman like Brice without the commitment phobia.*

She exhaled. *I should stop massage and go back to what I do best. Open my own law firm. Bury myself in work and get massages instead of giving them.*

She turned back to the drink the man bought her. She traced the edge of the circular coaster under her glass. *Thirty years old. No relationship. No children.*

Time ticked faster as her life seemed to slow to a halt.

"Evan?" Dr. Derek McGregor, her guy bestie, asked. The warmth of his hand on her back melted a small amount of the veneer holding her *I'm fine* façade in place.

She gazed up at him. *I need a nice man like you. A loyal man. A faithful man. A kinky man who wants a family and another man to share our bed. I need a man like Dylan Russo, but one who talks through problems instead of ignoring them...ignoring me.* "Hey, Derek. What are you doing here?"

"Jerry Wynn and I are having a drink." Derek leaned closer. The usual short, dark hair he normally kept meticulously trimmed had grown out and brushed against her cheek. "Jerry is taking the mic at midnight. His brother Highland's birthday would have been today. He's going to sing a song and give everyone in the bar a round in his honor. Want to join us?"

"Thanks, but I think I'll cheer him on from here and let y'all reminisce together." She'd probably flirt like she always did with Jerry only to feel like his best friend's annoying little sister when he gave her the usual *go away* pat on the back. *Not up for that tonight.*

"If you change your mind, come on over. We can celebrate your birthday too. I haven't forgotten about taking you to your parents' house tomorrow for the family throw down." Derek kissed her cheek and patted her on the back like a father would a child, exactly like Jerry would end up doing if they spent any time together.

Her friendly outer shell cracked. "I haven't told my parents you're coming with me. I haven't told them about the breakup. Rachel is five months pregnant. Just found out that tidbit tonight."

"Are you going to tell your parents?" He frowned and that disappointed grunt he always made when she avoided confrontation came out.

"Yes. No. Maybe?" She exhaled and slouched. "I don't know. The only plans I have tonight are to drink until the place closes and walk home alone."

"They're not worth destroying your liver." Derek put his arm around her and squeezed. "I'm sorry about Rachel and her pregnancy. There are other men out there. Men who would do anything to love you and make lots of babies with you." He waggled his eyebrows. "They'll be lining up to get their kink on with you."

"Yeah, well, I'm taking a vow of celibacy right now." *I'm almost ready to ovulate and Henry decides he's done with me too. It's for the best. He's been acting more and more unstable lately.*

Derek laughed. "That is not going to work for you."

I'm changing my ways. No more sex until I'm married. I'm not calling Brice for sex every time my relationships falter or fail. I'm turning over a new leaf. She pursed her lips and gazed into his eyes. "I'm being serious."

"So am I." His hazel eyes twinkled. "You're going to be fucking some guy's brains out before midnight."

She glanced down at her phone and tapped the screen. "I'd have to be partially naked already and with someone single in the next four minutes in order for that to happen." *So much for making a scene at the wedding or the reception.*

"Fine. I'll bet that you can't keep those sexy legs and pussy untouched for twenty-four hours."

"You're on." She turned to her beer. *Happy birthday to me.*

"You're coming with me." Derek took her drink and her hand. "We'll play a drinking game before Jerry takes the stage."

"I'm really not in the mood."

"Which is exactly why you're coming with me." Derek tugged her hand, and she slid off the bar chair.

"Do you want two miserable evenings with me?" She inhaled and dug her heels into the plank floorboards. "Do you?"

"An evening with you is never miserable. Worst case scenario—I get you tipsier than you already are and throw a few contracts at you. You'll willingly give me free lawyerly advice, and I'll carry you home and tuck you into bed before you pass out."

"I don't do free. Not when I've been recently screwed over."

He tugged, and she shuffled forward. "Maybe you'll end up getting it on with some guy here and your disposition will change… And I'll win the bet. I'll claim my winnings, which means you'll be photographed nude with your new exhibitionist lover under the watchful eye of my camera."

"The only sex I'm getting is from a dildo I haven't bought yet."

He laughed. "And that is why we are besties. You tell me things I really don't need to know but want to."

She continued to resist, but less so, as he tugged her toward the man whose presence sent her off balance. Drinking with Derek and Jerry would not work. Derek—the happily married man—and Jerry—the bachelor married to mixed martial arts—would dole out dating advice like it was candy.

I have to get out of here. Go back to my empty house. Figure out how I'm going to tell my parents they were right, and I was wrong. All I need is one good, solid, sexy man who doesn't mind that I'd rather deal with a scandal than bow down to a blackmailer. But two loyal, faithful, sexy men who love that I enjoy some double fucking and kink would be ideal.

The frown on her face deepened. *Men like Derek, Garrett, and Cade are one in a billion. Ella is one lucky girl. I have zero luck.*

"I'm going to win this bet," Derek said. "I'm going to get Ella and the guys to help me. We're going to introduce you to every bachelor we know."

She yanked his arm. "I'm not interested in just anyone. I want someone who understands commitment. I want a man who doesn't want to change me. One who embraces my curves, my career choices, me. I'm serious. The next cock or cocks that penetrate my vagina are going to be my husband's or husbands'."

Derek pulled her forward into the crowd. "Get ready to bend over."

"I'm serious, Derek. I want a man ready for marriage and kids, and who needs another man to join our bed. I want an older man. I want…" She gazed across the room at Jerry. *A man like you, but who has a taste for men too.* Her chin tensed and she had to pull in her bottom lip in order not to pout. "I'm never going to find what I want. I should head for the nearest nunnery."

"Stop with the melodrama and come on." Derek

tugged at her arm. "You'd get kicked out of a nunnery anyway."

Yeah. I would. Evangeline acquiesced to her demanding friend but made him work for every step she took toward the man she wished she could have.

Chapter Two
Dylan

Dylan Russo slowed as he passed by Evangeline's beautiful historic home in Memphis, Tennessee. She had changed since they were juniors in high school and he'd moved away. The girl who couldn't keep a pound on her bones had filled out into a woman with curves that made his cock throb and ache more than ever in anticipation of their reunion. His desire for her hadn't waned in fourteen years, and now that he'd seen her again, he wanted her all the more.

He had some bridges to build. Expecting her to come over to his table at the bar seemed unrealistic now that he'd had time to reflect. He'd grown seven inches the summer he'd left, but he'd always been muscular. His face hadn't changed...much. He had changed. No part of him looked like the heavyset, short teen. *I waited too long to move back. I'm starting at square one with her. Again.*

The evening he'd expected to have talking at the local bar she frequented hadn't worked out, but maybe, with a sample of the dominant man he'd become, he could win her away from the pansy assholes she planned to marry in eight weeks.

His phone vibrated in his jacket pocket. He shifted the shoulder straps of his backpack and grabbed his phone. *Matteo Zanipolo.*

He swiped the screen. "Dylan Russo." *Why are you calling so late?*

"I need your help. My daughter's good-for-nothing fiancés emptied her house and left her. They're married. They married Rachel Innis. Remember her?"

Mean girl, Rachel Innis? The tormentor of innocents. She's why I followed my father's footsteps into law. To punish bullies like her. "I remember her. When did this happen?"

"Rick told me a few minutes ago, and I immediately called Ella Winthrop-Jackson to find out exactly what happened. Gelie isn't answering her phone. Those bastards took everything. Her laptop, her security safe, her files, her office furniture, her plates and…" As Matteo talked, Dylan fumed.

Evangeline is no fool. There was either a mistake in what was being moved or she got targeted by criminals.

He opened his car door and took off his backpack. He continued to listen and learn why Evangeline's expression had stayed sad at the bar.

"I'll swing by the reception and start cleaning up the mess," he said.

"If I went over there, I'd end up in jail charged with assault," Matteo said. "I don't know what she's thinking anymore. She hasn't been herself since she quit the firm."

"You offered partnership to a man who lost more cases than he won. A man who cost the company money. You chose him over the top grossing attorney in the firm—your daughter. Why? Why did you do that?"

"She's been *openly* sleeping around with men, women, and both *at the same time* since she graduated high school. She had a sex tape that went public. A *sex tape*. And then another and another. What was I supposed to do? Invite *her* to be partner when Joseph is an upstanding member of the community, married with children, and loyal to the firm? He's a good lawyer, and he's brought in a lot of new business and retained it."

"I would have sued your ass if I were her, family or not. What she does behind closed doors is none of your or anyone else's business. Period."

"She does it in public. She's been caught nude at parties. I've had to pay off men and women who were going to give home sex films, with Gelie in them, to the local news outlets. She said to let them do it and show them that it didn't matter. She didn't care about my law firm, my reputation, or hers. She wouldn't have one client if those other films came out. If they came out tomorrow, she'd lose her job at the spa. She would end up penniless."

"Bullshit. The one sex tape that was *conveniently* released the day before you asked Joseph to be a partner didn't hurt her professionally or personally. It hurt your bottom line because she quit." *She didn't break any laws. She didn't do anything to compromise her career. I bet Joseph was the one who made a profit from that sex tape.*

"All her clients fled as soon as those tapes became public."

"She quit working and because of that they looked for other representation. I've gained her ex-clients. They don't give a shit what she did or does off the clock because when she's on, she's all business." *Once she's mine, she'll be in my office after hours on her hands and knees with her skirt over her ass begging me to fuck her.*

He grabbed his cock. *I'm going to make her so wet her pussy is going to suck my cum out with every one of her sexy orgasms. Maybe one day, we'll have a beautiful little girl with Evangeline's innocent brown eyes and sun-kissed skin. We'll be lovers, sexual explorers, and possibly parents together. Forever.*

Matteo huffed. "If Gelie had stayed at the firm, she could have made amends to the women in the office. They were as upset and embarrassed about her escapades as the men. It damaged our firm."

"Give that crap to someone else, Matteo. *You* damaged your firm by passing her over for the promotion when she was bankrolling the damn place. You should have been her fiercest advocate. You betrayed her."

Dylan could imagine the man dropping his head in his hands in defeat over the new dark granite counter of the repurposed desk his wife designed.

"She defied me."

"If I were her, I would've sued your ass and then some. I'd never speak to you again. I'd—"

"You'd come in and force me to sell my life's work for pennies and demand that I wave the white flag of surrender because of some wrong you think I did. Instead of dealing with the truth, you decided to ignore her constant lapses of judgement, her choice to give up a lucrative career rather than fix her problems, and come here to convince her to take over *my firm*. She's to blame, not me." The fire seemed to be back in Matteo's belly. Always ready to kick someone he'd knocked to the ground.

"You are hell bent on fucking over two men who

chose another woman to marry, but you can't tell Evangeline you're sorry for promoting Joseph?" *That is so fucked up, I don't even know how to—*

"She slept with Joseph's brother. He caught them in her office. I'm not rewarding that behavior."

I don't believe that for an instant. That's something you would do, not my angel. "Why didn't you tell me that before now? Did you ask Evangeline about it? Did you talk to Joseph's brother for confirmation? Or, did you want to believe it so you could punish Evangeline for being transparent about her love life? For being fearless in the face of blackmail? God knows you can't be transparent or honest about yours. Have you come clean about the love child you've kept a secret from your kids? Don't you think Rick and Evangeline would like to know they have a half sister? What are you afraid of?"

Silence fell on the other end.

Dylan pushed harder to force Matteo into submission. "I've met Joseph's brother. She wouldn't fuck him, not if he were the last man on earth."

"Dylan, you're overstepping your—"

"You want overstepping? Here you go. I bet you didn't think I'd find out about your dick's adventures and conquests, did you? Didn't think I'd find out about the string of women you shoved your cock in. Or about my mother and *you*. I'm thorough in my background checks, Matteo. Twenty-three years of lies about your *passione,* about your one-and-only true love. How would Trish feel if she knew you spent your Monday mornings for the last twenty-two years in bed with Faegan Fairchild, not at the gym with the guys?" He paused.

"I exercise at the gym Monday mornings."

"Oh, right. Because Faegan passed away six months ago. How much longer will your illegitimate daughter continue to keep the secret that you're her father?" *Thank God my mother never got pregnant with your child. You ruined her life, but at least my mother was smart enough to use birth control.*

Dylan tossed his backpack into the backseat and slid into the driver's seat. "Kicking your secret daughter out of the only home she's known isn't going to give her those warm fuzzies that a dad is supposed to give his daughter." *She'll either tell the world what an asshole you are, or she'll be so ashamed of you, she won't acknowledge your side of her DNA.*

"How I handle family business is none of your concern."

"You're going to lose your family, and you won't have anyone to blame but yourself."

"You better not tell my children anything."

"What are you going to do, Matteo?" He typed the address of the reception into his phone and started the engine. "What leverage do you have with me?" *None. I'll tell Evangeline and Rick about their half sister, Sally. I'm not keeping your secret any longer. If you're not careful, I'll air my own truths about the day my mother died and your involvement. I will never forgive you for what you did to me, to my father, to my family because of your lack of sexual restraint.*

"I'm telling my kids, not you, and I'll do it when I'm ready."

Dylan pounded the steering wheel. "Tell them tomorrow after dinner or I will. They deserve to know. Sally Fairchild deserves a family." *Evangeline will have a chance at a familial connection to nurture with someone who desperately needs and wants one.*

"Sally has me."

"You? You're going to take care of her? How is sending her onto the streets because her mother isn't around to fuck anymore something a loving father would do?" *Care about someone other than yourself.* "Get your shit together, Matteo. Where is the decent man you once were? The one who treated everyone like family. What happened to you?" *I remember when I was six and you invited me to join my parents for dinner at your house for the first time. I thought you were a great man back then. Was it all an act to get into my mother's pants? Have you truly ever cared for anyone but yourself?*

"Sally hangs out with whores. I warned her I would take everything away. I'm following up on my threats. I didn't do that with Evangeline, and she went boy crazy. She left my firm to give strangers massages, and she's terrible at it. What I'm doing for both of them is called tough love."

"You're a fool, Matteo."

"Think whatever you want. You get those two idiots Gelie almost married to give her back everything *I gave her.*" The commanding tone in Matteo's voice made Dylan's blood boil.

Because it's all about you. It's always about you. You. Your firm. Your reputation. Your money. Your things.

"Since you're incapable of advocating for your eldest daughter, I'll take care of her from now on." He hung up on the man. *Evangeline is mine to love. First thing in the morning, I'm finding Sally to discuss her*

17

future, and see if she needs me to protect her from her father's wrath.

He sped along the interstate until he turned onto the road leading to the rustic farm where the wedding reception was held. Henry, Todd, and Rachel's names were written on signs made out of planks of old, unfinished wood which showed the way to the party.

He parked behind the black limousine and strolled into the crowd at the reception.

A slender blonde wearing a beautiful white lace gown with gold sashes wrapped under her breasts and another sash under the pronounced baby bump highlighted the bride's condition. She shoved two big pieces of cake in two handsome men's mouths as guests cheered them on.

His heart fell to the floor for Evangeline. *Betrayed by your father. Betrayed by the men you loved. Betrayed by your friend.*

The blonde wiped her hands on a handkerchief as one of the men in a black tux with a white rose on his lapel was handed a microphone.

"We wanted to share some extra joy with you today," the man with dark, curly hair said. He placed one hand on her belly. "We hadn't said anything, but I know you figured it out. We're five-and-a-half months pregnant."

Rachel kissed the man with light brown hair standing beside her and took the microphone from the curly-haired man. "We decided six months ago to make our seven-year on-again-off-again relationship permanent, to work on having a family, and to get married. Here we are at this beautiful reception, a testament to dreams being fulfilled."

Manipulator. Liar. Cheat. How did Evangeline get mixed up with you? He strode forward with his phone in his hand recording the event. "Sorry to interrupt."

The three honorees stood staring at him with their smiles deepening into what he recognized as confusion.

"Hey," the light-brown-haired guy said.

"Hi," Dylan replied. "So, the three of you have been in a relationship for seven years and have been planning this party and ceremony for the last six months?"

"Yes, we have." Rachel's condescending tone hadn't changed in all the years he'd been gone. The woman didn't recognize him. All those years she'd called him names, and she probably never gave him a second thought.

Dylan continued recording the interaction. "Great. Thank you. I am just clarifying your actions, your plans, and your timeline."

"What's going on?" the curly-haired man asked.

"I'm the Zanipolo family attorney." He caught the fear radiating through the threesome and exploited it. They might have thought they could trample over Evangeline, but they were about to find out she had someone to protect her. He would fight to his last breath to do just that.

The sound of shoes shuffling behind him along with car doors opening and closing in quick succession brightened his mood. Engines roared to life, and the noise of wheels hitting gravel forced him to raise his voice. By the time he finished telling the liars and cheaters about their criminal behavior, the amount of guests in attendance had decreased substantially.

"The movers screwed up," the curly-haired man

said. "It was an honest mistake."

"I want her laptop in my hands tonight. The rest within twenty-four hours." He loved the smell of their fear. He would ruin them, destroy them, if they didn't do exactly what he ordered. For what they'd done to Evangeline's heart, he would make them pay and pay and pay until he found satisfaction in their suffering.

A couple interrupted them. "The relationship was an open one with the four of them."

"No, it wasn't," Dylan said. "Henry and Todd planned this wedding with Evangeline Zanipolo. All this…" Dylan slowly pivoted in a circle as he pointed at all the decorations at the venue. "Everything around you was paid for by Evangeline Zanipolo and her family. The gold-rimmed china and gold utensils on each table are real and the property of Matteo Zanipolo. They have been used at every wedding reception the Zanipolo family has planned, three generations back."

Rachel's conniving eyes widened. "What?"

There it was. Recognition that she wasn't getting away with this one.

"Yes, you've stolen tens of thousands of dollars of property from my clients. The Zanipolos are willing to give you a chance at making this right."

"Shit," the curly-haired one mumbled.

"I'd have used a curse word with a little more weight than that, if I were in this predicament," Dylan said. "But it's not me looking at criminal charges. It's the three of you."

The innocent couple who'd stood up for the threesome backed away. "Y'all should go straighten this out. Evangeline is honest and fair. She'll give you a chance to explain."

"Yeah," the curly-haired one said. "Yeah. Hey, what's your name?"

"Dylan Russo."

"Do you have a card?" the guy asked.

"Yes, I do. Would you like one?"

"Yeah, man," he said. "I would." The man stepped forward and puffed out his chest as if Dylan would retreat or back down.

Dylan tapped the screen of his phone and ended the recording. *I don't see what Evangeline saw in—*

The man exhaled and the bravado he'd shown minutes before evaporated into thin air.

Submissive. They are both submissive. Oh, Evangeline, you found two men who would never push you to surrender to them. Rachel wanted what you had and took it. She was always jealous of you. This time, she did you and me a favor.

He slid his phone into the inner pocket of his jacket and pulled out a few business cards. "Here. One for each of you."

"I'm calling my attorney," Rachel said.

"I'd highly advise you to do that." He walked to the cluster of staff eavesdropping. Not even his name seemed to ring any memory bells for Rachel. The woman was as shallow as ever.

A heavyset woman wearing a black pantsuit stepped forward and shook his hand. "I'm assuming the evening is over?"

"Yes, ma'am. Who do I speak to about delivering the borrowed items to their rightful owner?"

"That would be me. I'll need the wedding party to sign off on the change in delivery," she said.

Dylan turned and looked at Rachel as she spoke

into her phone. Her face drained of color and her phone dropped from her hand to the ground.

His phone vibrated. He took it out and answered.

"It's Cal Westland."

"Cal, it's pretty late for a social call." *Rachel has friends in high places.*

"I've instructed my clients not to talk to you until we meet at Rachel's home. I can be there in thirty minutes."

"Text me the address. I'll see you soon." Dylan ended the call. He faced the woman in charge of the venue and handed her a business card. "If anyone besides a man with the last name Zanipolo attempts to take the items loaned to this venue for tonight's festivities, call the police and then call me."

"Yes, sir." She walked toward the rustic bar.

He opened a text from Cal and set the GPS for the meeting place.

"Mr. Russo?"

Dylan turned toward the man's voice.

Rachel and the curly-haired guy were gone, but the larger of the two men with straight, light brown hair and blue eyes stood beside a waiter next to the cake table. "I think I need to sign off on a few things and then I'll ride with you to the house." He lifted his hand and motioned for the woman in the black suit.

Dylan strode forward with the woman and stopped beside the man whose name he didn't know.

"I'm Henry Westland," he said, shaking the woman's hand and then Dylan's. "Everything here, except for the cake, should be delivered to the Zanipolos. If there are any additional charges, I will pay for them."

"Of course, Mr. Westland," the woman said. She pivoted and marched back to her staff.

"Are you Cal's nephew?" Dylan asked. *Why isn't Cal here?*

"I'm his son." He walked toward the parking lot with Dylan. "My dad will kill me for talking to you, but I want you to know that the movers fucked up. Evangeline's office and bedroom were off limits. We took all the furniture, but Todd and Rachel said that Evangeline told them to take it all. If that isn't true, I'll make sure she gets the items she wants back as soon as the movers can deliver it."

Dylan stopped at his car. "I hope that you're willing to apologize." He thought there was regret in the big guy's eyes. "If you want out of this relationship with Rachel and Todd, say the word."

Henry nodded. "This was a mistake. Rachel told me that I was the baby's father, but I'm not. She legally married Todd. I'm just the—" He paused, his hand on the hood of Dylan's car. "—Apparently, I'm disposable, like Evangeline."

"Henry, we all make mistakes. What you do from here on out matters," Dylan said.

"Yeah." Henry slid into the passenger side of Dylan's car and buckled in. "Rachel and Todd have a savings account together. They were supposed to have paid for the wedding out of it. The way they were acting, I don't think they did. In fact, I'm going to see if they took anything from me."

Dylan followed Henry's directions to Rachel's latest acquisition from a recent divorce—a mansion in the suburbs.

Chapter Three
Jerry

Gazing into the dark ale he would pretend to drink didn't stop the ache in Jerry Wynn's heart over the loss of the Wynn family. They had been blood related, but it was the day Major and Mae took him into their home and treated him as a second son, not their nephew, when his life changed for the better. Adopting Jerry after his mother passed away had been the best suggestion his cousin Highland had ever made. From that moment on, Jerry had a strong, solid, loving family who believed in him, in his future. He wore the name Wynn like a badge of honor.

The family he loved was gone—Highland, Major, and Momma Mae. Years had gone by since they passed away, but the heaviness of the void in his life continued to weigh him down. The wounds of their untimely deaths opened as the memories of the family he loved flooded his vision.

Highland's hand seemed small in his. "I need you," Jerry whispered. "Please don't die."

Momma Mae curled her arm around his and clung to him. "I've let him go. It's your turn, Jerry."

The same thoughts ran through his head tonight as they did that night. *Who am I going to talk to when I need advice? Who can I trust to love me? Stick by me?*

He searched the room for Derek, but his friend had

already disappeared into the crowd at the bar. *I shouldn't have told Derek about Dylan. I shouldn't want to reconnect with the man. Not when I'm not willing to move. Not when I want a woman to marry, to love, to have children with. A woman like Evangeline. She'd never go for a man like me for the rest of her life. She'd never want a man like Dylan, either. Dylan. A man who enjoys men as much or more than women. The only man I ever wanted to do something other than beat the hell out of when I looked into his dark and sexy brown eyes. The man who I can't get out of my head.*

He adjusted his cock that had sprung to life. He'd never been interested in a man until Dylan. The only other man who'd given a rise to his cock had been Brice Loffiten, and Jerry didn't know what to think about that reaction. Not tonight. Not when his life seemed empty.

Loneliness and lost dreams had taken hold of Jerry and dragged him down a rabbit hole he couldn't get out of alone. He and Dylan had come together over that loneliness, and he wanted Dylan tonight. He wanted someone who understood real loss. Someone who fought with raw emotional isolation. Someone desperate to fill the unrelenting need to be soul close. *I'm tired of living this life alone.*

He gazed at the singer on stage. Out of the corner of his eye, he thought he saw the man he'd fallen for three years ago. *Dylan?*

The man's hair was longer, but the jawline, the strong and athletic body of a tri-athlete, and the gait seemed intimately familiar. The man grabbed a black backpack and slipped it over a shoulder. He walked toward the exit without looking Jerry's way. Maybe seeing the lookalike was a sign to call him. To see how Richmond, Virginia was treating him.

He's probably with someone—or several exclusive someones. Maybe I'll ask him to be my attorney. Being friends with him would be better than not having him in my life. I'll let him know I'm retiring. Maybe, if he hasn't already found someone, he'll want me. Maybe he'll move here. No. He wouldn't move here. Not with his painful history in Memphis. I can't leave. Not yet. Not until the court declares the couple who took Momma Mae's life guilty of murder. Not without the one person I trust as much as Momma Mae, Major, and Highland—Ella Winthrop-Jackson. She can't leave with her three husbands' businesses and family based in this town, and her business based here too. I'm never going to have the future I want—a woman and Dylan to share my bed, babies in the house, and love. Real, undying love.

He looked around, and a jolt of energy sent his body buzzing at the sight of her. No one, not even Dylan, sent his cock into the *must fuck* zone like she did.

The naturally tanned beauty he refused to get a massage from shuffled as if she wanted to be anywhere but heading toward him. A slight tug from Derek, and Evangeline Zanipolo's mocha eyes closed for a second before she picked up the pace. The normally easygoing smile that lit up a room seemed weighed down into a frown. The perfect posture she'd always exhibited warped into a deep slouch.

Without thinking, he stood up and pulled out the chair next to him as she approached. "Sit."

She slid into the seat, and her flowy, scoop-neck

shirt shifted, showing more skin than usual. The woman had curves he would give anything to dive into. *Too young. Engaged. Never going to happen.*

He pushed her chair closer to the table and nearer to his. She might be off-limits, but she always smelled like vanilla and honey, and everything about her screamed sexy. She'd be a great mom and wife and... *She's engaged and too damn young.*

"Hey, Jerry," she said.

"What's got you all frowny-faced?" He shouldn't have, but he slid his arm around her back and rested it on top of the chair. He leaned over and breathed in the aroma of stout beer. *You don't drink beer.* He tensed. *Why are you alone?*

Derek cringed.

Evangeline leaned against his side. "I'm surprised Ella didn't tell you."

Jerry curled his fingers around the edge of the corner of the backrest. He pulled her chair closer until it touched the edge of his and pushed her softness against his side. "Who upset you, and where can I find him?" *Women are not to be toyed with. I will teach your client a lesson.*

"Todd and Henry officially moved out today, and they took everything with them instead of only their belongings. And on this lovely evening—" She picked up the beer Derek had put on the table and took a sip. "—They married my ex-best friend Rachel. She's five months pregnant."

Jerry sat in silence. *Holy shit. Rachel is a skanky bitch. I never understood why you two were friends.* "Ella was upset when I talked with her earlier but wouldn't elaborate." He glanced at Derek. *You didn't*

27

say a word about it.

The tall, lean redheaded waitress walked over holding a green serving tray with a pitcher of beer and three glasses. She stopped beside him. "You're up in five."

"Thank you, ma'am." Jerry gazed at Evangeline's perky breasts. *A twist to the right and I'll see your nipples through that lacy bra. Show me.*

As if she could hear his desires, Evangeline shifted, and her loose shirt dipped forward just enough to show him the pretty pink nipples he fantasized about sucking. *I want you. Why do you have to be so young?* He adjusted his cock. *I'm not getting involved with a woman barely out of college.*

"They couldn't wait for a different day to do it, either. My birthday will always be tarnished because of them," Evangeline said. "They gave me the biggest 'fuck you' of my life." She lifted her chin and caught him damn near drooling over her breasts. A miniature curve in her lips lightened her frown.

"They're fucking idiots. You're better off without them and that skank."

She huffed a laugh, but only a small portion of the sunshine he loved to see in her eyes appeared in the darkness. "She is a skank."

He kissed her forehead and slid his fingers over her shoulder. The flimsy material shifted and uncovered her left nipple. *Hard and red, the way I like them. I'd suck and fuck them. You'd be mine. Mine.* "You deserve better." *I'd keep you in my bed until we made a bunch of babies. No. It would never work. She's. Too. Young.*

She placed her hand on his thigh and lifted her chin. "Thanks."

He covered her hand with his and glided it closer to his hip.

Her lips parted and those sexy lips, that mouth...

I'm going to take you home with me and fuck you all night long.

"Jerry Wynn." The waitress's voice calling his name stopped him from taking Evangeline to the nearest hotel.

"Shit," he mumbled. He slid her hand to his cock, and son of a bitch, she squeezed with the perfect amount of pressure to draw precum to the tip. "Do not go anywhere. Do not drink anymore. I'm going to give you a birthday present you will never forget."

"I—I—You—" Her mouth gaped.

He moved her hand to his balls. "Yeah, me and you. In ten minutes or less, we're going somewhere private."

"We are?"

He pressed his cheek to hers and whispered in her ear, "If you decide to join me, you're going to find out what it's like to be taken by a *man*." He held back from kissing her. If he touched her lips, he wouldn't make it to a hotel or home without having eased the ache in his balls.

"I want to," she moaned. "I'm ready."

"Unzip your jeans and show me." He drew the edge of her earlobe into his mouth as she unzipped and guided his hand down her panties.

She shifted her hips, and he slipped two fingers inside her drenched pussy.

"Evan, my cum is going to be inside you very soon. You want that, don't you?"

"So bad..." She spread her legs. "I want you so

badly."

Derek kicked Jerry's leg under the table. "Are you going up there?"

Damn it. "Ten minutes, Evan."

He stood up with a hard-on that he couldn't hide and walked to the front of the bar near the entrance, leaving her with Derek. His body tingled with excitement like it did when he entered the ring. *Fuck her age. Fuck the reasons not to. I'm making her mine tonight.*

Chapter Four
Evangeline

"Oh. My. God," Evangeline mumbled.

"Yeah," Derek said. "I'm so glad he and Ella don't have any chemistry. He is like an atomic bomb ready to explode." He exhaled.

"Does he date guys?" *Please let him be into threesomes. Maybe that would be bad. Two Jerry Wynns? No. Please don't let him be into anything other than traditional relationships.*

"He doesn't date. At least, he hasn't in the time I've known him." He took a swig of beer. "He sure does want you."

"I'm used to two men. One will never be enough." *Don't even call me out on that lie.* Juices trickled onto her panties as she zipped up her jeans. "Jerry Wynn has talked to you about me?"

The doc nodded. "He has. He thinks you're one sexy woman."

"Not possible. He'd take one look at my stomach and his cock would deflate." She gazed at her empty beer glass. *I probably drank my daily caloric intake in beer. I'll belch and fart if I lay down. I might even throw up. Even if he doesn't mind my curves, he'll be totally turned off if I vomit on him.*

"You're beautiful, and there is nothing about your belly that would make any guy's erection vanish.

You're going to have sex with him tonight, and I'll win our bet."

I don't know that I could handle a man like Jerry. I'm the one in control with other men, but around him—I crumble into submission. He's too much like Brice. Much too much like him. He's like two of Brice. If Brice ever joined us it would be like fucking three men.

Heat rushed to her belly. *Heck, yeah. Three men in my bed, dominating me... I. Want. It.*

Wanting something wasn't going to make it happen. Jerry was a one-woman guy. She was a two-or-more-men woman. *Jerry wouldn't be enough.*

She tried to inhale happiness then exhale negative thoughts, but her adrenaline kicked in and her brain shifted into hyper drive. *What if Jerry Wynn is too much of a man for me? He doesn't even have to touch me and I melt around him. I'm melting. I'm freaking out.*

"Are you okay?" Derek asked.

"I'm fine. Thanks for saying what you did, but it's been a long day. And I have a bet to win and an empty home to..." *Jerry Wynn touched my pussy. I squeezed his cock. I. Squeezed. His. Cock.* She panted. "I'm—"

Jerry's voice stopped her cold. "I'm Jerry Wynn. Thanks for being here tonight with me."

She glanced at him and caught him smiling at her. Visions of their future babies—his green eyes, her dark hair, and his smooth, porcelain skin—swam in circles around his gorgeous face.

"Highland sang like a rock star," he said as if speaking directly to her. "I don't, but I'm following our family tradition in his honor by singing an old Irish song in remembrance of his life."

The entire pub fell silent.

She swiveled in her chair toward the stage to get a better view.

Jerry moved the mic stand to the side. The twinkle in his green eyes died as he hypnotized the crowd with a song she'd never heard before.

Singing a cappella, his voice rose and fell as he pulled her into a world of strife, determination to make a better future, and the lady who loved him so much that he conquered all in his path to make her his.

His voice captivated her. The Irish lilt, the beautiful tone, and the depth of emotion drew her forward, following the others mesmerized by the cage-fighting champion with a voice straight out of heaven.

She navigated through the crowd until she faced the man with a voice as enchanting as his presence. *You're out of my league. So far out of my league. I'm the one who would never be enough for you.*

He took her hand and pulled her against his hard body and ended the song. "This round is on me."

She gazed up at him.

The emerald eyes that dominated all his competitors in the ring locked in on her. "Evangeline."

"Oh, shit."

Those Irish eyes came back alive and sparkled under the spotlight.

The coals smoldering in her belly for the intense man flared into uncontrollable flames. *You're into me. Holy shit. You're going to make good on that birthday promise.*

She'd held the alpha position in her recent relationships, but with him, she wasn't even a beta. If she let her guard down, she'd surrender with his slightest command. He'd break her heart. *I'm never allowing anyone to control me again. Never. Not after Joseph.* "I've got to go."

He curled her into his powerful arms. "Happy birthday, Evangeline." In those three words she'd heard the gentleman in him. He'd never force her. He'd never hurt her. Once he had her, he'd never let her go. Handling that kind of man... She couldn't. She'd never come across a man like that.

She parted her lips, but the words she wanted to say—*Take me. Love me. Kiss me*—didn't come. "You can't be my rebound. Rebound relationships never work."

He stepped forward with her in his arms, guiding her into the darkest corner of the bar. "Don't insult me."

She hadn't intended to feel him up, but as she tried to find an exit from touching his broad back, she dipped low and moaned as she found exactly what she'd fantasized about.

He gripped her hand and held it, cupping his balls. "Say you're scared, if you're scared. Do not lie to me."

She gazed up at him, trying to avoid eye contact, but failing miserably. "You scare the hell out of me."

The sexy, dominating smile on his lips flipped every damn switch God installed in her when she was born and glued her feet to the floor.

"When you're ready for a real man, call me. You have my number, don't you?"

She nodded. *I'm so drunk I'm hallucinating. I have to be hallucinating. Jerry Wynn is not asking me to call him for sex. He wants me to make a booty call. Oh, my God. I'm definitely hallucinating or dreaming.*

He leaned over. "I'm a patient man, but the way you're massaging my balls is testing my limits. You sure you don't want to come home with me?"

Yes. I want to go home with you. Yes. Yes. Yes. "I can't. Not tonight."

He brushed his lips over her cheek. "We'll celebrate your birthday another time, then."

She nodded. "Another time."

He squeezed her hand cupping his groin and pulled her hand from his body. "See you around, beautiful."

She waved. She actually waved like a virgin would to the boy she hoped would be her husband someday. "Bye."

He turned and walked away like he did when he left the octagon as the champion.

"How on God's green earth have you not been snatched up?" she mumbled.

Derek's laughter brought her into reality. The man had somehow snuck up on her.

"He's been waiting for the right woman. I think that right woman might be you." Derek took her hand and led her to the exit. "I'll walk you home."

"I can walk home myself." She turned to leave alone, but he joined her outside.

"You made the right decision back there. Don't get involved with another man until you're truly ready." He slowed their pace and hooked his arm around her as they continued down the street. "Jerry wants certain things—marriage, fidelity, respect, kids. He doesn't want to wait, either. If you can't give him that, don't even consider giving in to his charms. He's been hurt enough. Don't be the one to tear him apart."

He's been hurt? Tear him apart? She nodded when

her mouth wouldn't open. *He's suffered loss, but what don't I know about the man whose life is as public as they come?*

Walking eased some of the sexual tension attacking her private parts. Maybe it was the distance from the man she claimed as her one exception. The man who she'd have sex with no matter who she was with—married, engaged, or other. *I turned him down. I turned down my exception.*

Derek walked her up the stairs to her front door. "Happy birthday, Evan. This is going to be a great year for you. Check your emails. The photos are spectacular."

"Thanks, Derek." She opened her door and walked in. "I'm not going to check my email tonight." *Sort of can't check it on a secure line. They took my damn laptop and canceled WiFi, cable…ugh. Pictures of my pussy and boobs on the cherry line of Oils by Ella will have to wait.*

"Check it." Derek closed the door.

She bolt locked the door and looked around her empty home. *They may have taken all the contents, but I own this place. If they don't return my stuff, I'm going to sue their asses.*

Chapter Five
Brice

Typing in Evangeline's security code to access her garage in the back of her house, Brice Loffiten second-guessed his decision to check on her well-being. The text he'd received from Cal Westland about Henry's sudden blow up with Todd and Rachel combined with Evangeline's phone silence forced him out of bed and into his car in the middle of the night in fear for her safety. When Henry went off the rails, he always showed up off his meds and high on God knew what at Evan's. The guy had a good heart, but he had issues galore.

The gate opened, and he drove forward. He pressed the button on the remote Evan had given him when she first purchased the property years ago. The garage opened and he drove inside, thankful to see the car he'd given her the day she finished law school. *You're home, and there are no signs of Henry's presence.*

He parked and slipped out of his car.

His phone vibrated. *Evangeline.*

—I'm fine. It's been a long day. Thanks for the birthday wishes.—

He typed back.

—I just arrived. I was worried. Mind if I come in?—

He sent the text and waited. Her answer came

immediately.

—Don't judge. I'm a mess and I have nowhere for you to sit or food to eat or anything.—

He hurried into her house and found her sitting against her front door wiping tears from her pretty brown eyes. *Oh, sweetheart, I wish I hadn't been so right, but I'm so glad you didn't make the biggest mistake of your life.*

He took off his running shoes and sat down in front of her. *I love you. You make me want to settle down and even have a child.* "Cal called me and told me what happened. Henry took off about twenty minutes ago. If he shows up—"

"I'll call the police and text you immediately. You've got nothing to worry about. He's not coming here. He's probably with his sponsor. He'll be back at the fire station to work his shift in no time. He loves his job. He won't do anything to jeopardize it." She lifted the neckline of her flowery, sheer blouse, but it slipped back down, exposing one bare shoulder and more of her chest in the process. "Henry talked me into starting fertility treatments and then he emptied out my house without saying a word."

His cock stood like a large pole supporting a tent in his shorts. "Want to spend the night in one of my hotels?"

She shook her head. "They left me a blanket. I'm going to camp out."

"I'll camp with you."

She raised her chin and met his gaze. "But you hate camping."

I love you. "I've never camped with you." *You don't need to be alone.* He stood, and precum made a mark on his gray golf shorts. He pulled the hem of his shirt out of his shorts and let it hang over the stain.

"You don't have to hide anything from me," she said. "I like that I still turn you on."

"Everything about you turns me on. Always has. Always will." He held out his hand. *Take it.*

The gentle touch of her hand in his made his heart swell with hope. He tugged, and she gave into his will and stood. *Nothing is as wonderful as your trust in me.*

The oversized blouse slipped down her shoulder and unveiled her left breast. The pale-yellow lace bra showed more skin than it covered.

The vulnerable way she stood before him, the rise of her chest with each audible breath, the unzipped jeans hugging her hips made him want to take her into his arms and make love to her forever. He parted his lips to speak, but she opened her mouth.

"Posing nude for Ella's Oils gives us a…" She dropped her gaze to his groin. "We're comfortable with each other naked, right?"

"Very comfortable," he said. "You still sleep in your birthday suit?"

She let go of his hand and lifted her blouse over her head and released it. "Yes, sir." She unhooked her bra and the strapless thing fell to the floor. "I'm tired, and I have a miserable day ahead of me."

"What's happening tomorrow?"

She led him through the house and up the stairs. "My family birthday celebration."

He opened her bedroom door.

She walked into the room with nothing but a folded comforter in the corner and pushed her jeans and panties down her legs.

Glistening pussy called to him.

"Undress and I'll get the bed...the blankets ready," she said.

"Are you sure?"

She glanced over her shoulder but didn't meet his gaze. "I'm sure. It's fine. A hard-on against my back doesn't bother me." Without waiting for a response, she moved to the corner and unfolded the comforter. "Imagine this as a soft, cushiony mattress."

He pulled off his T-shirt and shorts and watched as she made do with what she had. A new side to her emerged, one he'd never seen. For a woman born with a silver spoon in her mouth and who had made millions in her own right, she didn't complain about her circumstances.

She twirled around and smiled at him. "Your bed awaits, my king." She curtsied.

He bowed. "Thank you, my fair queen." He sat on the comforter, and she sat next to him. "You're amazing, did you know that?"

"I'm not. Another failed relationship. Another year wasted."

"You *are* amazing." He relaxed back onto his elbows and tried to ignore his erect cock trickling cum. "You got a few hits, but you're okay. You're dealing with it."

She looked at him and lay down on her side facing him. "I don't really have a choice."

"Better this happened now, than two years from now." *I don't have a condom. I doubt they left you condoms. We might make a baby tonight.* He adjusted to his side and placed his hand on her hip. He pressed his fingers lightly against her back, and she scooted closer.

"Yeah," she whispered. "Thanks for coming over and checking on me."

"I worry about you, Evan." He glided his hand over her hip and between her wet thighs. *You're as turned on as I am.*

"How long are you in town?" She glided her leg up over his hip, giving him full access to her pussy.

He caressed over her juicy pussy lips and dipped a finger inside. *You're tight. You haven't had sex in a while.* "We're filming that ad for Ella's Oils on Monday. I'll be here until Henry is stabilized and I know you're safe." In and out, he stroked her pussy.

She moaned and rolled her hips. "I don't have condoms."

"I don't either," he whispered. He added another finger and was rewarded with a soft mewl from her lips.

"Brice," she mumbled. She skimmed her hand down his arm over his hip to his cock and guided it to her sex.

He shifted and rolled over her. With her mocha eyes gazing into his, he pressed against her drenched entrance. "You haven't since we—"

She shook her head. "Henry and I made up. He moved back in and never spent more than an hour with me a day, usually an hour a week for the last three months. Todd..." She glanced away. "He moved in a week later. I was a cash cow for them. I guess Rachel gave them something I couldn't."

"Look at me." He retreated from her pussy.

Big brown eyes with bigger tears looked into his.

"They don't deserve you. They never did." He kissed her forehead. "You're precious. You're

41

gorgeous. You're smart. You're sexy. You're going to be a wonderful wife and mother."

She inhaled like she always did when she tried to control her emotions. Men had let her down throughout her life. He had let her down.

"Thanks," she whispered.

He thrust his hips forward, and his cock found its home inside her.

She wrapped her legs around his waist. Tears drifted down her cheeks. "I need you to love me tonight."

"I love you, Evangeline Zanipolo," he whispered. *I'm going to do my damnedest to get you pregnant. You've tried so many other times, but those men weren't right for you. I am, and I'm ready to step up as a lover, husband, and father.*

"Do that slow thing you do," she said in a sultry southern drawl. "I'm so wet and sensitive. I'm going to come fast. Really fast."

He spread his legs, and his balls settled perfectly against her dark passage.

"Oh, yeah," she moaned.

He swiveled his hips and ground her clit. With another thrust, he shifted so her hips curled up. Deep inside her, his cock grew harder than it'd ever been. He rocked forward and penetrated farther into her taut channel.

She parted her lips and raised her hands over her head. She flattened her hands against the wall as her pussy rippled around his cock. "You're right there. Do you feel that?"

Hell, yes, I feel it. "Yeah, baby. Yeah." He circled his hips and ground against her clit. Over and over, he lazily brushed the tiny bud which made her pussy clench and his cock tap against her sweet spots. He flexed his cock, and she shuddered beneath him.

"Brice, this feels different. You're so big. So deep inside me. It's so good. So…" She rolled her hips and arched her back. Her breasts pushed up against his chest and she let her head dip back. "I'm coming, Brice. Oh, God. You're making me come so hard."

With her pussy sucking on his cock, he began thrusting in and out. In and out. His cock dove in and out. Deeper and deeper and deeper.

She shook, thrashing her head and hips. "Fuck. Fuck. Oh fuck, yes. Yes. Yes."

He gazed at her and felt a rush of her juices squirting. She'd never done that with him before. Her lips parted and her mouth gaped. "Please," she begged. "Please."

He grabbed her legs and pushed them up and forward. His cock dipped in to the end of her channel. His balls buzzed and the vibration rose and shot up his cock, releasing his cum. He'd never had sex without a condom. Never wanted to. Never thought he'd ever meet anyone he'd even consider going unsheathed with.

Thoughts of beautiful little girls with dark hair and blue eyes filled his vision. *Please have my baby. Please make this night change our lives.*

"I love you," she whispered.

His body took over with a whole new need for her, for a future with her. He thrust as bliss consumed him. He emptied his cum inside her and nearly collapsed on her. "I love you, Evan."

"I made a mess," she whispered. "I've never done that before."

He rolled onto his back and pulled her to his side. "I want you to do that again." *And you will.*

"Mmm," she mumbled. Her breathing slowed to the steady sounds of sleep.

He inhaled the lovely scents of vanilla and honey mixed with sex. *I'm going to find a home for us. Somewhere far from the city. Somewhere with lots of land. A place where the memories of my childhood won't haunt me. Somewhere that's safe and secure, away from Henry.*

Chapter Six
Jerry

Holding his phone, Jerry stared at the photo of his best friend, Ella Winthrop-Jackson, and the young woman who gave him a new reason to sweat, Evangeline Zanipolo. His right hand drifted under his shorts to his aching balls. *I want you, Evan. God, I want you.*

Dark eyes he could fall into and never touch the bottom. Long, caramel hair he wanted to run his fingers through all night long. Plump lips he would guide up and down his thick cock.

He cupped his balls and panted like a hormonal teen. "She's too young. Too damn young."

"Dude," Jason Winthrop, his best friend's son, said. "Ask her out."

Jerry slid his hand from under his shorts and glanced at Jason standing in the doorway. "You're not supposed to be here."

He held out a small pile of ultrasound pictures. "The latest on the triplets. Mom is still waiting on the paternity results. The guys are on edge about who is the father. Looks like there is a set of identical twin boys. I'm not sure how Derek will handle the news if he isn't the dad of at least one of the babies." He walked in and leaned against the wall near the heavy bag.

"You okay?" Jerry asked.

Jason shook his head. "Katie is engaged to this really nice guy. Why does he have to be nice?"

"She likes nice guys. You're nice. This guy is nice. The next guy will be nice."

"Dude, they're getting married in a month," Jason said.

"I bet they won't. And the last thing you need is to be married to a woman who is concerned about what your mother does behind closed doors. That's fucked up. You'll find someone who loves you and could care less whether your kids are the same age as your half brothers and sisters." Jerry placed his phone, screen down, beside his boxing gloves on the bench. "Want to hit the bag? Work out?" *I could use a distraction.*

"Naw," Jason said. "You need to ask Evangeline out. She's single and into you. She's got the googly eyes and everything when you're in the room."

"She does not. She's too young. She's more suitable for you than me." Jerry ran his hand over the top of his damp hair. *I would have made love to her last night. I don't think she's into me enough for a relationship. She saved me the pain of a bad breakup by walking away.*

Jason laughed. "Dude, she's thirty. She's not too young for you. She's too old for me."

"Thirty? I thought she was twenty-three, maybe twenty-four." Jerry searched Jason's eyes for any kind of deceit.

"She doesn't look her age. You don't either. So while you're standing around jerking off thinking about her, she's actively looking for Mr. Right, which could be you."

"Jay," Kyle, Jason's identical twin brother, shouted

from another room.

"In the weight room. I caught Jerry with his hands down his shorts working his cock over Evangeline," Jason shouted.

Jerry groaned. "Really, man? Did you have to go there?" *Is nothing sacred with you two?*

Kyle strode in wearing a sweat-laden T-shirt and running shorts. "Ask the girl out. I caught her showing Mom the American flag tattooed near her pussy. Legs spread wide. Total exposure. Mom talked her into posing for the Sensual Oils by Ella line."

"What?" Jason huffed. "When? How did I not know about this?"

Jerry's jaw dropped. *She does not pose nude.* "Evan's on an oil bottle?" *Since when did she get a tattoo? I've seen her in a swimsuit and there were no signs of ink on her. You're so full of shit.*

Kyle nodded and waggled his brows. "Tits, pussy, ass. They're all there. She's modeling for one of the new lines."

"You're shitting me?" Jason said.

"Nope," Kyle said. "This is between us, but she's having another photo shoot with Derek tonight. Clamps. Dildos. A friend of Derek's is going to model with her."

"Model? How?" Jerry asked. *Not like Ella does with her husbands? Cock and cum and pussy. Fuck.* His heart accelerated into survival mode and his muscles tensed. *I'm going to kill anyone who touches my Evan.*

"She's totally cool with her body," Kyle said. "They're going on a lunch date first, hoping they're compatible and have chemistry for maybe more than genital modeling."

"She wouldn't fuck him?" Jerry asked. *People do things they would never do in front of Derek. Shit. She could. I can't let her.*

Kyle shrugged. "Maybe? I don't know. If things go well at the photo shoot, they'll travel to Atlanta to film an advertisement for Mom's products next month while Mom and Garrett are cheering you on in Vegas. Although, Mom might be cheering you on from home. She's close to having those babies."

"Evangeline is not getting naked with another man." *Shit. Shit. Shit. I can't cancel Vegas.* He grabbed his phone and dialed Derek. *You're not setting up my girl with another man. Not now that I know she's not too young.*

"Hi, Jerry. Have you seen Jason yet?" The tone of Derek's voice exuded so much excitement, it seemed palpable.

"The triplets are gonna be big babies. How is Ella feeling?"

"Ella is excited the babies will be out soon. Come over for dinner tomorrow and hang out."

"Dinner sounds good." Jerry rocked from side to side. "Not to get involved in your part in Ella's company, but—"

"But you're going to step over a boundary, aren't you?"

Jerry exhaled. "Yes, I'm going to step into an area that is none of my business."

Derek groaned. "This is not a good idea."

"I don't want Evangeline posing with a guy for Ella's sensual lines. Kyle told me about the photo shoot. Do not set her up on any dates." *It's one thing if she's posing by herself, but with a guy... No. I'm not allowing some stranger to touch my girl.*

"Why? Are you finally admitting you're *interested* in dating her?" Derek asked.

"Thanks for selling me out," Kyle huffed.

"It's Derek," Jason said. "He's going to be fine with us knowing."

Jerry glared at Jason. *You and Kyle don't keep secrets. You should have told me about this a long time ago.* "I don't want her with another man. She is not having sex with another man." *I went too far.*

"She's already in contract for the photo shoots and the advertisements. She is contracted with Troy and Ella for promoting and modeling the new wild cherry line."

"How long is her obligation?" *How could you and Ella do this to me?*

"Three years," Derek said. "She's open with her body and she keeps her mouth shut about it. She and Troy are friends and she works for him as legal counsel whenever he asks, which is often."

"She's not posing or having sex with anyone else. Do you hear me?"

"If you don't want her having sex with someone else, then get your ass to her house and pick her up. You explain why she won't be going on a date with my friend or enjoying a consensual fuck on or off the set. Happy?"

"Damn it, Derek." *No, I'm not happy. I know what Troy's promoting entails. I've been to his promos.* Jerry sprinted to his garage, grabbed his keys, and hopped in his minivan.

"Are you alone?" Derek asked.

"Yeah." He waited as the garage hangar opened.

"Did you call the guy you told me about?"

"I called his private line last night and left a message." He slid his hand beneath his shorts and gripped his throbbing cock. *I need to get laid. Bad.*

"Evangeline is expecting me to pick her up in thirty minutes to meet a potential husband, but I think she loves you and has for a long time. So, you better hurry and fight for her."

Jerry pushed the speed limits of his family-friendly vehicle. "On my way."

"You better be okay with her genital modeling and offering product samples. She's been doing it for a few months, and she likes it. Don't force her to give it up."

He swallowed hard. "Yeah, yeah. I know. Her business. Her body. Her choice. I have to be reminded it's only at Troy's parties and they're safe and consensual."

"I'm going to tell you something private. Will you keep it between us until Ella gets the nerve up to tell you?"

"What happened? Is Ella okay? You guys haven't done anything to hurt her, have you?"

"Ella's fine. You know we'd never hurt her. This is strictly something I want you to know so you can work it into a conversation so Ella can get this off her chest. She's afraid you won't approve and you're like a brother to her. She'd be devastated if you—"

"What is it?" *She couldn't do anything that would make me think less of her.*

"Ella is planning on selling the spa and expanding her business with Troy. She'll still work on you, but she's going to do that for free. She's retiring her license and concentrating on increasing our family and developing her sensual line of products."

"I'm fine with whatever she chooses to do. As long as she's happy, I'm happy."

"You need to offer Evan the same kind of love and acceptance for her position in the company, only Evan needs more support and approval because she doesn't get it from her family. Don't go into this relationship thinking you're going to change her. Be honest and tell her about Dylan. Tell her what you want for the future. Tell her you are proud of her. Tell her you support her in…" Derek continued the lecture Jerry had heard the man give Cade a time or two.

But Evan was Jerry's now, and potentially watching her and other men and women expose the private parts he planned to take for himself…both turned him on and made him sick to his stomach. *What if I lost her to someone else?*

"…Support, protect, and love her, and she will thrive as your wife or girlfriend."

"I'll see you later," Jerry said. His phone buzzed. He parked on the street in front of Evangeline's home.

"Look at the link I just texted." Derek hung up.

Jerry opened the text and clicked the link.

Evan's pink nipples glistened on the screen. The frame expanded over her sexy curves and shifted focus to her wet pussy.

A nude college-aged man crawled between her legs. "Smells like a fresh pussy," he whispered. He caressed over her thighs and spread them wider until her folds opened and her clit and pussy welcomed his calling.

Cream slid from her sex and the camera followed it down, showing the edge of a small American flag tattoo on her inner thigh. "I didn't mean to..." Evan whispered as her pussy contracted and another small rush of juices flowed down between her ass cheeks.

The man's tongue darted out and scooped up some of the juices. "Fuck, you taste good." His skin flushed and his breathing turned shallow. "Sugar and strawberries." He groaned as he fed from her pussy.

Jerry fisted his cock and moaned along with the man eating his woman.

The man lifted his face and licked his moist lips. "I need to fuck you. I need to suck your tits."

"Yes," Evan moaned. "Please."

The single frame divided into four. Four different angles focused on their sex. The man drove into her and Jerry's cock jerked.

Jerry grabbed napkins from his console and pumped his cock, lubricating it with precum.

The man's big cock slid into her pussy. "I'm gonna come. I'm gonna spurt my cum in you. You smell so good. So good." In, in, in, the man thrust and then pulled out. In. In. In.

Her pussy expanded and glistened. "May I come?" she begged.

"Not until I do," he grunted. His mouth closed around her breast and sucked as he arched and drove into her like a fucking machine. His legs trembled. His balls drew up so tight Jerry could see the moment the man gave in to the overwhelming need.

Jerry pumped his cock and covered the top with his other hand filled with napkins. He spurted as the man's body shuddered over Evan.

"Yes," Evan cried out.

The man sucked at her breast and smiled. His face

relaxed and his eyes half closed. He parted his lips and curled his tongue around her nipple.

The film closed to one angle at her pussy as his cock withdrew. Cum trickled from her sex. The man kissed her clit and rubbed oil all over the outside and dipped oil from his fingers into her pussy.

The camera angles focused on her pretty privates, but anyone who knew her would recognize her voice. Those who knew her intimately or fantasized about her—having seen a few flashes of her nipples over the years—would be certain she was the woman in the film.

The action ended and a nude photo of Evan spread eagle with a clear shot of her glistening pink pussy with a link to subscribe for more videos. A male voice Jerry didn't recognize said, "The best fuck I've ever had, Evangeline Zanipolo."

Jerry quickly tapped on the link and, there for the world to see, was his woman's pussy and tits on twenty or so films with both men and women. The last one available for viewing was filmed five years ago and had over a million views.

He clicked on the next clip as he cleaned up his own mess.

The same man that had been in the last film stood beside an older man with salt-and-pepper hair covered in soap in an open shower room made for ten.

Jerry slid his finger over the time bar and stopped as the two men fucked her in the shower. The camera angles showed everything. The three weren't faking it. They enjoyed every single moment. The moans were sincere. The moments were real. He couldn't stop staring at the screen. At her. *Mine.*

"I want to fuck three men," Evan said in a sultry

southern voice.

The young man grinned. "I can make all your dreams come true."

Jerry's jaw dropped. *I am going to fuck her hard. Hard and long and over and over and over again until she uses that voice for me.*

He looked down and his cock stood at attention. He pulled his shorts over the big bulge and tied the bag of dirty napkins closed. He inhaled. *I smell like cum.*

He squeezed his hands around the leather wheel. *Keep it together. Wish her a happy birthday again. She's most likely hung over from last night. I'm checking on her. I'm here to check on her, not fuck her like a madman.*

He stepped onto the sidewalk and took the stairs two at a time until he stood at the door. *She's thirty. She's going to be mine.*

A quick stretch of his neck to both sides and then he rapped on the door.

"You're early," she shouted. "I hate you."

The door swung open.

"Der..." Her mouth hung open. Not a lick of makeup on her pretty face. A simple white T-shirt that showed her pink nipples and tight white leggings left nothing to the imagination. "Derek called you to take me shopping and to my parents' house tonight, didn't he?"

Not quite. Would you go out in public like this? Everyone can see you're not wearing a bra or panties. Your nipples are pointing at me. "Derek can't make it. I'm your chauffer, date, whatever you need." He leaned in and kissed her cheek. "So, we're shopping for clothes? Visiting your parents? Birthday celebration with the family?" *I am not wearing exercise clothes to meet your parents for the first time. Momma Mae would roll over in her grave.*

She pinched the bridge of her nose and closed her eyes. "I can't believe I'm about to say this, but you can't wear that today. My parents go overboard with birthdays that end in zero. I'm thirty and, long story short, Derek was stepping in as a potential therapist to break the ice over my forever-single status. They love him and don't lose their shit when he's around."

"Derek is a great guy, but I'm better. Should I wear a tux? We'll need to stop by my house so I can change."

"Do you have a tux?" She shook her head. "Of course you have a tux. You probably have ten. And that kilt. Shit. No kilts today. Black tux. I need to…" She paused and looked over her shoulder.

He gazed into her empty house. No furniture. No lamps. He leaned forward and peered inside. "I'm jumping to conclusions, but—"

"Yes. I wasn't exaggerating last night. They literally took everything. A friend dropped off my laptop and office files this morning. Henry and Todd can have the rest. I'm not suing or wasting any more time on them."

She swallowed as she lowered her gaze. "I didn't see it coming. But I understand why it happened." Shaking her head, she seemed lost in her thoughts. "I'm not going to make the same mistakes again. I'm only dating a man who will support me, attend family functions, and love my friends. If they have a problem with my career choices, they're gone. If…" She rattled off an exhaustive list of "ifs," and he paid attention to every detail.

"…and if he doesn't like my excessively poochie belly, he's out the door."

He gazed at her torso. *You don't have a pooch. Who has destroyed your image of yourself?* "You've got curves where women should have curves. You're beautiful, Evangeline." *I want to see and touch every gorgeous inch of you. I want to get my mouth on your—*

"You're just saying that." She rolled her eyes at him and seemed defeated.

He cupped her face and bent over until they were nose-to-nose. "I have the luxury of being able to tell the truth. I look at you and my thoughts aren't innocent." *Don't kiss her. Don't…*

She parted her lips.

"Fuck it." He stepped over the threshold into her home and met her lips.

She moaned.

Electricity zigzagged through him and fired up his cock so much that precum seeped from the tip.

I'm going to fuck you right now. I don't have a condom. I don't even care. If you get pregnant, all the better. He kicked the door closed.

He slid his hands down her back and cupped her muscular thighs.

"Please, don't stop," she whispered against his lips. "I'm clean."

"I don't care if you're dirty."

She laughed, and kept laughing, and laughing, and laughing. She wrapped her arms around him and clung to him as she roared with laughter.

What did I say? He let go of her thighs and skimmed along her body until he stood gently holding her.

Tears flowed down her cheeks as she shook her head and smiled. The mirth that had exploded seconds ago, she managed to contain.

Is this still gonna happen? I'm hard as a rock and ready to get you in bed.

The sparkle in those mocha eyes took him in and held him.

"I haven't laughed like that with anyone in I can't remember when." Instead of shying away like most women he'd known would, she hugged him. "When I said I was clean, I meant I don't have any diseases. I'm clean, but I'm dirty because I hauled office boxes and climbed into the attic for old towels and supplies that weren't there." She giggled. "They did leave my toothbrush and toothpaste."

He nodded. "I tend to take things literally. I don't have any diseases, and it's been a while since I dated anyone worth sleeping with."

"It's not been long since I had sex." She let go of him and opened the front door.

He definitely said something wrong. Her mood shifted much too quickly for it to be anything else.

"I need to shop for a dress, shoes, and makeup for tonight. If we have time, I'd like to pick up an air mattress. I can probably handle purchasing the rest of the house items online. We need to be at my mom and dad's for family photos at three and dinner starts promptly at five."

He followed her out of the house and observed her attempts at taking control. She pulled the handle of his driver's door.

"Evan, you're not driving my car." He took her by

the hand and led her to the passenger's side. He opened the door.

She looked at the seat with the tied-up plastic bag in which he'd stuffed the cum soaked napkins.

"Sorry." He picked up the bag and helped her inside. "I was cleaning up before I came over." *Odor-resistant bags for diapers come in handy.*

"Please tell me there isn't a dirty diaper in there," she said. "I know you babysat Ella's kids yesterday."

"Not a diaper." *I'm not going to elaborate.*

"Thank the Lord."

He buckled her seatbelt in place and tested it like he did with Ella's kids before he realized his hands touched her breasts.

She dipped her chin, and a blush rose from her neck to her cheeks.

He strode to the other side, wishing for the first time in a long time that he had a sports car. The minivan worked perfectly for his lifestyle, but for a day of pampering like she needed, driving something other than a babysitter mobile would have been nice.

He stuffed the small trash bag in the door of the car and started the engine.

As he drove toward home, the flow of blood from his cock finally returned to his brain. *She's not shopping wearing a transparent shirt and pants. Not in public.*

"Call Jessica X," he said.

"Calling Jessica X," his car responded. The phone dialed.

"Who is Jessica?" Evangeline asked.

"I'll tell you in a sec."

"Jerry?" Jessica answered.

"I need a favor. My girlfriend needs a pretty dress for her birthday dinner and all that hair and makeup stuff that you handle so well. We don't have much time. Can you get your team together and meet at my house in an hour?"

"An hour? It's Saturday morning. I have appointments." Frustration laced her tone.

"This is important to me. She's coming to my fight in Vegas." He looked over at Evangeline and mouthed *Will you?*

Evangeline smiled and pointed to her chest. *Me?* She mouthed back.

"Ree-ah-lly?" Jessica exhaled. "Front row? Your seats?"

"Yeah. What better time to meet my girl than this morning, right, Jess?" He winked at Evan whose lips parted and her hand flattened over her heart. *You are going to be mine.*

"Tall? Short? Details??"

"Five-feet-six-and-a-quarter inches. Beautiful brunette with long black lashes. Red lips with a natural glistening sheen. Lightly tanned, smooth complexion. Muscular legs and arms. Curves that—"

"I need an hour and a half. See you soon." Jess ended the call.

"She's the owner of Jess's Boutique and married to one of my trainers."

"Call her back and tell her it's me. She knows me." Something in her tone made him hesitate, but he called anyway.

"Fine, Jerry, I'll be there in an hour. Sheesh," Jess answered.

"My girl is Evangeline Zanipolo. She said you two

know each other."

"Thank God she dumped those guys. I've been praying for her to come to her senses since she introduced me to those pricks. That Todd kept coming in with her friend who stood in for her fittings and added details upon details until I finally told him I was done and they'd have to find another designer to make crazy. Hang on, Jerry... What, Danny? Oh... Dang. I've got to go. Her father is on the landline. I love him. Like, I'd leave Danny for the man if he came on the market. I'm kidding, Danny. I'm kidding. I'm so not kidding, Jerry." She laughed as the call ended.

"Mom, may I speak with Dad?" Evangeline said.

Jerry looked at her.

With her phone to her ear, her nostrils flared with each intake of breath and a fiery red took over her face. "Tell Dad to drop it. Now. Please, Mom. I'm not coming home if it's going to be like this. I don't want Dad involved in my personal life. I'm fine. I swear, I'm fine." She dropped her head as she slouched over. "Oh, Lord, no. Mom, I haven't seen him since I was sixteen. Uninvite him."

With the accelerator pushed to the floor, Jerry glanced at the woman he wasn't going to let anyone else have.

"Is Dad on crack or something?" Her voice rose to a scream. "I'm bringing a friend. You're not making this a game of *Embarrass Evangeline until Everyone Leaves.* I'm not putting up with that anymore. Henry and Todd were smart to dump me. Dad's insults run off everyone I love."

"Don't you say that, Gelie," her mother shouted. "If this *friend* is interested in you, he'll do like Kaila did for your brother. He'll keep his mouth shut and put up with your father to keep the peace. And no more sex talk or—"

"I don't talk about sex. Dad does. *He* is the one who brings up *my sex life* in front of family and my friends. Stop taking his side." Evangeline hit the phone with every finger, slapping it over and over, then screamed. Her hands shook and smoke seemed to come out of her eyes and ears.

"So, your father is a verbal processor?" Jerry asked.

"He's an attorney. So, yeah, he is." She inhaled like she had been deprived of oxygen for most of her life, then with shaky hands placed the phone on the console. "You shouldn't come tonight. If this were any other day or time or season, you could meet my parents, but not now. Dad is probably going off on Jessica for not calling either of us about the wedding dress. He is going to burn every bridge I've ever erected." She shook her head. "My father can be a royal asshole."

"Don't worry about me, beautiful." He took her hand and kissed it. "I can handle tough situations of all kinds." *I fight for a living.*

He pulled into the driveway past Kyle's and Jason's jeeps and parked in his garage. *I have to get rid of them.*

"Jerry, you don't know how bad it can get." She stepped out of the car and followed him into his home. "I am not dragging you into this clusterfuck."

He led her into his gym.

Kyle held the heavy bag as Jason threw punch after punch.

"Ky and Jay, I've got some people coming over,"

Jerry said. *Get out now.* "Y'all have to leave."

"I should bring Jay." Evangeline sashayed into the room like she regularly worked out there. "They'll play nice with him in the room."

"And where are we going, sexy?" Jay asked. The kid pulled off his gloves like he had all the time in the world to hang out and visit.

"You're not going anywhere with her," Jerry said. "I am."

"Tell Jerry about my father," Evangeline said.

"You're going to love him," Jay said. "Better yet, he's going to love you. You know how Derek is about you, although he tries to keep it chill?"

Jerry nodded. *He's a fan, but not a stalker.*

"Mr. Zanipolo is like Derek on steroids. I think he might have a heart attack when you walk through the door. So, keep Derek on speed dial and brush up on your CPR."

"He is not like Derek," Evangeline said.

"Yes, Evan. He is." Jay glanced at his phone. His jaw clenched, and the muscles in his face and neck contracted. He lifted his chin at Jerry and gave him a tense smile. "Ky and I are leaving for a few days, maybe a week."

Jerry nodded. "Everything okay?"

Jay patted Jerry on the back. "I have a lead for that girl I've been searching for. I have a first name and a photo. I might be a dad. I might have a baby boy." He walked by in a daze.

Ky took her hand and squeezed it. "Don't worry. Jerry can handle anything. He's like Mom. He'll make sure you celebrate your birthday and forget about everything else." He let go of her hand and walked out the door. "Show her a great time, Jerry. I was playing you earlier. Sorry. I got put up to it."

"Yeah," Jerry said. *None of that matters.* "Take care of your brother and call me if you need anything." *I hope this girl is nothing like Katie. God, give him some answers this time. Give him a reason to stand up for himself against Katie's verbal barbs.*

"Will do," Ky yelled.

A door slammed shut. The boys were gone.

"My father wouldn't know a jab from a hook. I'd know if he were a superfan like Derek." She walked around the room, touching everything.

"Derek isn't a superfan."

She glanced over her shoulder and raised her brows as she smirked. "Derek has Jerry Wynn underwear and plays you on that video game. He has all the Jerry Wynn action figures, and they are displayed in his home office. He's a superfan, Jerry. My father is not."

"Derek helps me decide what my followers might like. He hasn't bought any of that stuff. And the underwear is comfortable. Jay and Ky wear them too. Millions of men wear them."

"Really?" She seemed genuinely surprised.

"Yeah. Now, why are you opposed to me meeting your dad? It might be good if he doesn't know who I am. Lots of people have never heard of me. Billions of people don't know who I am. I'm always surprised when someone does."

"I'm not opposed to you meeting everyone I'm related to, and to state for the record, millions of people know exactly who you are. I'd wager a bet that billions know who you are." She tapped the wooden bench where he left his gloves.

I need to put those gloves away. "What kind of bet?" he asked. *Am I making you nervous?*

"A hundred dollars," she said.

He shook his head. "Not money. And let's make it a bet that's winnable. I'm goal oriented."

"I'll bet you my father doesn't have a clue who you are."

"Okay. Like I said, most people don't. But I'll bet you that he recognizes me and calls me by name." *He will by the end of the night. So, I'll win.*

She rolled her eyes. "He has to ask to take a picture with you."

He grinned. *That will be done almost immediately since they scheduled a photo shoot for your birthday.* "Okay. If I win, you spend the next two nights with me in my bed in my house. You travel with me to Las Vegas in three weeks, go to the fight, and sleep every night in my bed…" *For the rest of your life.*

She huffed. "Sex?"

He shrugged. *If you're willing, I'm all for it.* "If that is what you want for your win, I'm good with it."

She threw her hands up and shook her head. The soft curls he was ready to run his hands through lifted and fell and drifted over her shoulders to her chest and back. "No. That is not what I'm asking for. You're going to take me on a date to one of your events."

"Deal." *I'd do that anyway.*

"And, you're going to dance with me tonight." She puffed out her cheeks like a chipmunk and exhaled. "And, you're going to kiss me afterward. I want a real kiss. Tongue. Teeth. Hands."

"Want to practice?" He crossed the room toward her.

"No practicing." She avoided him and hustled to the door. "When is Jessica going to be here? Do I have time for a shower?"

"Jess will wait." He grabbed her hand and strode out of the gym and led her to his bedroom.

With little more than a gentle tug, she followed, which sent his confidence skyward.

"I use Ella's ginger products," he said. "If you want a different soap or shampoo, I can run next door to Jay and Kyle's and get whatever you need."

"Ginger is good. I'm not picky."

"Towels are on the shelf near the shower. If you have any questions, ask or feel free to search the cabinets and shelves." He pushed open the door to his bedroom and flipped the switch on the wall.

"Do you sleep in this room?" she mumbled.

He searched the room for anything out of order. The books were neat, dust-free, and organized on the built-in bookshelves on either side of the fireplace. The bed was made. Nightstands clear of clutter.

"Yeah, this is my room. Is there something wrong?" *Ella and Jess like my room.*

"It's just so…clean and…organized." She let go of his hand and walked to the bookshelf next to the fireplace. "Are you a reader?"

"Yes, ma'am. Are you?"

She nodded and traced her fingers along the edges of several books as she explored his room. He watched and followed, noticing her stop and glance at the bed and continue around the room.

"Are you obsessive-compulsive?"

"No, but I do like things neat and orderly at home. I was pretty poor growing up, so I take care of the stuff

I have."

"Huh. I didn't know that about you. You're so polished in public." She opened the doors to the bathroom. "Wow. Aren't you afraid people will see you?"

He laughed. "No. If I have guests, I grab the remote and blinds come down, covering the windows to the backyard. A select few know where I live. I've yet to have anyone show up who hasn't been invited."

Big brown eyes gazed into his. "I'm messy. I don't make the bed. I leave cups and bottles of water everywhere. I do put my clothes in the hamper, most of the time. I don't iron, and I burn almost everything I cook or bake, or grill."

"Is this the 'are we compatible?' portion of our date?"

She huffed and turned away. "No. I'm making observations and statements. That's all. We are not on a date."

"I dust and clean. I have a private chef, although I cook and bake successfully—without burning anything. I do my own laundry. A maid comes about once a month or so." *I've got to buy condoms. I should have changed the sheets this morning.* He closed his eyes and inhaled. *Calm down. Control the situation.*

"You can go now," she whispered. "No peeking in on me."

He opened his eyes.

She held a towel and washcloth in her hands. "Go on. Close the doors. Yell when Jessica arrives."

"Maybe a quick peek?" *Shower sex? Bubble bath?*

She shook her head. "No, Mr. Wynn. Peeking leads to touching which leads to *sinful things.*" She straightened her posture and batted her lashes. "Normally, I like sinful things, but the kind of sin you offer scares me."

"Too bad." He walked out of the room and closed the doors. He cupped his groin and held in a moan. *She's fucking perfect.*

Chapter Seven
Evangeline

"Crap," Evangeline mumbled as her father stood up and raised his glass of champagne in the air. *Don't embarrass me because I was late for pictures or whatever else you think I did wrong tonight.*

"My little Gelie Belly is back on the market," her father said.

Under the table, Jerry placed his hand over hers and squeezed.

Teetotaler Dad was three sheets to the wind when they arrived, and Jerry seemed to immediately understand the "Matteo Zanipolo shit-storm about to destroy everything in its path" situation.

"Thank God, those punks she lived with for the last two years knocked up her good-for-nothing best friend and not her."

"Dad, it all worked out." She glanced over at her mom and glared on contact. *Make some excuse and put the man to bed before he says anything worse.*

"They stole from the family, and that doesn't go unpunished." Dad leaned over the table, and the bubbly her father typically turned his nose up at spilled over the rim of his glass onto the gold-threaded tablecloth. "They took the earrings my mother, God rest her soul, handed down to you as they were handed down to her from her grandmother and her grandmother before her."

Fury emanated from every square inch of his body. He drew his empty hand into a fist and pounded the table. "They will pay for what they've done."

Evangeline's brother Rick rose from his chair. "Dad, the family heirlooms have been returned. Let it go."

"I'll never let this go." Dad swayed as he walked his glass and hands backward on the table and stood up straight. With all gazes on him, he looked at her with the saddest brown eyes she'd ever seen. "You'll always be my princess. Always. Happy birthday, my sweet little princess."

He raised his glass. "To my baby, my Gelie, may this year bring you happiness beyond your wildest dreams, health for a long life, and love, true love, for *one* man who will live and breathe to see your eyes light up when he enters the room."

Rick put his arm around his father. "To Gelie."

Jerry stood and coaxed her up. "To Evangeline."

One by one, her family stood and joined in the toast.

Her father downed the champagne in his glass and sat. Everyone followed the patriarch's lead.

Waiters switched the glasses and filled goblets with wine and served the first course. Dad's focus rested on her instead of the gourmet food.

"I ordered your favorites, Evangeline."

"Thank you, Daddy." She smiled as she picked up her salad fork. *No one in their right mind will ever want me enough to deal with you.* "You always make my birthday special." *Lord, give me the strength to get through this.*

"One man from now on, princess. Fall in love, real

love. Lasting love."

She nodded. *It's not a one-sided choice. I need someone who will love me as much as I love him. Someone who is as kinky as I am. Most of all, I need someone who will put up with you.* "Yes, Daddy."

He reached across the table. "Stop throwing your life away with that massage business. I need you to carry on the Zanipolo tradition at the firm. No more of that embarrassing lifestyle. No more sex scandals. No. More."

"Let's not talk about this now," she whispered.

"What better time than now?" He leaned back in his chair and crossed his arms over his chest. He gazed around the room like a king ruling over worthless peasants, and she watched as everyone except Jerry looked away.

"Not in front of my friend," she said.

"Your client?" Dad pursed his lips and dropped his chin. "What's his name again?

"It's Jerry. He's not a client. He's a friend." *Here we go. Run him off too. But if you do, I'm never coming to another family gathering.*

"Derek should have come. He would talk some sense into you. This kid." He rolled his eyes and scrunched up his lips as he frowned. "You've never mentioned him before. I know all your friends."

"Sir," Jerry interjected.

She grabbed Jerry's arm and squeezed. "Not the time."

Her father rocked his head back and forth as he narrowed his eyes, bit his bottom lip, and moved his lower jaw forward in his trademark court challenge gesture. "Did I call your name?"

"Sir, I believe you referred to me as 'the kid.' "
Jerry smiled. "I haven't been called a kid in a very long
time."

Evangeline tugged on his arm. *He's not predictable
when he's drunk. When he's sober, he'll eviscerate you
with words to prove he can.*

"You will speak when you are spoken to, and only
then."

"Since we are in a discourse, Mr. Zanipolo, I'd like
to say for the record that I am not a client of
Evangeline's. Your daughter and I are friends."

"Which means you're fucking my daughter," Dad
replied.

"What I do or do not do with or without your
daughter is none of your business." Jerry squared his
shoulders and sat up straight. He placed his fingers on
the edge of the table. "You've had a lot to drink today. I
suggest you end the night now before you stick your
foot down your throat so far you start choking."

Dad's mouth gaped open as his eyes widened. "Did
you say your name is Jerry?"

"Yes, sir. I did."

"Jerry Wynn?"

Jerry nodded. "Yes, sir."

"*The* Jerry Wynn?"

"Yes, Dad. He's *the Jerry Wynn*." *Are you finally
embarrassed by your actions?*

Jerry's phone buzzed, making his jacket vibrate.
He reached into his jacket and withdrew his phone
while staring at her father.

Dad's face contorted with what seemed like
absolute disbelief. "You're interested in *my daughter*?"

"I'm disappointed she introduced me as her friend

instead of her boyfriend, but she's the one making the choice whether I'm worth her time." He set the phone on the table as it continued to buzz and the stare-down between the two men continued.

She placed her hand on his thigh and squeezed. *You're more than worth my time.*

"She has had sex with women and men and everything she can—"

"Sir, it's time for you to end this line of conversation. You're not going to make me go away. Words don't bother me. I'm somewhat immune to them, but the others at this table aren't like me. They are hurt by the kind of conversation you're driving. You have a choice to either stop venting your anger on those you say you love or to continue to break their hearts. What's your choice?"

The truth which exited from Jerry's mouth produced absolute silence. No one spoke to her father like that. No one interrupted him without some kind of immediate and miserable blowback.

The phone stopped buzzing and started up again, but Jerry kept his focus on her father.

A smile grew on Rick's face as the only sound in the room came from the buzzing of Jerry's phone on the wooden table.

She slid her hand between Jerry's legs and found a rock-hard bulge. *I love you, Jerry Wynn. No one but Rick has ever stood up for me with Dad, and he only did it once and paid dearly for it.*

Dad tilted his head in a slight nod and lowered his gaze in acquiescence. "I apologize. Please, answer your phone, and we'll continue dinner."

She'd never seen him apologize to anyone. Ever.

Jerry picked up his phone with one hand and slipped his other hand over hers and squeezed.

"Yeah?" Jerry answered.

"Where the fuck are you? Everybody is here. Unlock your door and let the crew in to set up for the interview," his publicist said.

"That's tonight?"

"Yeah. Back-to-back interviews. At your house. Tonight. Come on, Jerry. Don't fuck with me."

Jerry guided her hand to his thigh. "Sorry. I'm not home. I'm texting you the code for the front garage. Stall for me. I'll be there as soon as I can." He ended the call.

"You have to leave?" she asked.

He gazed at her. "Beautiful, I forgot all about these interviews when you invited me over today. I'd love for you to come with me and meet my team. It shouldn't take too long."

I'd like nothing more, but I can't. "You go," she said. "I'm going to stay here." *And have a miserable evening with my family.*

"This was set up months ago. Other people are counting on me. I'll come back as soon as it's over and make good on that bet you won."

"If you say so," she whispered.

He pushed his chair out from the table and squatted beside her. "I'm sorry, but I agreed to these interviews leading up to the fight." He kissed her cheek. "Save a dance for me."

"My card might already be filled." *Please come back. I do not want Rick to drive me home.*

"I'll cut in," he whispered. "I want that kiss I owe you." He stood up and walked to her brother and sister-in-law, mother and then father, thanking each one for having him and apologizing for leaving early and for the language from the phone call.

He crossed the formal dining room toward the hallway.

The gorgeous man who'd bought her a drink last night strode in holding a small, red velvet box with a bow around it. He stopped in front of Jerry.

"Jerry Wynn?" The man held out his hand. "I'm Dylan Russo."

Jerry accepted his hand and spoke but too quietly for her to hear.

Dylan took out his phone. "Do you have time for a picture?"

"A quick one," Jerry said.

Dylan wrapped his arm around Jerry like they were best friends. He started snapping pictures.

Jerry patted Dylan on the back. "Man, I've got to go. I'll see you later." He strode out of the room as though he ruled the world.

"Please tell me he's one of our clients." Dylan's delight carried straight up to his eyes.

"No," Dad answered.

The excitement in Dylan's dark eyes vanished. "If he's not a client, why was he here?"

I can't believe you're the same Dylan Russo from high school and you're in this house again. She glanced around the room, and all eyes rested on her.

Sobriety seemed to fill her father. "I thought he was a lookalike until a few minutes ago. Since when does he live around here?"

"He's lived here for a couple of years," Evangeline said.

Dylan sat down next to her, taking Jerry's seat. "I hope one of you pitched him some business. It's not every day someone like Jerry Wynn shows up at a birthday party."

"Maybe you can talk Evangeline into hitting him up for business," Dad said. "Oh wait, she is playing massage therapist, not doing what she was born, raised, and gifted to do." He glared at her. "You should have told me who he was."

I did. You didn't pay attention to anything I said.

"Matteo, that's enough," Dylan ordered.

"Are you the one taking over the Zanipolo Law Firm?" Evangeline asked. *At least you'll notice how much he's changed since you moved away. Everything is my fault now.*

"I'm the one who bought the firm." Dylan placed the jewelry box beside her plate. "Happy birthday, Evangeline." He gazed into her eyes. The geeky teen who hid his dominant side to everyone but her had turned into a sexy man who didn't seem to be hiding much of anything.

"Thanks." She lowered her gaze to the bulge in his pants. *You had some kind of total transformation since we were teens.* "Thanks for the drink last night."

He slung his arm over the top of her chair as if they were an item. "I hoped to talk to you, but you didn't look like you wanted company. You didn't recognize me, did you?"

"It's been fourteen years. I'm sorry." *You've really changed. No longer the husky kid with a super brain who turned me on with a raise of an eyebrow. I've changed too. I'm heavier with so much baggage I can't carry it all. And Dad will be happy to tell you all about it.*

"You look the same, only more beautiful. I missed you."

A piece of their past friendship came loose and, without thinking, she leaned closer and whispered in his ear, "Are you visiting?"

He cupped the back of her head and held her as he whispered, "I bought the firm last month and plan to absorb it into my national brand. I had hoped your father would tell you. Clearly, he didn't."

Heat poured into her from his touch. Her nipples hardened, her breasts seemed to perk up in remembrance of his masterful mouth. Her sex gushed with need for an orgasm like the ones he'd given her so often when they were young and in love. She slid her leg against his, falling into the training he'd given her so long ago. *I don't blame you for not coming back to Memphis, but why did you drop me? Why didn't you return my calls, my texts, my emails, my letters?*

She crossed her legs, closing off the offer she'd given him seconds before. "Why didn't you tell me about buying the firm?" *Why didn't you come over and talk to me last night at the pub?*

He slid his hand from her head to her shoulder. "I'll explain when we're alone."

"Yeah. Okay." She returned to a proper posture and caught her father glaring at her. *I should have canceled dinner. Dad's an ass, and Dylan isn't going to tell me shit.*

The waiters served dinner, replaced Jerry's water glass with a new one for Dylan, and added a glass of wine.

Taking control away from her father, Dylan guided

the conversation to focus on sports, music, and business—not her, her birthday, or her slutty sex life.

By the time dinner ended, Dylan's chair cuddled hers. The side of his body fit as comfortably against hers as it had as a teen. His hand caressed up her thigh and under the slit of her dress. The boy experimenting with sex and scene play had turned into a man skilled in seduction and probably a mastermind of kink.

He gazed at her as his fingers slid over the edge of her wet panties.

"You two go and have dessert outside," Mom said. "I'm taking your father upstairs. Rick and Kaila need to get home to the boys." She stood up and escorted her father out of the room.

Rick and Kaila walked over and hugged her.

"Call me tomorrow," Kaila said. "Happy birthday."

"Happy birthday, Sis," Rick said. "You always have my support in everything you do."

As long as it's me being an attorney for Dad, I'm sure you'll voice your support—otherwise, you'll stay silent. "Thanks for being here tonight."

"Wouldn't have been anywhere else." Rick tried to fake a smile but gave up and walked Kaila out.

So much for family love and a ride home. Dessert with Dylan is going to be interesting and probably a big mistake. I need to text Brice for a ride home. And I've got to stay away from having sex without condoms. No more sex. Not with Brice. Not with Jerry. Not with Dylan.

Dylan enclosed her hand in his. "Want to open your presents first?"

"You didn't have to get me anything."

He handed her the velvet box that had sat on the

table unopened. "This is for show. But this"—he reached into his inside jacket pocket and pulled out a small envelope—"is the real present."

She pulled the black ribbon and opened the small jewelry box. A large ruby with diamonds framing the gem set on a platinum band nestled against white satin. "I can't—"

He plucked the ring from the box and slid it onto her right ring finger. "Your father is handing over his clients to me, and I'll be distributing them to some of my attorneys. He'll announce his retirement next week. I've fired many of his employees but retained a handful. I'd like for you to consider joining my firm as a partner."

His gaze skimmed over her chest as he made no attempt to hide his perusal of her body. The gentleness in his brown eyes disappeared and a *take no prisoners* dominance filled its place. "If that doesn't appeal to you, I'd like to hire you as a part-time consultant. Whether you decide to work with me, for me, or not at all, I'd be honored if you'd date me and see what the future holds for us."

"I might give an occasional consultation, but only if I'm interested in the case. As for the date—"

"I've been married to my work for years. I'm ready for that to change." He removed the jewelry box from the palm of her hand and placed it on the table behind him. "Don't say anything until you read the letter." He slipped a piece of paper into her hand and walked toward the hallway.

She opened the letter.

I vow to marry Dylan Russo if I'm not married by the time I turn thirty. We're going to have lots of wild, kinky sex and have a houseful of kids.

Forever Dylan Russo's sex kitten,

Evangeline Zanipolo

Fired burned her cheeks. *He kept that?* She whipped around toward the hallway.

The man loosened his forest-green tie and leaned against the door frame. "There's more. Turn it over."

She turned the college-ruled paper over.

I, Evangeline Zanipolo, promise to play sex poker at Dylan Russo's house for Dylan and anyone else he chooses on the night of my thirtieth birthday party, whether I'm married or not.

Love,

Evangeline Zanipolo

She folded the note and slipped it back into the envelope. "I don't think so." She took her time as she walked to him. She shook the letter at him. "I can't believe you kept this."

He snatched the letter from her hand and tucked it inside his jacket pocket. "I keep all legal documents that have to do with me and my sex kitten."

"Hey." She snapped her fingers. "Give it back."

He shook his head. "A woman like you doesn't come along but once in a lifetime." He stepped forward into her personal space.

She dropped her hand to her side and retreated until she was backed against the wall. "My father would lose his shit even more, if he saw that."

"He'll never see it." He pressed his hands flat against the wall behind her. "Like he never found out you sucked my cock during our study sessions. Like he never found out my face was buried between your legs every damn chance I got. Like he never found out I gave you the taste for multiple men and women fucking you." He lowered his gaze to her lips. "I've seen your advertisements for Oils by Ella. I know it's you. I'd like a sample to lick off your pussy."

I can't believe you're here, seducing me. "I don't think so."

"I do. I bought the entire line of oils. I plan on tasting each one of them on you in the privacy of my home."

She held her breath. *Why are you really here? It doesn't make sense that you'd buy Dad's firm. The place can't be very profitable with Joseph taking over.* "You bought each oil to try?"

He nodded. "Yes. Of course I did. They have to be top-of-the-line if you're modeling for the company. Which flavor will be my favorite?"

"If your tastes haven't changed, which I bet they have, I'd say the one that will be on pre-order soon." *I need to stop playing your game. You love the chase, and I'm being an idiot allowing you to chase me.*

"Should I expect a new advertisement soon?" He reached into the outside pocket of his jacket and drew out his phone. A quick swipe and glance. "Ahh, I see a notice for a new product line coming soon. Wild cherry?"

Her pussy clenched. "Yes." *Brice and I are modeling. I bet you'd like to watch. I bet you'd encourage Brice to fuck me.* Her voice fluctuated into a deeper tone of sexual need.

"Mmm," he whispered. He slipped his phone into his pocket and pressed his lips to her forehead. "Why will it be my favorite?"

She shuddered. "You always loved cherries."

"I loved your cherry. I can recall the moment it burst and my cock tasted its juices. Nothing has ever been sweeter."

That moment changed my life. You made my...our first time magical. But you left and I had to look elsewhere for the magic. I found it with Brice, but he'll never settle down. Will you? "Sex has been just as sweet since you left...actually sweeter, like a magical cherry in the wilderness that's prime for plucking...over and over again."

"By two or more men and seen by many."

He hadn't forgotten her preferences for at least one man in her bed and another watching. "Some things never change." *I'm about to combust.*

He slid the back of his hand over her breast. Up and down. "Mmm. I want to watch and then fuck you with another man's cum in your pregnant pussy."

The air in the room seemed to evaporate with him nearby. She needed oxygen or she would do things. Things she wouldn't take the time to think about. Naughty things.

He licked his lips. "I want to kiss you. May I?"

Yes. Hell, yes. "Why should I let you?"

"Angel, you're single. I'm single. We're alone. You're blushing exactly like you used to when you loved me. I'm losing my mind thinking of all the fantasies we need to play out." He slid his hand behind her neck and into her hair.

Her nipples were so hard they hurt. She wet her dry lips, but her mind began to race with all the mistakes she'd made with men. *I'm not the same girl. I'm tired of being left for greener pastures. I want marriage and children.* "I'm embarrassed, Dylan."

"You have nothing to be embarrassed about. You love sex, and you're great at it." He stared at her lips. "What do you say to that kiss?"

She rubbed her lips together. *Slow down.* "We don't even know each other anymore."

"One kiss. See if there's chemistry." His other hand curled around her back. He pulled her against him. His rigid cock pushed against her belly.

She dipped backward under his complete control.

"There's chemistry," she whispered. Her pussy clenched. Her stomach quivered. Her throat refused a moan clawing to escape. *I'm going to regret this.* "I give you permission to kiss me."

His lips met hers, and sparks burst from her toes to the very ends of her hair. His tongue welcomed hers and moved instinctually. No hesitation. No mistakes.

Strong. Confident. Experienced.

He lifted her leg over his hip. He thrust his pelvis in sync with his tongue.

You know exactly what you're doing. Dominating. Controlling.

He broke the kiss and gazed into her eyes. His hand at her thigh traveled to her soaked panties. His fingers pushed the wet fabric aside and dipped inside.

She lifted her leg higher. *I don't want to stop but I have to.* "As good as this feels—"

"It will feel much better with my cock inside you."

You always said that, and it was true every. Single. Time. But you left me.

"Angel," he whispered. He pumped his fingers in and out of her, making her pussy juices lubricate her passage for his cock. "You're going to love what I have planned for us."

She moaned. *You left without a goodbye. You stayed away. No explanations. I grieved for your mother's death alone. Why didn't you contact me? I loved you. You moved on. You discarded me like Joseph. Like Todd. Like Henry. Like the other men in my life.* "I can't. Not here. Not tonight."

"Okay. Okay, Angel." He slid his fingers from inside her and circled her clit. "Dinner and a movie tomorrow night."

"I'm working." She closed her eyes and slid her leg down his muscular thigh, ending his fingers' musing. *I swore I'd never let anyone control me again. Not my father. Not you. Only someone who doesn't care what anyone says or does. Only Brice. Only Jerry... Shit. I should be doing this with him. With Brice.*

Shivers as cold as ice skimmed over her flesh. *I'm not cheating on anyone. Neither Brice nor I talked about exclusivity. Jerry and I haven't even kissed. Jerry is not my boyfriend. I don't know what he is, and he left. He probably won't be back. I'm not having sex again. Not tonight. Not tomorrow. I want marriage. I might have lost the bet with Derek, but I'm renewing it now. Celibacy until my wedding night.*

She moved from the comfort of Dylan's arms and hustled out of the room.

He followed. "What's wrong?"

"I'm single, but I'm not ready to jump into another crappy relationship based on sex. The next relationship I'm in will be for the long haul. I don't want to be your toy."

"Most women want to be my toy and love my presents."

"Yeah, well, I can buy my own damn toys and

presents. I don't need yours." *Which is probably why you're not married. You don't trust anyone. You probably make everyone sign contracts that are painfully one-sided before you agree to have sex. Toys and presents are all you can offer them. Well, Mr. Dylan Russo, you can't buy me.*

She took off the ring he gave her and handed it to him. "It's lovely, but I don't want anyone thinking we're something we're not." *I'm not your possession.*

She stepped outside, and the vision she'd shared with her mother when she was a little girl lived and breathed in front of her eyes. *A special celebration under the stars for the bride and groom.*

"Your mother did this?" Dylan asked. He led her from the patio along the white-and-pink rose-petal path lying over the lush grass her father meticulously landscaped to the white-satin-wrapped circular table with a six-inch white-frosted wedding cake on a gold stand in the center.

Her chin quivered as she spied the gold-rimmed china placed elegantly on the table—china her grandmother had passed down to her mother and would have been passed down to her on the day of her wedding. The hand-blown Irish crystal Evangeline had fallen in love with on the last family trip abroad but hadn't purchased sparkled in the candlelight. The gold utensils her father had splurged on for her mother lay like pieces of art against the shiny tablecloth. Her grandparents' wedding bands were strung separately on pink velvet ribbon and wrapped around white linen napkins that had been placed atop each plate.

"Your mother has always been a romantic," Dylan said.

She nodded. Her heart drowned in regret as she gazed at the future she had dreamed of—a future that had seemed attainable as a child, a future she'd let go of after that man…the man who *used* her and lied. Lied. Lied.

She stared at the engraved words on the utensils and regretted wasting years of her life on relationships that remained more about protecting her heart instead of true love.

I will love and marry the next man I take to my bed. I'm going to have a faithful, lifetime, soulmate-love like my grandparents had. Love, honor, and respect will form our union. Honesty will hold us together through the ups and downs of life.

Dylan picked up a fork and held it near the cluster of candles beside a bouquet of pink and white roses in a crystal vase. "Did your father buy this?"

"No." She picked up a knife from her mother's set and handed it to him. "Mom saw the one-of-a-kind utensils in a shop when my parents were on their honeymoon in Italy. Back then, they couldn't afford them. But last year, Mom found the artist who designed them and asked if he'd reproduce the pieces in a set for twenty and add the words *Ti amo, la mia passione* onto the extended handles. They were supposed to be a gift for me and my husbands."

Dylan tilted his head as the small letters came to life. "That sounds like something your mother would do."

"Yeah, she rarely says anything but when she does, her words speak to the heart." *Loyal, faithful, honest, and kind. Obedient to a fault.*

"Very true." He placed the forks back in their

rightful places on the table. He slid the gold candlesticks off to the side, closer to the cake. "Your father isn't the man he used to be."

"You noticed?" *You seemed quite comfortable with him.*

"Negotiations for the law firm were challenging, but as soon as we ended business matters…" He paused and looked into her eyes as if he were searching for something. "He told me I'd become one hell of an attorney."

That's a compliment, Dylan. Dad likes you. Always has. "Congrats on the *coup d'état*. How's your father? Still fighting the good fight as a state prosecutor?"

"Thanks. He's good. No, he's been working for me part-time doing legal research." Dylan pulled out her chair. "About six months ago he married a nice woman who has two young children. She's twenty-eight. She's pregnant. My dad is the father. It's good and awkward."

She sat. "Do you think it will last?"

He chuckled. "You don't hold back, do you?"

"No, I don't." *Maybe I should.*

"I'm pretty sure it's going to last. She's solid and loving. She asked me if I would accept her into the family and be more of an uncle than stepbrother to her kids, not just be an older brother to the ones she'll have with my father. She wants a big family and to have me involved as much as possible."

"That's considerate. Please tell me she signed a prenup." She slid the pink ribbon with her grandmother's wedding band off the napkin and placed it at the base of the cake stand.

"Nope. True love doesn't require one. When you meet her, you'll see why my dad fell hard for her." He cut a slice of cake and placed it on her plate. "Happy birthday."

"Thanks for rolling with this."

"Tell me what this is all about."

"It's probably either a plan B for my mom and dad, if I didn't show up for dinner. Or, more likely, it's a reminder not to settle for a man who wouldn't consider me his passion, his true love." She stabbed the cake with her fork. *I don't know that I'd recognize true love if it came and bit me in the ass.* "Dylan, are you running away from your father's new life?"

"I'm not running away from anything. I like my dad's wife. I like my stepbrothers. I miss everyone, but I want to be with you." He sat. He placed the ring from the pink velvet ribbon next to hers and served himself a slice of cake. "Why aren't you working full-time as an attorney? I get why you're doing the advertisements, but that wouldn't preclude you from practicing law."

She smeared the white frosting around the rim of the plate. *I can't handle walking into my father's building, lobby, office... I'm sick of hearing the accolades of my father's favorite employee—the man who lied his ass off and yet my dad believed him over me.*

"I work for a handful of clients. But I needed a change. I thought becoming a massage therapist would be great. And school was great. I loved getting massages, but I think I might hate giving them, which would explain why I spend all my time selling Ella's products at the spa instead of giving massages." *That, and the people who do come to me want legal advice, not someone touching them. Thank God, because I don't want to touch them.*

She sighed. *I need to change my life. Move. Start over. Go to an uninhabited island where my only contact would be electronic.*

"Open your mouth," he said.

She opened her mouth and, before she thought about anything else, she'd chewed and swallowed two pieces of cake he'd fed her. Obedience came naturally to her, clearly a genetic trait carried on from her mother.

"I'm going to tell you something I don't want you to tell anyone else." He placed his fork on his plate and stood. "Promise not to tell?"

"As long as it's not illegal," she whispered.

He turned her chair around where the back rested against the table and placed his hands on the table's edge on either side of her. "It's not illegal."

I might be in over my head with you. "Carry on." Inside she trembled with the desire to fall under his control, but she knew where that would lead—to a broken heart.

"I like things my way," he stated. "I'm demanding. I don't accept excuses. I will push and push and push until I get what I want, exactly the way I want it." He wet his lips and lowered his gaze to her chest. "I know what you are. I know what you're hiding from everyone else."

"And what do you think I am?" Her voice came out like a sexy purr. She hated that she wanted to give him exactly what he wanted. And she loved that, with the desire to obey his every command, she would please him and find pleasure herself. She had followed him down a path of sexual enlightenment a long time ago, and she would still follow him wherever he led.

"Angel, you're one submissive I need to dominate and own," he whispered. "And I will."

God help me. She opened and closed her mouth. Over and over, she tried to form words. No sounds. No denials. No lies.

He slid his hand down her shoulder, over her breast, to her lap, and gathered her skirt up until the slit at the front uncovered her panties. "Show me your pussy, Angel."

She inched her legs apart and slid her panties down her thighs.

"Open those wet kitty lips for me."

She obeyed.

"Push two fingers as far as you can inside the pussy which has always been owned by me."

"Dylan." She moaned as she slid her digits inside. *I need to come. I need some kind of...*

"Add another finger," he whispered.

Without hesitation, she surrendered to his authority. Her walls contracted around her fingers, and juices slid from her center. She panted as her pulse thundered in her ears.

"Remember when I spanked your ass and pussy, then made love to you the last night we were together?"

She had come so hard she'd scared the both of them. She nodded.

He pressed the side of his cheek to hers. "I know what I'm doing now."

She gasped. *If that had been instinct, I'm scared of what I'd do—*

"When I finally get my cock inside you, you're going to fall into bliss like you've never known." Hot lips brushed against her ear. "Once I have you, I'm never going to let you go."

A squeak escaped as she took a quick intake of air. *Fuck me now.*

"I love your hunger, Angel." He dragged his stubbly cheek across her smooth skin until his lips brushed against hers. "You're not allowed to come. If I taste you coming hard, I'm going to punish you."

She gazed into the eyes of a man who could and would do just that. "Punish me," she whispered.

"I will," he whispered. "I'll enjoy it." He slid down to one knee and nuzzled her neck. "Don't come."

"I can't promise I won't." *I might come before your mouth gets down there.* She pumped her fingers in and out of her pussy. *You've got me surrendering to you without even—*

"Bad girl." He gripped her thighs and forced them wider. "This is mine."

Her heart thumped and thumped so hard she could feel the vibration in her feet. Frenzied, she thrust farther in, attempting to find the spot where she would blow apart in bliss. *I can't control him. I can't do this, but I want to. I can't go back there. I can't let him—*

He pulled her hand from her pussy and licked the tips of her fingers. "You have to earn my mouth on your clit, my tongue inside your pussy, my fingers in your ass, my cock in your mouth."

She trembled.

"I'm going to strip you bare and dress you in raw confidence. You'll remember who you are. You'll remember you're mine. You've always been mine." He closed his mouth around two of her fingers and sucked as his other hand glided up her thigh, sending electrical currents into her bloodstream and branding the memory of his touch into her brain.

"Dylan." Her body craved his touch, his voice, his control. Her mind had shut down for the first time in…since he moved away.

Her fingers slipped from his lips as he rose. "I'll pick you up for dinner tomorrow."

Her brain immediately switched on and ran through her work schedule. "I have to work." *I'm taking over control.* She cupped his groin.

He pushed her hand away. "I told you. You have to earn my body. I'll take you out after work."

She huffed as she reached under the skirt of her dress and pulled her panties up where they belonged. Without control, he would take and take and take until she had nothing more to give. *You're not getting in my panties again. No sex. None. I'm not falling into the same pattern. No more games.* She slammed her thighs together and bolted up onto her feet. "I'm busy."

The corners of his lips curled into mild amusement.

"I'm not into the dominant-submissive lifestyle." *I'm not getting another mind screw.*

He stepped aside and blew out the candles. "Don't lie, Angel. You're smarter than that."

"I'm not lying." She couldn't take her eyes off him. He stood like a shadow in the garden, not real, but not fake. She ached to touch him, to have his hands on her, to hear his voice demanding her obedience. *I want someone to love me, all of me, not just the sexual parts.*

He shook his head as his lips fell into a line of disappointment. "I see we'll have to start with a lesson in honesty."

"I'm plenty honest. I'm open about my lovers, what I'd like for my future, and the type of sex that I'm willing to participate in."

The moon shined a spotlight on him as he stepped forward. "You have been fucking two men who hadn't a clue what they're doing. You have closed off your heart. You didn't catch your lovers cheating because *you didn't miss their touch.* You didn't miss anything about them but the space they took up in your cold mansion of a house."

He knew. How he knew, she had no idea, but he saw right through her appearance straight to her soul. He was a real man like Brice, like Jerry.

Shit. Jerry. He won't understand how weak I am around a dominant man. "Dylan, you couldn't be more wro—"

"You're starting at a reward deficit. Do you really want to lie about something we both know is true?"

"I don't know what you think we are, but I haven't agreed to anything." She turned away from him and stared at the simple cake symbolizing an easy life with the man of her dreams. A sexy man who would dominate her in bed. A man who would calm her mind, lessen her nightmares, protect her when the places and people in her past tried to swallow her whole.

Memories of the controlling man who she'd thought was kind and honest—until she found out in the most public way he wasn't—inundated her thoughts.

Cold shivers crept through her veins, freezing everything in its path. Stiff limbs held her in place when all she wanted was to run away, run so far the fear that held firmly inside her heart and mind would have no choice but to leave, to exit, to release her.

The world that was stripped away four years ago seemed insignificant against the chasm eating away at her future.

"Life was simpler when we were kids," she said. "Choices seemed to have logical consequences. Lies were easily discerned. The truth mattered..." *Then Joseph came along and changed everything. He targeted me. He took my thoughts and twisted them. He exploited my weaknesses. He set me up so not even my father would believe me. He took my heart and stomped on it. He took the position I should have held. He took my office. Took my friends. Took the hearts of the people I worked with and turned them against me. He undermined my credibility.*

Her chest ached with the betrayal. Marriage was sacred, and he had made her a mistress without her ever knowing. Not until he showed up with his wife the night her father promoted him and demoted her. *His wife had to know the truth. She had to have been a part of the scheme to discredit me. I was naïve. So naïve.*

"Angel, it's going to be okay. I'm here, and I'm not leaving you," Dylan said.

His hand touched hers.

A spark of electricity shocked her. She jerked away, but he held on. *I'm not going to be your secret submissive. I'm done with secrets. I'm living my life on my terms.*

Dylan led her a few feet away from the table and faced her. "Life has ups and downs."

She gazed into his eyes, finding the honest boy she'd loved all those years ago. "Yes, life does, but let's not talk about the ups or the downs anymore tonight."

His gaze fell on her lips. "Tomorrow evening?"

"Maybe." She closed her eyes. Being with him made her miss the bond they had. *I can't trust you like I used to.*

"Angel," he whispered. His lips touched hers as if he already had her.

Sparks of energy burst inside her belly, melting all the ice in her veins, and formed a closed circuit of arousal inside her clit and pussy walls.

He moaned as if his body reacted the same way to her touch. Maybe it was his confidence that pulled her back into his world. Maybe it was the master in him. Maybe it was the power exchange she craved and hadn't experienced in years that had her falling into submission.

He bent his knees and gathered the skirt of her dress. He drew it up her thighs as his tongue demanded her acquiescence as much as his hands had.

She gave in to her memories of their love. The energy buzzing in her center spread like medicine through her blood.

Hot to the touch, his hands gripped her thighs. He lifted her up.

She curled her legs around his waist. *Push my panties to the side and fuck me.* She unraveled his tie as the need to feel something deep inside her body overtook all reason. With nimble fingers, she removed his belt and unearthed his cock from his pants.

Yes. So big. So hot.

He broke their kiss. "I know what you need, angel. You need to feel control, but even in this, you don't have it. I do."

Damn it. No. She held the girth of his cock and wished it wasn't real. *I should be home masturbating until I am tired of trying to get some kind of orgasmic relief. Not running headfirst into a mistake I don't know how to get out of.* "I don't have protection. We can't do this."

He trembled as he labored to breathe. "I told you, my cock is not getting inside you until you earn it."

"I don't plan on spending enough time with you to *earn* it."

"Evangeline?" Jerry's voice cut like a knife deep into her heart. "Are you out here?"

"Shit," Dylan mumbled.

The man moved and shoved and smoothed down their clothes until they posed as the pinnacle of proper. He kissed her lightly on the cheek. "Why did he come back?"

"I'm here with Dylan," she said. "We're getting ready to leave."

"Good cover," Dylan whispered.

"It's the truth," she said. *And I'll tell Jerry how I would have been sexing it up with you, if you hadn't been the one demanding control.* "And I'm not in a relationship. I don't have to *cover up* for anything I do or say."

"I see you now," Jerry said. "No dancing tonight?"

"Not tonight," Dylan answered. "We spent most of the evening around the dinner table talking. It was a typical birthday dinner at the Zanipolo house." He led the way toward the patio where Jerry waited under the lights.

As they neared, she slowed.

Jerry stood like a man who knew exactly what she'd been doing and had considered doing. No questions existed in his green eyes. Shoulders square. Back straight. Muscles contracted and pumped. Arms crossed. Controlled fury sheathed every molecule in his body. She'd seen the look the moment the bell rang at the beginning of every one of his fights. That calculating flat stare that stayed in his eyes during every round and only lightened once his name was announced as the winner.

"I didn't realize you were coming back," Dylan said. "Angel and I were just catching up. We haven't seen each other in a long time."

Jerry nodded. "That explains why you two were alone."

"We haven't been out here long," she said.

Jerry took a step to the side and opened the door. "Nice seeing you, Dylan. I'm sure I'll see you again." He offered his hand.

Dylan shook Jerry's hand. "I hope so."

Dylan walked inside, but Jerry closed the door behind him, stopping her from entering the house and leaving her alone with the world champion fighter.

"I promised you a dance," Jerry said.

She glanced through the windows at Dylan's confused expression and then at Jerry's softening jaw. "I'd love a dance under the stars."

Jerry enclosed her hand in his and, with strides both strong and graceful, he led her to the dimly lit west section of the lawn. He extended his arm and guided her in a quarter circle to face him. "How far did you go with him?"

Chapter Eight
Jerry

The calm and collected nature of the woman who he'd learned from Danny and Jessica had been one of the highest paid and most sought-after celebrity attorneys in the country made his cock harder than ever.

"Were you spying on me?" she asked.

"When I opened the door to the outside, you were wrapped up in him." *You make me want to do things I shouldn't. Not here. Not with Dylan watching.* "Spying isn't really the word I'd use. It was more like stumbling into an intimate moment and wondering if an interruption would be appreciated or not."

"I was close to having sex. Thank God for the lack of my sexual readiness and his..." she paused as if she wanted to tell him something but decided at the last minute to change her mind. "Actually, we weren't close to doing it. He is not into public sex. Me?" She shrugged. "I've been known to do almost anything, anywhere." She didn't shy away from the truth. She didn't sugarcoat it, but she also didn't elaborate as much as he wished she would.

He stopped you and it wasn't because he wouldn't fuck in a discreet public place like this backyard. Why? "How interested in him are you?"

"Jerry"—she shook her head as she raised her chin toward the sky—"I don't know."

"Come here." He patted his chest with his right hand. "It's been a long day."

She averted her gaze as she curled around him and buried her head against his shoulder. "I'm not normally like this. Well, I am extremely sexual, but I'm not usually this…this…needy for a man."

He rested his cheek against the top of her head and held her. "Sometimes we have to take a detour to get where we want to be."

She nodded and seemed to cling more tightly to him.

"Your dad is nicer sober."

She let out a soft chuckle. "He knows you can kick his ass." She glided her hands over his firm ass and under his jacket, along the waistband of his pants. "I'm sorry about tonight, but dinner conversation was over-the-top, even for him."

"That's pretty much what your brother texted me. Ella gave him my number. Then your mother called me as I was driving over here and repeated the same words. Then Kaila? Is that your brother's wife?"

"Oh, jeez, Kaila called you?" She seemed to shrink as he held her.

"Yup." He held silent for a few more seconds. "She asked for tickets to Vegas for you, Rick, and the boys."

"Please tell me you're joking."

He laughed. "I am. She didn't ask for tickets, but she did call." He swayed with her in his arms and she easily fell into his rhythm. *Your family loves you. They need to stop judging your relationship choices. You don't go in their bedroom. They shouldn't go in yours. They won't when we're married.*

"I don't think I can go to Vegas with you."

"I'm not going to force you, but I'd like you to join me." *Say you will. I want you to be there for my last fight. It's going to be the start of the rest of our lives.* "You could bring a friend, but you'll have to celebrate with me privately after I win."

"That sure of yourself, are you?" The serious look on her face almost made him laugh.

"Yes. If you're there, I'll end my opponent's misery quickly." He smiled and her shoulders dropped an inch. *You're worried I'm not going to win. Are you anxious that I might get hurt?*

"How can you be so confident?" She shook her head, and the soft curls he would have tickling his thighs—hopefully tonight—drifted over her shoulders and down her arms.

"I've done my research. I know his weaknesses, but he doesn't know mine. No one does. Not yet. I intend to keep those a secret."

"Will you tell me?"

He leaned forward and whispered in her ear, "You and Ella."

"How are we weaknesses?"

I love both of you. "One special secret for you today," he whispered. "I need to know you can keep this one before I dole out more."

"I'm an attorney. I can keep secrets." She seemed to coil up like a snake about to bite.

"Is it Dylan that has you all tense? Is it this house? Family? The intimate table for two that I wasn't supposed to see? Is it that you feel slighted because I won't bare my soul to you without you baring yours to me?"

He questioned his choice to lay it on the line and

call her out. *She's going to either be up for taking me on, or I'll end up running her off.*

"Yes," she said. "All of the above. I want you to tell me everything."

"You're used to one-sided relationships, Evangeline. I want a full partnership with you. One where I'm in control."

She fell silent.

The gentle sway of their bodies stopped.

"Tonight seems to be a night for truths. So." She slid her hands from around his waist to his hands. "Here's the truth as I've seen it throughout my life. When I'm not in control, I'm not happy."

"You haven't been with the right men. In fact, you tend to choose boys who will cheat and enable you to say that men suck and continue whatever bullshit you say in your head about your body. You're a smart and sexy woman who needs her mind to shut down and surrender to a man…" *A man who loves you.* "I know it and so do you. A person doesn't become good friends with Derek if they don't want to shut off their brain for a while and let him make some decisions."

"Maybe he does that for you, but he doesn't do that for—"

"Cut the bullshit." He let go of her hands and shoved his hands into his pants pockets. *This is why I don't screw with younger women.* "He does it for me, and I do it for him. Derek knows his limits with me, and I know mine with him."

"You guys have sex?" Her mouth gaped.

"No. We're friends. We talk about life and being an alpha male in a world that either vilifies us or puts us on a pedestal to worship." *Maybe you're not who I think you are.*

She closed her mouth and lowered her gaze.

Nope. You're exactly who I think you are. A submissive who is scared to trust.

"Derek tiptoes around you. He holds his tongue. He isn't like that with anyone else. He knows you're more dominant than he is." She rubbed her palms over her stomach twice and dropped her hands. "I bet your mind shuts down with him because he's loyal and you trust him to have your back."

You're observant. "I can see how that might be true."

She glanced toward the house. "Are you going to kiss me or take me home?"

Am I that hard to read? I hope to kiss you and take you to my house, not yours. "Are you going to date Dylan?"

"I'm pretty sure I agreed to dinner tomorrow night with him."

You're going to fuck him before you ever see food. He'll make sure of that. "Did you date him when you were in high school?"

She clasped her hands and kept her gaze at the house. "I wasn't allowed to date." She fidgeted and kept staring at the house.

He followed her gaze.

Dylan stood watching them. He waved.

You two had some kind of heavy relationship in high school. First love? Sex for the first time? Jerry nodded at him. "I want you to remember something, beautiful."

"What's that?"

"The minute I enter a competition, I expect to

come out a winner." He gazed at her. *I should have listened to my gut when I first met you. We'd be married with a baby on the way by now. I wouldn't have been wishing for relationships that—*

Her chin lifted. Her eyelids rose until those big brown eyes stared at him like an innocent doe. Her red lips parted. "You're not in a competition."

He nodded. *Yes, I am, and the man waiting for you is a real competitor.* "Let's be honest with each other. Dylan thinks you're his. Part of you believes he's right. The rest of you, the biggest part of you, knows you're mine." *I hope you want to be mine.*

He took one step and filled the empty space between them. Fire burned in his blood to take her right there, right then. He cradled the back of her head. "No denials?"

She shuddered. "None."

He gently closed his fingers around her silky curls and tightened his fist. "I want all of your heart and soul." He carefully tilted her head until her mouth parted and she accepted his position of power.

A hushed moan rumbled from those supple lips.

His cock throbbed in preparation for action. He stepped forward as he guided her to arch her back.

She melted in his hands as he gently allowed her to depend on him, trust him to keep her from falling. The more she softened, the more his heart opened to her.

Babies. I want lots of babies with you.

Her eyes drifted shut. "Jerry."

"Happy birthday, Evangeline." He brushed his lips against her warm mouth but withheld a full kiss. "Stay the night with me."

She inhaled. "I can't."

He kissed the corner of her mouth. "You're going to have to wait for that kiss I promised you."

"I don't want to wait." She grabbed the lapels of his jacket.

As she pulled up for a kiss, clinging to his jacket, he closed his fingers around a thick rope of her silky hair and silently demanded her to stop.

"Please," she whined.

He swatted her ass. "No whining."

She gasped.

"You're not going to make me do anything," he whispered. "You'll either acquiesce because you want me, or you won't have me. You can think about what I have to offer and whether you believe it is something you want to have for the rest of your life. I told you yesterday, if you're interested in a real man, not some boy or boys, I'm available. If you want to continue playing games with men whom you can manipulate, forget my name and delete my number." He released her curls and quickly maneuvered her until she stood on her own and could follow him. "Take your time and think about it."

Dylan opened the door as they approached the house.

Jerry moved Evangeline in front of him. She stepped inside first and then he walked forward, ignoring his competition and ex-lover.

"Hey, Jerry, do you have a minute to talk?" Dylan asked.

Jerry strode through the house to the front door and opened it.

She walked out.

Jerry turned around. "What would you like to talk

about?"

"Are you happy with your current attorney?"

You want to talk business? Now? "Why?"

"I'd like to talk to you about what I can do for you as your potential attorney," Dylan said. "Late lunch tomorrow? Two o'clock?"

"I'll check my schedule and get back to you."

"I'll put you down on my calendar for two tomorrow. I'll have my assistant confirm the details tomorrow morning."

Jerry laughed. "Yeah, you do that." *Had you checked your messages, we wouldn't be having this conversation.* He turned around and walked outside.

Dylan joined him. "I'm a big fan. I have tickets for your fight in Vegas. How long do you think it will last?"

Evangeline sat in the back of the black limo waiting with the door closed.

Jerry's cock hurt from being hard for so damn long. He stopped and faced him. "Are you serious?" he whispered. "Cut the shit and tell me what your game is."

"I live directly across the street. You and Evangeline should come over and the three of us can hang out and talk."

"Dude, why are you acting like we don't know each other?"

Dylan kept his mouth shut.

Jerry huffed and joined Evangeline in the car. He closed his eyes and regrouped. *What's the big secret? You're acting like I'm going to announce to the world you and I had a thing. I don't do that.*

Dylan knocked on the window.

Evangeline rolled it down.

"Why don't you and Jerry come over to my house for a drink or two?" Dylan asked.

"Not tonight," Evangeline said. "I don't want to hear any business pitches."

"No business pitches," Dylan said. "I promise, no business at all. It will be casual. We can catch up." He glanced at Jerry. "All of us can catch up."

Evangeline grabbed Jerry's hand. "Nope. He's mine, and we're leaving now."

Dylan jerked his head back as if he'd been punched.

"Jerry, I'm ready to go home." Evangeline started rolling up the window.

"See you some other time, Dylan," Jerry said.

Dylan composed himself in a millisecond. "I'll see both of you soon." He stepped away from the car.

The tempered glass met the frame of metal and the outside world was shut out from the cocoon of the car.

"Derek, please take us to Evangeline's." He gazed at Evangeline's delicate hand gripping his. "So, I'm yours?" He skimmed up her body until his eyes met hers. *The slit in your dress is torn. Did he do that?*

"Yeah, you are. Dylan is hot for you. I can see it in his eyes. He's not taking you from me." She tightened her grip on his hand and raised her other to his chest. "I know you're not into guys. I know you think there is no way it would ever happen, but Dylan... He's a guy's guy and a woman's guy, and he always has been. I don't think he's changed in that regard. He's probably only honed his skills and become even more selective."

"You're worried *he'd* take me away from *you*?" *Never going to happen.* "But you're the one who is going out with him tomorrow night."

She let go of his hand and climbed onto his lap. Straddling him, she untied his bowtie and slipped it from around his neck. "You've fooled around with at least one man, haven't you?"

"Why do you think that?" *How perceptive are you?*

"Most men would be angry or argue or blush, but you're as calm and controlled as always. Words really don't faze you, do they?"

"Not so much. Would your feelings for me change if I told you I had or hadn't been with a man or multiple women and men?"

Her breathing accelerated. As she lowered her hips, the slit in her skirt ripped up past her panties. "No."

"What if I told you I'd only been with one man and I could count the number of women I've slept with on two hands?" He pushed the fabric of her dress behind her hips and slid her panties down her thighs.

She held onto his shoulders as he slipped the panties off one leg and then the other. "If you were a virgin, I wouldn't care."

Those mocha eyes staring at him seemed to bare a fragile soul, one he would love and cherish. He'd make her stronger. He'd protect her. He'd heal her wounds and she would heal his.

He cradled the back of her head. "I'm yours. But you need to know that I am particular with what I will and won't do in and out of bed. I'm the one in control. I stay in control in every aspect of my life. I don't play with toys or ropes or devices. I dominate naturally and you will submit automatically. I won't force you to do anything, but if you decide you want forever with me like I do you, I expect you to follow my rules. All of them."

Evangeline's eyes grew wide, but she didn't say anything.

Speechless? "The truth of my past is that I have had consensual sex with ten women and one man as an adult. Jessica X is a past lover, and Dylan Russo is the only man I've slept with. I expect you to keep both of their names between us. I'm telling you this only because those are the only two people who you will most likely know."

"Oh, my God," she mumbled. "She's older than you. A lot older... You and Dylan. But he acted like he didn't know you." Her jaw dropped, leaving those luscious lips parted. She inched her thighs farther apart and lowered her hips until her pussy pushed against the top of his cock.

That's it, baby. Get closer. Show me you want me. "Yeah, which is one of the reasons I'm telling you. Secrets ruin relationships. I don't mind that you've slept with other men or women, but I want to know the ones whom you loved."

Her mouth dropped open and her butt hit his lap. "You..." Her lips parted again to speak but she tilted her head to the side and stared blankly at him.

The vehicle jerked to the right.

Jerry wrapped her up in his arms and instinctively shifted to protect her with the sudden movement. He enclosed her safely under him across the long line of seats.

"Sorry," Derek shouted. "Obstruction in the road."

Derek's voice seemed to jar her out of her thoughts.

"Why did he act like he didn't know you?" she

asked.

"I don't know," Jerry said. "I rolled with it, but it was weird. We left our relationship as friends—or at least I thought we had."

She exhaled against his lips. "You slept with Dylan."

"Yeah. I did. I haven't been with any guy since."

"I've heard that before," she scoffed and turned her head, leaving him staring at her reddening cheek.

"It's true. I'd been physically and sexually abused by men when I was a kid. Believe me, I've never been into guys. Never. Not until three years ago, when I randomly met Dylan at a restaurant bar. The last person who I felt that comfortable with had been Jessica and I almost married her. So, don't act like I'm a liar. That is one thing I'm not." *Although I am leaving out my attraction to Brice. But you probably don't even know him, and I don't ever plan on acting on it. I can't even explain it to myself. It makes no sense.*

She nodded. "Sorry." She exhaled and the color in her cheeks lightened to pink. "I'm sorry." She faced him. "I'd like to sit up. May I?"

He rotated and shifted to the seat across from her as she adjusted her dress and position.

"I'm surprised and truly sorry you've had to deal with abuse. Were the men who assaulted you prosecuted?" She lifted her hands, lowered her gaze, and shook her head. "Please don't take that as judgement, if you didn't tell anyone or if there were other circumstances surrounding it that prevented prosecution. It's a devastating situation to be in, and I would never have thought anything like that had happened to you."

"They weren't prosecuted, but they all died in a fire that I was lucky enough to survive. That night is still a blur, but somehow little Ella pulled me and my mom out and got us to the broken-down barn on the farm between her land and my mom's. Ella was as brave then as she is now."

Evangeline hugged her stomach and leaned over her knees. "Holy shit. Did your mother start the fire?"

"Yeah, she wanted everyone to die, me included. The sheriff called it a tragic accident, but they knew what had happened. My aunt Mae and her son, my cousin Highland, came to the barn and took us home to Oklahoma with them. My mother passed away less than a year later from a drug overdose. Aunt Mae and her husband Major Wynn adopted me. Highland was an adult and became more like an extra father than a brother or cousin. They gave me the support and love of a real family. Ella, her husbands, and Dylan are the only people, besides you, who know about my real past."

She rose to her elbows and covered her eyes. "So, your mother's sister or father's sister adopted you?"

"Mother's sister. The first year after the fire, Major Wynn took me everywhere with him when Momma Mae was working as a financial advisor. Major didn't let me be alone with my biological mother. He homeschooled me at the boxing and wrestling training facility he owned. He and Highland taught me how to fight, and Momma Mae taught me how to run a profitable business. Once my mother passed away, he opened a new facility in Memphis and we moved. This is where I went to high school." *What is going through your mind? Is my past going to end things with us?*

She inhaled as she raised her head and leaned back against the seat. "I'm speechless. I thought…" The exhale that exited her lips seemed to take forever. She stared into his eyes. "No one ever questioned your past, did they?"

He shook his head. "Nope. Momma Mae, Major, and Highland scared the shit out of most people. We all shared flaming red hair, green eyes, and damn near transparent white skin. The house fire burned my past, and my biological parents were dead. Ella could have made a ton of money selling me out, but she didn't. She stayed the same loyal girl she'd always been. I would do anything for her. I love her."

Her shoulders lifted and the pulse in her neck bulged as it throbbed. "You love her?"

"I love her like a sister," he qualified the previous statement. "We've always been best friends. Nothing else. Ever."

Her shoulders dropped and her face seemed to relax. "Momma Mae called you her miracle baby in interviews." Tears filled her eyes and she swallowed hard. "The Wynns loved you."

He cleared his throat. "Yeah. It's been tough without them." *I want a family like that. I want to be a dad like Major was to me. I want a wife to love. I want you to be my wife, Evan. I want you to be the constant in my life.*

"Do you think you'll ever talk about any of your past publicly?"

"No, but when I see signs of abuse, I step in and get involved. I have a fund for kids who've been abused and/or bullied set up with four inner-city gyms and with all the fitness facilities my company owns. The kids have a safe place to go every day of the week. They get food and clothes, whatever they need. All they have to do is stay off drugs and alcohol, don't join a gang, and show up. I stop in unannounced and whoever is there gets a group exercise session with me. The kids who are there, year after year, get their technical training or college paid for by me. It's a great program. I finished putting a kid through med school last year. He's the first doctor out of the kids I've sponsored."

She spread her legs and slapped her chest over her heart, letting out a soft sigh. "Why don't you tell anyone?"

"I don't want kids showing up with the sole purpose to meet me. I want them to go regularly because they want a better life, a group of people who want to see them succeed, and they're willing to sacrifice in order to get it. The kids I meet are going to be successful and happy because they recognize and take the opportunities offered. I'm just there to help facilitate their success."

She asked question after question about his personal and mostly anonymous charity. The more he told her about the kids, the more she opened her body and moved closer to him, until she ended up on his lap straddling him again.

"You have a heart for kids," she whispered. "You're going to make a great father." She lowered her eyelids and moaned. "I want to go home with you…but I can't."

"How about we make it another night? Plan to come over and stay for dinner or longer."

She nodded. "You might not be interested in me after I tell you something." She leaned forward and rested her head on his shoulder.

"I doubt it, but tell me."

"I'm one of the girls who poses for Ella's oils. I am close with my modeling partner and we had sex last night. It was unexpected, and I feel like you deserve full disclosure. I love him. I have for a long time, but he's a bachelor and travels. He's older. Fifteen years older than me. I doubt he'll ever settle down."

"I don't have a problem with you posing for Ella's oils, but we'll have to discuss exclusivity in our relationship. Once you're with me, you might find that you're less interested in having sex with other men and more interested in having sex with only me." *Once you sleep in my bed, you'll want to stay.*

Derek stopped the car at the back gate.

She kissed Jerry's nose and climbed off him. "I'm going to be honest. I love sex. I have been told I have a borderline sex addiction which, most likely, is why I end up in sexual relationships with multiple partners. If we decide to give a long-term relationship a try, which I would really like to, I'd need you to decide on one or two other men you'd allow me to fuck regularly. You can set the rules. I will follow your rules. All of your rules. But I do need this one allowance."

Before he could wrap his mind around her ultimatum, she opened the car door and typed in the code for the door gate beside the car entrance and disappeared behind the heavy foliage blocking the backyard from any passersby.

She's the one. She's going to be the mother of my children. Evangeline Zanipolo, you're mine.

Chapter Nine
Brice

Brice tossed and turned in his bed. He wrestled with the T-shirt and pajama pants he'd worn in case Evangeline decided at the last minute she wanted company tonight. She hadn't called to talk or let him know she got home safely. She always called to check in at least once a day, but she hadn't yesterday and now instead of sleeping nude, he was ready to leave at a moment's notice to get any amount of time with her.

I should have called her. She's probably avoiding me because we had unprotected sex. I should call now. Tell her I love her and I'm ready to commit. He unplugged his phone on the nightstand and picked it up. *I could start off by asking how she fared at her parent's house? Did the birthday dinner festivities go well? Did your father verbally abuse you as usual? Did your mother sit there and watch? Did your father have her call whoever you brought and apologize for him to test their personality? Did you bring someone who will continue to forgive or make excuses for your father's behavior?*

He tugged the bottom of his shirt down. *That man is an asshole. I should have gone with her. I should have protected her. I should stop overthinking all of this and call.* He swiped the screen of his phone. *Four in the morning. It's too early to call. She's probably sleeping in her bed at her parents' house. I should have asked her to marry me last night. If I had, I wouldn't be here fully dress and alone, I'd be naked and asleep with my smart and sassy Evangeline snuggled up asleep next to me.*

The phone vibrated in his hand.

Evangeline. Yes.

He slid his finger across the screen. "That must have been one big, thirtieth-birthday bash with the fam," Brice teased.

"Henry is here," Evangeline whispered. The panic in her voice sent him out from under the covers and running to his safe in the closet. "I need help."

"Where are you?" he asked. *Is he at your parent's house? Did he show up at your birthday dinner? Did you invite him to stay? Did he stalk you? Follow you home?*

"I'm at home," she whispered. "He's got a gun. Hurry. He's out of control. I called Cal and my friend on the police force and—"

"Evangeline," Henry screamed.

"Shit. He's found—" The call ended.

He grabbed his gun and holster and raced out of the penthouse and into the elevator. He hit the button for the garage level. *Go. Go. Go.*

He slid the holster over his shoulders and checked his gun. He dialed her. *Come on Evan. Come on and answer.*

The call rolled straight to voicemail. He dialed again. *Answer the damn phone.*

The elevator doors opened, and he sprinted through the garage to his car. *I'm not losing you, Evan. I'm not. I can't.*

After he tried for a third time, he left a message. "I'm on my way," he said. "Get somewhere safe." He didn't want to alert Henry to the secret safe room in the house in case Henry had confiscated her phone and checked her voicemail.

With his bare foot pushing the accelerator to the floor, he practically flew out of the hotel parking garage onto the street. The tires screeched as he turned down one road to another, racing toward her house. *Go to the safe room. Please, this is why I added it to your house. Please, please, please, don't try and talk him down. You're his target, Evan. You're the one he wants to hurt when he's out of control.*

His phone rang.

He answered before any of the information popped up on the screen. "Evan?"

"It's Cal. Evangeline called me. I'm on my way to her house. Henry is there. He's had another psychotic break. It's been coming for a few months now. I think Todd and Rachel have been supplying Henry with drugs. Henry loves you. Will you come and help me get him? I've got a team for backup meeting me there, and I've put in a call to the police."

"I'm already on the way. Cal, if he hurts her, that's it. I'm making her press charges. I love her. I am going to marry—"

"I know you love her, but he needs help, not jail. Listen, I've got everything in place to keep him out of the system. He needs rehab and to stay away from Rachel and Todd. He's not going to hurt Evangeline. He is dangerous to himself, not—"

"He's got a fucking gun," Brice shouted. "Where did he get a gun?"

"I don't know, but I'll find out. If you get there before me, talk him down," Cal said. "This is the last time. I promise." Cal ended the call.

Brice had heard that same promise the last five times Henry showed up at Evangeline's. Henry didn't mean to break her door. Henry didn't mean to break her window. Henry didn't mean to slap her. Henry didn't mean to toss her down the stairs. Henry didn't mean to slice her arm with the kitchen knife. Henry didn't mean, didn't mean, didn't mean. The excuses seemed to never end. Henry was dangerous to others, and to himself.

It had been different when Henry was a boy. Cal had managed his medication, kept him on schedule, brought him regularly to a psychiatrist. It hadn't been easy, but Henry was just like every other kid in school as long as he was on the right meds. When a prescription needed changing, they learned quickly that a short stint in the hospital to adjust dosage and medication kept Henry safe from his self-destructive tendencies.

Brice had been there for Cal and Henry through the years. Henry was on the path to success, but then high school ended. Henry got sucked into a dangerous crowd during college. Illegal drugs and alcohol became his life. Then rehabs, psychiatric hospitals, and clinics became a quarterly occurrence. Cal stood by his son, and eventually Henry began to manage his mental illness and stay sober on his own, finding new ways to cope and new friends. On his meds, Henry had found his passion for life, for coding encryption, for fighting fires with a team of guys he could count on. He had a bright future ahead with Evangeline by his side, but then Todd joined them—conniving asshole Todd who brought narcissist Rachel into their lives. Those two fed Henry's paranoia, sent him on an emotional rollercoaster of pain and heartache, drugs, and sex. They lied to Evangeline about their true intentions and drug use. They lied, lied, and lied some more while Evangeline believed and when she found out the truth, forgave.

Rachel and Todd had torn friendships apart, wrecked marriages, and conned their way into financial security, while stepping on the backs of good, trusting people. *I hate what they've done to you. I hate what they've done to Henry. I hate that I'm scared that something horrible has happened to you. I can't live without you, Evangeline. I love you.*

Brice took a right onto Evan's street and slowed as he approached her house. The night sky clung to the cream-colored mansion's exterior and tricked the eye into seeing shapes of creatures behind the overgrowth of plants and shrubs. Darkness reigned tonight. Everywhere he looked, brought his mind back to the same place.

He methodically scanned the area, hoping to see at least one police vehicle and Cal's SUV.

The street remained deserted. No sign of Cal, Cal's team of professionals, the police, or Henry.

How did Henry get here? Hitch hike? Did Rachel drop him off? Did he park his car somewhere else and walk? This time is different.

There was nothing indicating Henry or Evangeline were there.

He parked in front of Evangeline's historic home. *Could Henry be hiding in the bushes? Could those shadows be him?* He took a second to assess his view.

The normally secured black iron gate outside the front entrance of her property had been broken off its hinges and tossed aside. His gaze followed the walkway up the concrete stairs to the white porch. The front double doors that had always stayed closed and locked were gone. A large rectangular hole served as an entrance for anyone who dared to enter. It wouldn't take long before street dwellers or criminals decided to wander into the mansion. The gate and house alarms should have been ringing so loud all the neighbors would have called the authorities or at least checked on Evangeline, but the silence surrounding him became deafening. *Where are the police? Did Henry disable your security system? Did he cancel your service? Why aren't any of the lights on? Did he cut your electricity? Did he dismantle the backup generator?*

Fear like he'd never known rushed through his veins. *Please be safe. Please be safe.* He sprung from the car in a mad dash to find her.

Taking the stairs two at a time, Brice's rapidly beating heart remained the only sound he heard. Entering the home, he searched for any sound of movement, any sign of life.

As he crossed the cold marble floor of the foyer, he removed his gun from his shoulder holster. The missing doors lay on the floor inside the empty entrance. *Henry took off the damn doors. Those things are heavy as shit. What the hell are you on, boy?*

"Henry," he shouted. "Are you here?" He held his breath, hoping to hear something, anything that might indicate Evangeline was alive.

If Henry was still inside, the kid wasn't giving up his location. *I should have come over earlier. I should have house-sat for her. I should have insisted she stay with me. I should have hired a bodyguard until Henry was found and placed in a rehab facility.*

He hugged the walls as he made his way through the first floor of the enormous house. *I should call 9-1-1. Cal and Evangeline never call the cops on duty. They call friends to help them keep Henry out of jail. The kid needs to stay on his meds and away from relationships and drugs. Maybe a stint in jail would scare him into staying clean for good and remaining on his fucking meds.*

Ascending the stairs to the second floor, he tightly gripped the handle of his pistol. The last time Henry went off the rails, Brice found him on the second floor pacing the hallway swinging a hammer at some invisible adversary. This time, the young man had a gun.

"Henry," he shouted. "It's Brice. Are you okay?"

The house remained eerily quiet.

He stopped at the top of the stairs. "Henry? I'm here to help."

"Brice?" Henry yelled.

"Yeah, buddy. It's me. Brice. Where are you?" *Please don't have Evan. Please don't make me hurt you.*

"I'm in her office. I can't find Evan. She was here, and now she's gone."

Brice peeked down the hall and saw a revolver close by on the floor. He slid his gun into the holster and grabbed his phone from his front pocket. He typed a text to Henry's father Cal, giving their location in the house.

"Help me find her, Brice," Henry yelled. "She's in

the house. I know she's in the house."

The banging of metal against wood kept Brice from moving. *What do you have now? Evan doesn't own any guns. You cleaned out her house of fucking everything. What could you have?*

"Where. Is. She?" Henry screamed. "Where. Is. She?"

"I don't know, Henry," Brice said. *You better be in the safe room I built you, Evan.*

"Hen-ry," Cal shouted. "Henry, it's going to be okay." The scuff of leather, the light footsteps against wood was entirely too familiar—Cal in rescue mode as Henry brandished a weapon threatening to hurt himself or, since he met Evangeline, her.

Cal nodded and stood by Brice.

"Thank you. Thank you. Go find Evan," Cal whispered. "Make sure she's okay. I'll get him out and in the hospital. I've got help downstairs and at all the exits. He won't get away. I should have forced him into a facility when he told me about marrying Rachel. She's the one who gave him the gun as a present for being an integral part of the wedding and leaving Evangeline for them. Do you fucking believe that?" His hands shook. "That bitch has been systematically ruining my son's life. Her antics are going to kill me." He inhaled, his demeanor calm and collected, and walked toward Henry's voice. "Henry, it's going to be okay. I'm here."

Brice gazed down the hall and saw Henry come out and drop an axe on the floor.

"Dad, I can't find her," Henry said. He rubbed his face and cried. "Dad, I can't find her. I can't find her."

Big Cal Westland showed no fear as he opened his

arms to his son. The man loved his boy fiercely. "I love you, Henry."

Like a child needing his father's protection, Henry walked right into his father's arms. "I'm scared." Henry sounded like a lost little boy. "I'm scared."

Brice raced up the stairs to the safe room in the attic. *Please be here.* He typed in the code and the door opened.

Evan was crouched naked in the darkest corner, shaking.

"Oh, my God," Brice mumbled. *This can never happen again.* He took off his shirt and walked toward her.

She rose slowly. Bruises on her legs. Her arms. Her face. Wet hair.

"Is Henry okay?" she asked.

How could you even care how he is after what he did? He nodded. "Cal is taking him to the hospital."

"Good." She picked up her phone from the floor. Her hands shook so hard, the phone dropped to the hardwood. "I'm cold. Not scared. I'm just cold." Her hands trembled as she fumbled to retrieve her phone again.

He nodded as he picked up her phone. *It's a thousand degrees up here. You're in shock.* "I've got it. Take a minute and breathe."

His phone buzzed. *Cal.*

—I've got Henry in the car. My team got the front doors back on the hinges and locked. The electricity is on, and the alarm has been reset. The gate in the front might take a day to get fixed, but a temporary one will be up in a few hours. Tell her to change the password to the alarm and to stay somewhere else until I call her.

I don't know what he's on, but he's crashed hard in the back of my truck. I'll pay for the damages and any therapy she needs. I'm sorry, Brice. I know you love her. Let me know she's okay.—

He texted back that she would be with him for the rest of her life, and if Henry ever came near her again, the police would be called.

"Was that Cal?" she asked.

He closed his hand around hers. "Yes. You're staying with me for a while."

She looked up at him with blank eyes. "I was in the shower. I fell." She touched her cheek and winced. "He *hit* me."

Looks like he flung you around too. "Did you lose consciousness?"

"No. I don't know. I didn't throw up. I ran…and slipped. He kept screaming. Over and over. There was nothing I could say to calm him. I kicked him, but he kept coming at me. What was he on? Where did he get it?"

"I don't know. We'll let Cal handle all that." He wiped the perspiration from his face as sweat gathered and trickled down his cheeks and neck. *It's hot as hell. Why didn't I add a separate air conditioning unit for this room?*

"He came up here. He couldn't find me." She closed her eyes. "Thank you for building this room. I thought you were crazy for doing it, but you might have saved my life tonight." She opened her eyes and a spark of life flickered inside her beautiful brown irises. "Am I making any sense?"

"Yes, my love," he said. "You're making sense."

"I don't want to stay here tonight," she said.

"You're staying with me, Evan. You're not coming back here." He helped her into his T-shirt and guided her out of the house as she talked through the events of the night. The dinner. Jerry. Her father. Dylan. The almost sex. The semi-ultimatum she gave Jerry. Her plans with Dylan for dinner. The call from Jerry about scheduling their first real date. The hot shower. Henry. The gun. Henry. The axe. Henry. Henry. Henry.

He buckled her securely into the passenger seat of his car and drove to the hotel on autopilot. The memories of his own childhood with a father who lashed out when work had pushed him to his limit flooded his consciousness. His father coming home to a scrawny, sensitive son with a curiosity that couldn't be contained. The curiosity his mother had indulged, loved, laughed about, and his father had too, until she died that horrible day. Maybe if his father had taken medicine, he wouldn't have been so angry, so bitter, so mean. *Maybe I would have married Evangeline years ago instead of guarding my heart for so long.*

He parked the car and looked over at her. *You snuck inside anyway. You do that to people. They love you. I love you.*

She gazed at him. "I'm okay." A pained smile parted her swollen lips. "I promise, I'm okay. And I'm going to sell the house. You were right. I never should have bought the place. I thought I would change the history with love inside it, make it better, but I didn't." She placed her hand on his cheek. "You helped change it a little. Putting in that room saved both my life and Henry's."

He covered her hand on his cheek and held it there. *I need you to be in my life for the rest of it.* "I can't lose you, Evan."

"You're not going to lose me."

"Let's go inside." He kissed her palm and released her hand.

To his irritation, she opened her door and got out.

He quickly exited the car and met her at the front of his car.

Hand in hand, they strolled into the building through his private entrance and rode the elevator up to the penthouse. He led her inside to his bedroom.

"You want me to stay in your bedroom?"

"Yes. You're moving in with me here until we find a more suitable location to live. Somewhere we can build a house, our house. I have land near Austin, Texas. It's close to Cade's ranch there. Have you been? Would you consider relocating?" *If you want to be with Dylan and Jerry, they both have ranches in the same area. When I travel, one or both of them could take care of you. I bet both of them would move for you.*

She took off her shirt and walked into the bathroom.

He followed. He'd been through this before with her, only this time she wasn't Henry's anymore. Henry had hit her, wrestled with her, fought her. She might have fallen, but the man's large handprints were left on her skin like tattoos in the form of bruises. Nothing indicated a more serious injury.

Her shoulder muscles tightened as she ran her hand along the darkened circle of black and blue on her face and neck that marked Henry's anger.

Brice walked into his closet on the other side of the vanity and typed in the code on the panel inside his tie cabinet. The wall slid on a track to the right, and the safe room he installed opened. He typed in the code for the safe and opened it. He placed the shoulder holster and gun inside and locked the safe again. He rarely brought his gun anywhere, but he didn't want Henry to be the only man armed in a room. He stepped out and closed it up.

"Brice?" she called.

"Just locking up my gun." He undressed and joined her in front of the vanity. He washed his hands and face.

"Are we… Are you asking me to move in with you?" she asked.

He dried his face and picked up his toothbrush. He opened the top drawer of the middle cabinet and handed her a pink toothbrush and mint toothpaste.

She took the items and opened them.

"Yeah," he said. "You move in, and I get to take care of you. Win-win." *When are you going to try and forget about what happened with us having unprotected sex?*

She squeezed a dollop of paste onto her toothbrush and handed him the tube. "What about other men in our lives?" She shoved the toothbrush into her mouth and brushed as her gaze met his.

"So, you haven't gone to your therapist lately, have you?"

She rolled her eyes, lifted her chin, and stopped brushing for a second. "No. I don't see how using sex to deal with my problems is a bad thing. Now, answer the question."

He glared at her. "Don't order me."

She looked away. "Sorry. I don't want a therapy session right now. I'd prefer to make love to you. To talk about the future, not dwell on a future I might not have had the opportunity of living, if you hadn't built me that room and come to my rescue tonight."

He added paste to his brush and twisted the cap back on the tube. "As long as we're all in agreement and willing to work together, I'll allow two other men into our relationship. Two at the most. I know you need some things I don't do." *I'm going to need at least one more man to keep you happy sexually. Dylan and Jerry would be perfect, but Jerry might not go for it. Not the Jerry I know.*

Honesty kept them together as friends all these years. Total truth in private had been what changed his perception of her, what pushed him into an intimate and loving relationship with her. Their sexual compatibility kept their chemistry at a constant boiling point. That they both processed everything with sex deepened their understanding of each other's needs.

She spit into the sink and turned on the faucet.

He continued brushing as she finished up.

For all the times they'd spent the night together, this would be the first in *his* bed. The first sharing his bathroom. His sink. His shower. The first with an expectation of marriage.

"You're really okay with me and other men?"

If she didn't have the purple bruise on her cheek, he would have laughed at the disbelief in her wide-eyed gaze. He walked to the shower and turned it on. "Come here." He held the door open for her.

She walked in. "Are you going to answer my question?"

He stepped in and poured body wash onto a cloth. "Yes."

"Yes, you're going to answer the question, or yes, you're okay with me bringing other men into our bed for sex and more?" She took the cloth from his hand. "You should use Ella's soaps for your hotels. They're better than this crap."

He laughed. "So, you think my hotel has crap bathing products?" *When you recover, you really recover.*

"Yes. I keep telling you to talk to Ella and Troy about getting their body products into your hotels and spas, but you seem pig-headed about changing." She slid the cloth from his forearm to his shoulder, raised his arm and rotated the cloth under and down in a smooth massage stroke.

You massage so nicely when you're not skin to skin. The pressure is firm and gentle, loving. "I'll talk to Ella and Troy. Why don't you set up the appointment?"

She caressed his skin as she glided over his chest with the cloth.

The way she stroked him was like no other woman had. His cock rose, and as she reached it, she leaned against him.

She transferred the cloth to him and stroked his cock. "I'd love to do that for you."

Carefully, he slid the soapy cloth over her back. "Does this hurt?"

"No," she whispered. "My right hip hurts a little. Not too much." Her lovely hands slid up and down his shaft.

He added more soap to the cloth.

"You wouldn't have to do that if you used Ella's body wash," she said.

"The hard sell," he said. He glided over her shoulders and leaned back to wash her chest and—

"Just sayin'. If I'm going to be living with you, we might as well improve your company's bath and body accessories." She raised her arms and widened her stance. "You should be using her products anyway. Your abs and ass are on the tangerine bliss oil."

"I appreciate your input. I have a lot of hotels, and she can't accommodate the increase in production at this time. I have a standing appointment with her once a year to discuss business opportunities." *If she moved to Cade's ranch in Texas, she could expand her manufacturing facility and supply my hotels.* He glided the soapy cloth over her and nudged her backward into the line of water.

"Mmm. I didn't know." She leaned her head back and inhaled as the cleansing fluid cascaded over her hair and back. The suds disappeared as she shifted side to side and the water sluiced along her skin.

Brice stopped the soapy caress at her hip. "He didn't attempt or succeed in…?"

She shook her head. "No. He wasn't interested in that."

He slid the bubbly cloth between her legs and moved forward into the water. He let the cloth drop and dipped his finger inside her. "No one else?"

"No," she whispered. "I'm actually very responsible when it comes to sex. Condoms are a must."

"Except with me," he said. "You want my cum here." He wiggled his finger inside her pussy. "Don't you?"

"Yes," she whispered.

He slid his finger from her sex and turned off the water.

She squeezed the water from her hair and placed her hand in his.

"Me and you," he said. "No one is separating us. You sleep in bed with me. Every night unless we agree on another man living with us. Then you can stay with him instead of traveling with me when I'm working." *Most of my hotels are in Texas. I could cut my traveling in half if we lived on my ranch there. The house is plenty big.*

They dried off and climbed into bed.

She lay on her back, the bedcovers turned down at her feet.

He kissed her shoulder. "I love you." He kissed a straight path down her body to her pussy and crawled between her legs. He opened her folds and gazed at her.

"Brice, we could actually..." She exhaled and splayed her legs wider, opening her heart and body to him.

"Want my tongue or cock?" *Pick my cock.*

Juices glistened at her entrance.

"I'm the only girl you will ever have sex with again. Only me. No other woman. Are you really okay with that?"

"Yes. Hell, yes. Have no doubts that I am good with having you in my bed every night for the rest of my life. I want this. Right now. Forever."

She wove her fingers through his hair. "I want whatever you want."

He moaned and kissed her pretty pussy. "That's the right answer, Evan. You always give me the correct answer." He laved along her slit. Up. Up. Up. Over her clit. He licked in short, driving bursts, plumping her clit until she was about to explode.

She gasped and tensed.

He spread her folds wide and tapped her clit with the flat of his tongue.

The muscles in her thighs flexed.

You're close. So close. He licked along her entrance and dipped his tongue in, teasing her.

Her moans grew louder.

He rubbed his stubbly cheek against her clit and went back to licking up her center to her clit. Tap. Tap. Tap. He thrust his tongue hard, lashing her clit.

"Brice," she squeaked. She gripped his hair between her fingers and pulled his face to her pussy. "I'm coming. Oh. My. God."

A gush of pussy juices squirted on his face. He lapped at her pussy and rubbed his face against her entrance.

She gasped and ground her hips. "I need your cock. I need your cock. In. Me. In. Me. Brice. In. Me."

He lunged forward and slammed his hard cock into the woman he loved. Her pussy gripped him and set to pumping his shaft.

"Yes," she shouted.

He thrust and backed out but left the head of his cock inside her. He powered into her. In. In. In. Her walls opened and closed, massaging his dick, pulling him deeper, giving him what he desired—a person to call home. *Mine. You're mine. You'll always be mine.*

"It's happening again," she gasped. "I'm coming again."

He let go and his cock jerked. Her pussy heated and surged with her luscious juices. He came with a roar. His cock spurted inside her. *I love you, Evan. I love you.*

He rocked his pelvis as he shuddered with each glorious release of cum into her pussy. He gazed down and his beautiful Evangeline gave him a sexy, sleepy smile. "Good?"

"Never had better," she whispered.

He kissed the side that wasn't swollen. "Flattery will get you everywhere with me." He rolled to her side and relaxed onto his back. His cock perked up as she shifted and snuggled against his side.

"Thank you," she whispered. "I needed that."

"I know, my love," he said. "I know."

He caressed up and down her back, avoiding the bruises, as she swiftly transitioned into the land of dreams.

He had some work to do to keep her from having unprotected sex with Dylan or Jerry for the next week or two. He needed to find out if her wish of a multiple-partner relationship like she wanted would be possible with the other two men. He was pretty sure Jerry tolerated him because of his friendship with Ella and Cade. The guy might beat the crap out of him for even suggesting something like sharing Evangeline or joining the two of them in bed. He had a pretty decent chance with Dylan agreeing, but moving? Would Dylan move from Memphis when he just got here? Would Jerry ever move? He needed help—Cade Jackson's help.

Chapter Ten
Dylan

Finding the warehouse in the middle of the country where Evangeline was shooting the latest Oils by Ella advertisement and product photos had proven to be an ordeal. The GPS locked up. The old landmarks he expected to see were gone. One dirt road led to another and another until Dylan wanted to scream. By the time he found the location, one custom-made sports car—Brice's—and one unknown SUV were the only ones in the parking lot, instead of the five cars Evan had told him would be there.

Assuming he'd missed the photo shoot, he entered the building. A dimly lit, empty lobby greeted him, offering a choice of opening two black doors—one marked *Boudoir*, the other *Classic*. A white note with his name was taped to the boudoir door.

Please be quiet as you enter. Session in progress.

He opened the door and entered.

Cameras, monitors, microphones, and spotlights filled the open design with three different styles of bedroom suites. Sexy moans resounded in the room. He strode forward, catching a nod from a short man with a baseball cap turned backward standing behind a camera. The man pointed to a chair a few feet from the director's chair.

Approaching the designated chair, he spotted a

large monitor turned on to the right. *Is that for an audience? For me? Is this your apology for canceling on me last night?*

A close-up of an older man with blond hair licking Evangeline's glistening inner thigh appeared on the screen.

She lifted her hips and moaned.

"Tastes so good," the man whispered.

Dylan recognized the voice but couldn't place it. Strong jaw. That tongue... *I know that tongue. What is his name?*

"Need your cock. Need you," she begged.

The man launched forward and shoved his big cock into her wet pussy.

"Yes," Evan shouted.

Dylan slid his hand over his groin. *Brice Loffiten. That cock belongs to sensitive and private billionaire mogul Brice Loffiten. This isn't part of Ella's ads. What is going on?*

The man's cock shuttled in and out of her. In and out. In and out. His heavy balls drew up against his shaft. The man was going to come and come hard.

"Yeah, baby," Brice grunted. "Squeeze my cock. Squeeze it."

She gasped as he thrust into her and froze.

They shuddered and moaned in unison.

Dylan's mouth dropped open. *First I find you with my ex-lover Jerry Wynn and now Brice?* He cupped his cock. *I want to join in. I want to fuck both of you. I love you so much more now, Evangeline. So much more. You've picked the two men I fell in love with years ago. But Brice doesn't do threesomes. I doubt Jerry wants that with you, either. Definitely not a foursome.*

Brice inhaled and slowly blew out an exhale. "Did you get close ups of all her orgasms, Pete?"

"Yes, sir," the man behind the camera shouted.

An arrogant grin spread across Brice's face as he sat back on his heels. "Watch my cock exit your pretty pussy."

"Oh, yeah," she whimpered. She lifted her head and curled into a crunch.

Brice's cock slid semi-hard from her channel.

"Hold that position for a sec," Pete said. "And, it's a wrap."

Brice lifted her leg and kissed her foot. "We're still modeling for Ella or are we ending that now?"

"We're modeling, but only as a couple," she said. "You're going to have to keep putting the temporary tattoo of the American flag on my inner thigh for the camera."

He lowered her leg to the mattress with a gentleness that showed he cared for her. "Okay, but once the contract is over, we're done."

She glanced away. "We'll see."

"No. We're done. You're done."

"Yes, sir." She sat up and hugged him. She shifted and lowered onto his cock.

"God, I love it when you do that," he mumbled.

Slowly, she rocked her hips back and forth. "I need to come again. It's building inside me."

His breathing came hard and fast. "Do it, baby. Come all over my dick. I want to hear it. I want you to scream."

"Brice," she cried out. She arched her back and shuddered.

He trembled. "Fuck, yeah." His arms shook and his

muscles clenched.

Her shoulders dropped and her head hung low. "You hit that spot and I unravel."

"Benefits of a big cock in a tight pussy." His chest rose and fell in deep respirations. "I'm kidding, sort of." He kissed the top of her head. "You have no idea just how special you truly are."

She lifted her head and gazed at the man. She opened her mouth, but the mics on the set switched off. The monitor cut to black.

What did she say? Does she love him? Is she planning a life with him? Only him? Surely not only him. Could he have become open to the possibility of having a husband too?

Dylan stood in the relative dark with a clear view of the two, while the bright lights probably blinded her and Brice from seeing him.

The two stayed connected for longer than he thought appropriate, but instead of walking in and taking control, he waited and observed.

Evangeline and Brice parted, but they strolled to the open shower together. Brice stepped behind her and she bent over. He fed his cock into her again and, as the water sluiced down over her back, he lazily fucked her as if he had no other place in the world to be.

"Hey," Pete said.

Dylan shook the man's hand. "Hi. I hope I didn't interrupt the shoot."

"It was fine. We usually have some friends on the set when we work. Evan and Brice are great. This wasn't part of the work session. This was a private filming for the three of you." The man turned around and tapped on his tablet. "This is the last scene. They'll be done soon."

Brice's voice grew louder and louder. Evangeline's moans lengthened.

The black screen came to life.

"They are insatiable," Pete whispered. "I had no idea the photo shoots did anything like this to them."

Brice's cock retreated from her. He caressed her ass and then slammed into her, burying his cock balls-deep. The man stiffened and raised up onto his toes. His legs shook.

"That is one hell of an orgasm," Pete said.

Yeah. Sure was. She wasn't kidding about being a sex addict. I bet Brice has the same addiction.

Brice stepped back, and cum dripped from the tip of his cock and drizzled from her pussy. He gently rubbed her ass and the backs of her thighs. "You okay?"

"Yeah," she said in a sultry drawl.

He picked up a bar of soap and washed her back and bottom as she seemed to rest in the bent position. Bruises appeared as he washed her. Large hand prints, but not as large as Brice's, littered her side and upper back. A nasty bruise covered her right hip.

Brice's cock rose again and entered Evan's pussy. He rocked back and forth as he grabbed the shampoo and washed her hair.

She dropped her head and he rinsed her hair.

This is too natural. How many times has he done this with you? The intimacy of the moment caught up with Dylan. *You're allowing his cum inside you. You love him. You love him and he loves you. Are you trying to tell me it's over before it's even begun between us? Why did you invite me here?*

Brice lifted the long, thick strands of her hair and flipped them over her back.

Dylan gasped as the evidence of violence claimed her cheek and neck. *Who did that to you?*

She shuddered again.

Brice stepped backward, his cock still hard and erect.

She stood up and faced him. "It looks worse than it feels."

He wrapped her up in an embrace. "It's probably good Dylan didn't show up. He'd want you to prosecute Henry too."

"Henry was out of his mind," she said. "Cal will get him detoxed and back on meds. Henry will have enough guilt over what he did to last a lifetime. He'll stay on his meds and not take anything else after he sees the pictures of what he did."

Brice took his time drying her off. The mic stayed on as they talked and stole sweet kisses here and there.

Pete patted Dylan on the back. "She's okay. The makeup we use covers everything. She'll look pretty normal other than some swelling on her cheek by the time they finish. I'm done filming. I've got to run to another appointment. Tell Brice I'll call him in a couple weeks when I've finished editing everything."

"Okay. Nice meeting you." Dylan handed him a business card.

Pete looked at it and nodded. "Thanks. See you around." He slung a camera bag over his shoulder and walked out of the room.

Dressed in a suit and tie, Brice strode forward with a strong swagger as Evan, wearing a black pantsuit and sleeveless turtleneck, sashayed across the set. Beside

Brice, she held a confidence and sense of pride she hadn't the other night.

Evan's gaze drifted toward Pete's chair and then to his. She halted midstride as his gaze connected to her.

"Angel," Dylan said. He strode forward, took her hand, and kissed it. "You're a naughty kitten today."

"When did you arrive?" she asked.

"Right before you showered. I'm sorry I was so late," he said. "Mondays and court. Lack of competent employees. Lost in the boonies."

Brice offered his hand. "Hey, Dylan. I haven't seen you in a long time."

Dylan shook it. "Good to see you." He looked at Brice's big bulge.

Brice adjusted his cock and grinned. "Interested in coming to my penthouse to talk?" He curled his arm around Evan's back.

Dylan nodded as he adjusted his cock. "I'd love to. Which hotel? Downtown?"

"Yes." Brice held out his other arm. "Come here."

Dylan walked into Brice's embrace like he had several years ago during their last hookup. He raised his chin.

Brice kissed his lips. "Evangeline knows we've been together."

Dylan slid his hand down Brice's back and cupped his ass. "Is the invitation you just offered going to include sex?" He thrust his pelvis and bumped Brice's bulge.

Brice leaned to the side and brushed the tip of Dylan's ear with his lips. He whispered, "Depends on what kind of sex you're interested in. Evan's not up for bondage for a few weeks. If you can adhere to my rules and boundaries, I imagine the three of us will spend some time getting to know each other again. If not, or if our discussion takes an unexpected turn, then the evening will be cut shorter than intended."

"Sleepover?" Dylan whispered. *You never do sleepovers.*

"Sleepovers aren't an option unless Jerry Wynn joins us as a permanent lover," Brice said. "That's not negotiable." He ground against Dylan's cock and moaned. "I don't think he'll be interested, but I believe in your skills of seduction. I also believe that you love me, Evangeline, *and* Jerry."

I'm surprised you remember our last conversation about the man I was heartbroken over. Jerry Wynn, the reason I cut off our occasional dates of convenience when we were both in the same city. He kissed the corner of Brice's forehead and turned his attention to Evan. "And where do you stand in all this?"

"I don't want Jerry to see me like this. I want him focused for his fight. I want him as my husband like I want you and Brice to be my husbands too. Without Jerry, I don't see the three of us working. Jerry is the one each of us needs. He's the center. He's the leader, the glue, the only one who can keep us all from falling apart."

"And you know this from what? One date with him?" Dylan could barely tolerate the absurdity. *I can keep us together. Jerry would make things better, but I can—*

"I've known him for two years. I've babysat with him at Ella's, countless times. I've spent a lot of time with him. Sure, it's been mostly him listening to me bitch about giving massages and my love life, but he talked too. Not much. He's not a big talker, but when he does speak, what he says is worth stopping whatever I'm doing to listen to every word. He is exactly what I need, what Brice needs, and what you need too. Or I assume you do from the way you acted with him the other night."

The truth packed a heavy punch, and Dylan wanted to cry from the direct hit. Always marked as the most dominant man in the room in all his business and personal circles, Dylan hadn't expected to find Evangeline with the only other men he'd ever encountered who were more dominant than him. He could compete with Brice, but not Jerry. If Jerry wanted Evangeline as his wife, he'd get her one way or another. And Jerry wanted a wife. A wife who—in a perfect world—Jerry would share with Dylan and more.

Faced with being the odd man out in a room where he should have been the man calling the shots sent him retreating for a chance to regroup. Brice had made his move and won. Evangeline had made hers too, but the result hadn't been determined yet. To get Jerry committed or to try a relationship on the order Evangeline wanted, she and Brice would need him.

Dylan kissed Evan's forehead and turned around. "I hadn't planned on a vanilla date tonight. I'll call you later, Angel." He walked to the exit in the waiting area and pushed the door open. He glanced back at the couple.

Brice's gaze softened and a slight smile lifted his lips. The man seemed to recognize and enjoy the game Dylan was playing. Evan's gaze fell to the floor with what appeared to be defeat.

Challenging Brice was one thing, but Dylan didn't

want Evan to suffer in their game of dominance. "Thanks for the sex show. I enjoyed it."

Although her gaze refused his, Dylan captured a ray of hope in the softening of her cheeks, the lowering of her shoulders, the gentle lean of her body against Brice's side.

"You don't have to call first," Evan said. "You can show up at the hotel and ask for access to the penthouse. You are always welcome. No matter what you choose to do or not do."

Brice kissed the edge of her forehead. "If we don't see you tonight, come over when you've made a decision."

"I'll call." Dylan walked out and let the door close behind him. *I'm either going to get everything I ever wanted or nothing at all.*

Chapter Eleven
Evangeline

Phone to her ear, Evangeline tried to ignore the cum making her panties sticky. "I'm sorry, Jerry. I…" She touched her cheek and wished she'd listened to Brice and taken more precautions for potential problems with Henry.

"I've got a lot going on, and I don't want to play games," Jerry said. "I'm—"

"I'm not playing games. There was a situation at my house the other night, and I have a meeting with realtors in a few minutes to sell my house."

The doorbell rang.

"*You're* Cade and Garrett's appointment," Jerry said like an accusation that she'd lied. "I'll be at your house in a few minutes." He ended the call before she could say another word.

Dang it. She called him back as she walked toward the front door. *Answer, Jerry.*

The call rolled into voicemail as she crossed the foyer. "Don't come over." She hung up. *Brice is all the I'm-worried-about-you alpha man I can handle today.*

Waiting at the door, two plain looking women dressed in business suits held clipboards pressed to their chests and stood beside Garrett Winthrop, a drop-dead gorgeous blond wearing all-black, military-style clothes.

You're supposed to be at the penthouse in an hour, Garrett. Not. Here. She opened the door and her shoulders sprang up like a geyser to her ears as the intense stare of Garrett's blue eyes zeroed in on her cheek.

"Thank you for coming, ladies." She clenched her teeth as she smiled. "Garrett, you're early."

The ladies plastered on a grin and walked in.

The flat expression on Garrett's face didn't change, but his blue eyes scanned her and the rooms. He took it all in as if he were profiling and assessing the situation at the same time. Knowing him, he most assuredly was.

"I'm always early," Garrett said. Each step seemed to be planned. Each swing of his arm, spacing of his body in relation to the entrances, exits, and people. Garrett was a dangerous man. A very dangerous man. How Ella handled him, Evangeline had no idea.

Evangeline shook hands with the realtors and then hugged Garrett. "Thank you for coming."

"Cade is outside," Garrett said. "Brice called him." He frowned. "You were supposed to call him."

"I was going—"

"Evan," Cade shouted.

She glanced over her shoulder, but Cade hadn't appeared yet. *Please don't bring Brice with you.*

"In the foyer, Cade," she answered. She turned to the women. "The house is almost empty." She explained that the house would be completely vacant and cleaned by the following evening.

The realtors seemed to be giddy over the opportunity to list it.

Cade Jackson strode into the foyer and hugged Evangeline. "I'm upset with you." He shook the hands of the two women. "I'm going to give you the official tour of the house." In seconds, Cade and the women were out of the foyer, leaving Garrett alone with her.

"You need to tell Ella about this," Garrett said. "I think you should tell Derek too. But that is between you and him. As for coming back here to do anything without an escort and security, it's not going to happen. The alarm system in the back needs to be replaced with a more sophisticated system. Henry is a tech guy when he's not fighting fires and could disable this system in seconds." He continued explaining the lack of safety in the house, the new security issues, and how best to help Henry from losing everything good in his life while keeping Evangeline safe from harm.

The doorbell rang.

Garrett strode to the door as she followed on his heels.

Through the windows in the door, she saw her red-headed fighter.

"Finally, someone you will listen to." Garrett opened the door. "Get in here and talk some sense into her. She's injured. She's probably pregnant with Brice's baby, and she's here trying to act normal when she needs to be resting and…" He pulled Jerry into a hug. "Take her somewhere so I can help Brice pack and move the rest of her stuff out of here. Cade will choose one of the realtors to sell the house. I'm about to lose my shit over this. I swear she's got Ella-itis. The girl's been doing everything for so long she can't listen to reason or take the help she needs from the people who love her."

Garrett turned around, and he and Jerry seemed to form an impenetrable barrier. Their expressions could have been pictured in a dictionary for the words "concerned" and "frustrated."

Jerry held out his hand. "Let's get you out of here." The tone landed hard in her ears. No offer of a choice laced the notes in his pitch. Nothing but his solid and demanding order to obey him vibrated through her.

With a need to please him, she placed her hand in his meaty palm. Electricity sizzled when her skin met his. "I'm fine. Henry is back on his meds. Crisis averted."

Jerry guided her out the front door.

"Tell Ella about what happened," Garrett said. "Today." He closed the door, shutting her outside with the man she'd been avoiding.

Silence pervaded the walk to his minivan, the ride to the diner, and journey inside where they were seated immediately.

"The pancakes are good here," he said.

"I've heard that." She gazed at him as he looked down at the menu. He hadn't looked at her for longer than a few seconds at a time. "I'm sorry about canceling my babysitting duties."

"It was fine. Derek's mom and dad took the twins for the week. What are you going to get to eat?" He glanced up and quickly dropped his gaze.

"French toast and bacon. A side of hash browns."

The waitress came over and he ordered enough for an army.

As soon as the waitress walked away, Jerry looked at her like he had in the limo a couple nights ago.

"You knew that night in the limo. You knew you might be pregnant, didn't you?"

She nodded. "I'm probably not, but this is one of

those times in my life where one decision seems to propel me into…" *How do I tell him I wish things were different, but I'm glad things aren't?*

"Propel you into what?" he asked.

"A mess?" She unrolled the napkin and placed the utensils that had been trapped inside to the right and left of where the plate would eventually be set.

"Derek told me about you and Brice and the complicated relationship you've had with him and he with you. What's holding you back? Or is it him?"

"I'm in love with you and Brice, and I never stopped loving Dylan. I can't have all of you." *Can I?* She searched his eyes for any semblance of acceptance of an alternative relationship. Nothing but a brick barrier hiding all emotions showed in his gaze.

"I'm not willing to be anything but number two in your life." He tilted his head and raised his brows. "Your kids would be number one. I'd be number two. Your kids would be number one in my life also. You'd be two." He shrugged. "I don't see it working any other way."

Out of nowhere the floodgates blew open and she began crying.

"Don't cry," he whispered. "Please."

She kept nodding but couldn't stop.

"Oh, baby," he whispered and moved around the booth to her side. He curled his arm around her.

The warmth of his body, the safety in his arms, the gentleness in his touch broke her apart. She lifted her chin and blinked at the heartbreak in his green eyes. *You love me. You're trying to do the right thing by stepping aside, by acting more like a friend than a man in love.*

"I'm sorry," she whispered. With tears streaming down her cheeks, she wrapped her arms around his neck and brushed her lips against his. "You'd be my number one until a baby came into our lives."

He crushed his mouth to hers in a demanding kiss.

Her tears dried up as she parted her lips.

His tongue dove into her mouth, commanding her to do as he willed. And she wholeheartedly obeyed until he broke the kiss.

He cupped the back of her head and stared at her. "You might be pregnant. What exactly does that mean?"

"I'm not sure if I was ovulating, but I could have been or could be right now. I won't know for a few weeks if the fertility pills—"

"Fertility pills?" He pulled her out of the booth and into the restaurant's one bathroom.

"I struggle in the reproduction department. I started meds thinking...well, it kind of backfired, but didn't. I want children. I just hadn't planned..." *The situation with Henry or Brice or you or Dylan.* "Everything changed in a matter of days."

He kept hold of her until he checked the two stalls, but the room was clean and empty.

"Jerry, what are we doing in here? I'm not going to—"

He cradled the back of her head. "If you end up pregnant, I want a shot at being the father. You up for that?"

She opened her mouth to speak, but nothing came out.

He palmed her ass and lifted her up. "Wrap your legs around my waist."

She obeyed. Her skirt slid up her thighs as she curled her legs around his waist. "I've got panties on."

He pushed down his shorts and pulled her wet panties to the side. "You haven't fucked Dylan bare, have you?"

"No," she said. "We haven't—"

The wide head of his cock pushed into her.

She gasped. *Oh, my God. You're huge.*

"Evan," he moaned. "I've waited for you for so long. So fucking long." He thrust.

"Jerry." She sucked in her breath as her pussy stretched like she was a virgin—and she was no virgin.

"I know, baby," he whispered. "Hang on, Evan. Hang on, baby."

His fingers slid over the dark bruise on her hip, but he softened his touch as if he knew exactly what was there. Maybe he did know the feel of her injury and instinctively moved to the edges so he wouldn't hurt her. She couldn't be sure, but the deepest part of her believed they were connected on such a profound level that he could feel her aches before he ever saw them, before he ever touched her.

Pain morphed to pleasure. His eyes softened as his body began to take over, claim her, and merge his soul to hers.

"I'm fertility challenged, Jerry. I might never be able to have a baby. Don't get your hopes up. I told Brice the same thing. I—"

"I want you, Evan. I need you with or without children. I need you." He thrust. "I need you." He lifted her up and pulled her down onto his cock. "I need you."

The thick rod shoved into her pussy stroked pleasure nerve endings as he entered and exited. Over and over, he loved her from the inside out.

Each delicious thrust brought another shot of electricity, another bullet opening barriers she hadn't known she continued to hold.

"I love you," he whispered. "I need you to love me."

She *needed* him to *love her*. She was always the one hoping to be loved, but Jerry…her Jerry wasn't sure she loved him. *You're the catch, Jerry, not me.*

"I do love you." *Can't you tell? Haven't you known all along I would have dropped every relationship I ever had for you?*

"You do?" The green in his eyes shimmered. A layer of defense peeled away, and the worried boy whose biological parents hurt him peered back at her.

She nodded.

The boy vanished and the conqueror appeared. "You really do." He thrust. "You do love me."

Electricity surged through her sex, into her belly, and powered up and down her spine with the rhythm of his thrusts. "I will love you no matter what happens in the future. You have me, Jerry. You have held my heart for years. You captured my soul. You're a part of me."

He shifted his hands, and the world fell away as loving pleasure sent her into a new sense of peace…*his*.

She heard his grunts, felt his release inside her, but nothing took her away from the wonderful place her brain sailed. No one could hurt her heart or body or soul as long as he held her.

As she floated back to reality, the sense of safety stayed with her. Love and peace continued to pervade all thought. *You need me like I need you. I love you.*

His lips pressed against the corner of her forehead.

"I'm sorry. The bathroom is not where I envisioned our first time together would be."

"Sex in a restaurant bathroom is a first for me," she said. Her lips curved into a smile. "Bar bathrooms are another story altogether."

He chuckled. "I've never done anything like this."

The door rattled.

She dropped her legs and he carefully maneuvered her down until her feet touched the tile. Gazing at his semi-hard member, she licked her lips. "I want to taste you."

His magnificent cock rose, accepting the offer.

Someone pounded on the door.

"Are you two ever getting out of there?" a woman shouted. "Do not go for another round. My bladder is full and so is my daughter's diaper."

"Oh, my God," Evan mumbled. Heat rose from her chest to her cheeks. She raised her voice. "We'll be out in a minute."

Jerry shoved his cock in his pants as she pulled her skirt down and found her shoes.

"How much longer?" the woman said.

Rushing around the small room, Evan grabbed some paper towels and wiped up her inner thighs. "Thirty seconds."

Water splashed in the sink.

Jerry reached over her to the paper towel dispenser. "Stay behind me as we exit." He wiped his hands and threw away the napkin. "You look great."

She lifted her gaze and spied him through the spaces between her long bangs. "I'm sorry."

He winked. "I'm not. Not at all."

The red in his cheeks conflicted with his words and

actions. He swept her behind him as he smoothly crossed the cream tile floor. The lock clicked and the door swung open.

"Oh, my," a woman gasped. "Wow."

"Sorry, ma'am," Jerry said. He walked forward.

A burst of bliss shocked Evan's system as she passed by the woman whose face turned a brighter shade of red than Evan's. *That woman wishes she was me.*

Jerry turned around and faced the woman. "Order whatever you want. Your lunch is on me."

The woman stood transfixed, staring at him.

He turned around and guided Evan to the hostess. "The lady in the bathroom, whatever anyone at her table orders is on me, and give her a certificate for another meal for her and her family. And I need the table in the back corner away from everyone else."

"Yes, Mr. Wynn," the hostess said. "Give me one minute." She hustled to the kitchen and then into the out-of-eyeshot back corner. A couple walked with the hostess to a table closer to the front but that remained in the semi-private area of the restaurant. In seconds, a team descended onto the abandoned section.

By the time the hostess showed Evan and Jerry to their private corner booth, the table had been cleared and she assured Jerry the rest of his requests would be taken care of.

"Is there anything else, Mr. Wynn?" the hostess asked.

"No, ma'am," Jerry said. "Thank you."

The hostess walked away, and two waiters arrived with their food.

Evan slid into the booth as gold-rimmed platters of

eggs, pancakes, meats, and all the fixings were set out like a banquet feast for royalty. There was china with the Wynn name written in green and gold cursive that spiraled from the center to the edge, white cloth napkins with gold-threaded boxing gloves embroidered in the corner, and utensils made of silver with his last name in gold engraved in the handles.

The waiters nodded and walked out of view.

She gazed at the table. The wheat-stained oak table brought out the gold and green hues on the plates. The black leather booth closed them in, making the diner seem like a separate entity. They were set apart from the rest of the world in the space. His space.

She looked at him. *Are you trying to impress me?*

"Are you coming to Vegas with me?" He picked up a napkin and flicked his wrist. The cloth billowed out and floated gracefully to his lap.

"Is this your restaurant?"

With a nod, he picked up the platter of pancakes and served her. "What about Vegas?"

"Can I bring Brice? Possibly Dylan?"

He picked up the platter of bacon, sausage, and ham and filled her plate.

The napkin in his lap rose and tented. She couldn't tell if his erection happened because of the mention of her other men, or the food, or from the skirt of her dress rising up her thighs.

"You can bring Brice. I'm not going to punish him for loving you." He gently placed his hand on her thigh and pushed the skirt of her dress up over her bare pussy.

"Will you punish me?"

"No. You made it crystal clear the way you roll. I'm not sure I can be a full party to it, but we can work something out." His fingers inched upward. "Have you forgiven Dylan? Are you going to offer him a chance at fatherhood?"

She swallowed hard. "I never thought I'd see Dylan again after I graduated high school. It's not that I ever had to forgive him. Losing his mother the way he did…" *That he was the one who found her.* "When I think about what he went through, I don't need to forgive him. I wish he had chosen to lean on me, but we were teens. Brice helped me see that. Dylan needed his father, and his father needed him. Dylan's father has finally moved on and given Dylan the courage to do the same." She scooted closer to him, giving him easier access to explore her body. "I haven't done anything with him. He likes certain things, and he has to prove to me he wants the permanency of an exclusive relationship with me and Brice and hopefully you."

"I want a relationship with you," he whispered. He leaned over and kissed her neck. "I want you to sleep in my bed. I want you to be by my side."

"I will open my heart, soul, and body to you forever, Jerry. I will give you all my love. I will try to have your baby. No guarantees, but I will try. But you're going to have to sacrifice a few things, like we all will. You're going to have to share me in your bed. You're going to have to accept Brice and possibly Dylan. You're going to have to consent to me potentially bearing two other men's babies, God willing. You're going to have to…" She slipped her hand under his shorts and stroked his length to his balls. *So hard. God, I want your baby. I want you to love me enough to accept all of us.*

"Evan," he moaned. "I can't think straight when

you touch me."

She turned.

He shifted and slid her onto his lap. "I want to fuck you so badly."

She curled her arms around his neck. "Here?"

"Every damn where."

She squeezed her eyes closed. *Yes. Right here. Right now.*

"I'm not sharing my bed with anyone but you," he whispered. "I'll let you have your fun with the other two, but you're coming home to my bed, to me."

"That's not going to work, Jerry. It's all or nothing."

"You've never even tried being with me," he whispered. "Try it."

"I promised Brice I'd stay with him."

"Ask for sleepovers with me." He slid her hips forward and back over his raging erection. "You're going to have to try my way."

Brice is never going to go for that. Not until we've moved away. Far away from Henry. "What if—"

"Ask," he whispered. "One step at a time."

"Okay," she said.

"We're going to eat now," he whispered.

"But I want—"

"I know what you want." He thrust up against her clit.

She moaned as her sex contracted and pleasure shot through her veins. "Yes."

"Later, Evan. Remember, you're trying my way first."

With her clit buzzing and her body on fire for him, she rubbed along his length and extended the surge of pleasure. *You are in this to win me. But will you truly share? Will you watch me with Brice? With Dylan? Will you enjoy being watched by them?*

"Gorgeous, crawl off my lap and eat your brunch," he said.

She obeyed.

"That's my girl," he praised her.

She smiled. *Make me your girl forever.*

Chapter Twelve
Dylan

Listening to the voicemails Jerry left hadn't helped Dylan's anxiety about seeing him. Sitting in the man's living room surrounded by all things Wynn, Dylan lost the sense of control he cherished.

Jerry held the control.

Jerry held the power.

All the power.

All the time.

"Have you slept with Evangeline since you've moved back to Memphis?" Jerry asked. The man extended his arms along the top of the cream-cushioned couch and with it provided another barrier from fleeing from the truth, from him—as if Dylan would want to be apart from the perfect man. Jerry was the one man Dylan wanted to be glued to forever. The one man Brice and Evangeline wanted to be bound to for the rest of their lives. Jerry Wynn held all the cards in the love deck.

"Not yet. My plans got sidetracked." *You appeared out of nowhere. Evangeline has closed off so much of herself since I left. It's my fault. I should have come to get her sooner. Should have kept in contact with you. Should have asked you to join forces with me in snagging Evangeline as ours the moment I met you.*

"You know Brice?" Jerry asked.

"Yeah. We've been friends for a long time. Years. I had no idea he was in love with Evangeline or she with him. What about you? Know him?"

Jerry nodded. "My best friend Ella's husband is Cade Jackson. Cade and Brice are tight. They do a lot of business together. I've spent plenty of dinners at Cade's with him in the room. He's spent time here with me and Cade and the guys." He scooted back and stretched his neck from side to side. His thighs widened and the contracted muscles relaxed into thick supple slabs Dylan wanted to lick. "Cade keeps trying to get me to hang out with Brice, but they're friends. I don't think he likes me much. And I'm not sure I like him all that much either. He won't let Evangeline out of his sight. He's a pain in the ass."

"You don't like Brice?" *That's interesting. He's just like you. Private. Intelligent. Closet bisexual.*

"Besides demanding he chaperone Evangeline's dates with me…" Jerry squeezed his shoulders together and stretched his chest. "The man is always listening when I talk about business. The next thing I know he's adapted what I'd talked about to all his businesses. It's like he's in competition with me. There's no real downtime when he's around." Jerry looked away and the bulge in his shorts became more pronounced.

You're into Brice. You're upset that he is making you choose all of us or none of us.

"Are we friends? Have you forgiven me for being a jackass at the Zanipolos' home the other night?" *This seems too comfortable. Feels so much like when we were lovers.*

Jerry cracked a half-smile and nodded. "I was disappointed, but I'm over it. We're friends, if you want to be friends. It's up to you."

Dylan's heart fluttered with shock. *You aren't sure of my true feelings. I love you. I loved you since that first drink at the pub. I wasn't sure you would want...* "Jerry, I want to be everything to you." He hadn't meant to be so blunt, but the insecurity underlying Jerry's tone and inside the man's eyes threw Dylan for a loop. "You and Evangeline are what I want. Having Brice join the three of us, for me, would be icing on the cake. Besides you, he's the only other man I've ever loved. Watching Evangeline's belly grow big with yours and Brice's children..." He grabbed his cock. "I want that for her, for you, for Brice. One day, I'll want the same for me."

"I want Evangeline to sleep in my bed at night. Not yours. Not Brice's. Mine and only mine."

Dylan huffed. *There's the Jerry Wynn ego coming out. Always having to prove that you're number one when everyone already agrees you are. You're not going to push me away. You're going to face reality.*

"No." Dylan stared at him. "Absolutely not. We parted as friends in hopes we'd find a woman we could share *permanently.* All of us sleeping in the same bed. All of us sharing each other, exclusively. Forever. At least, that was my understanding."

Jerry didn't move. No muscles twitched. Nothing. He sat there staring at Dylan. The man gave no hint of what he thought or planned to do. The unreadable conqueror Jerry Wynn held everyone's future in the balance.

After what seemed like hours but was probably only minutes, Dylan decided he'd had enough. If talking caused him to lose whatever battle they were in, then so be it. "What do you want, Jerry? What do you really want for your future?"

"I don't know if I could live with Evan and you *and* Brice. I don't like him. It's always a competition with him." Jerry's cock poked right at Dylan, tenting his shorts higher each time he mentioned Brice. Like Pinocchio's nose, Jerry's cock became the litmus test for the truth. The more the man protested his feelings for Brice, the harder and larger the man's erection became.

"Brice isn't in competition with anyone. He's smart. He hears something that he can use in his companies, he implements it. That's just good business. He respects you. You should be honored, not threatened."

Jerry's chest rose as he took a deep inhale. The muscles he exercised every day showed their hard work in the perfection of motion as he shifted on the couch. Ripples of hard muscle under smooth skin. Memories of his time with Jerry emerged as the love he held for the man softened the hardest places inside his soul. In Jerry's arms, Dylan experienced love. Unconditional love. In Jerry's bed, Dylan slept in peace. No nightmares invaded his mind when Jerry was beside him. No worries. No stressing about the future. In Jerry's house, Dylan believed the evil world outside couldn't touch him or his family. With Jerry, he was happy. But they needed something else. Someone else to keep them together forever. They assumed there would be only one more. But Brice changed that. Each of them needed the others. Jerry might fight it, but as soon as he realized the truth, the man would join their team.

"I never thought of it like that," Jerry said. His eyebrows scrunched together, and he huffed, but the inkling of a smile appeared on his face.

Dylan stood and walked around the ottoman to the man he loved. He sat beside Jerry, hoping the man would make some kind of move toward being more than friends.

Jerry didn't.

Dylan nudged Jerry's side with an elbow. "You don't have anything to prove to me or to Brice. You don't have to admit you like Brice. You don't have to do anything, but if you don't do anything, the rest of us will be moving to Texas without you." *And the three of us will dissolve into another failed relationship because we need you. I need you.*

"What? Texas? Why?" He got in Dylan's face. Nose to nose. Fury and confusion formed wrinkles along his forehead and red spread over his face like an instant sunburn. "I can't move right now. I have a fight. I have a—" He shut his mouth without finishing.

"I have a few things to put in place before we move," Dylan said. "But it won't be long. A week, maybe three at the most."

"Are you serious?"

"Serious as a heart attack," Dylan replied. "We're ready to finally have a place to call home, to settle down and raise kids, to feel safe, to have some privacy and a community that will accept us as we are. It's not here. Not with all the baggage we carry from our collective history with this town and the people. We can visit and have a house or two here, but let's start fresh in Texas."

Jerry closed his eyes, and the burning fire that he'd

let out receded back to wherever he kept it. The man's jaw slackened. "Memphis. A place of extremes. The highest of highs and the lowest of lows. Elation that turns to misery and vice versa. Momma Mae loved it here. Loved the people. Loved helping the community. Loved making a difference. Then two fuckers took her away from me. Two pieces of shit, hired to not just kill, but to torture a sweet old lady already dying from heart disease."

Dylan wrapped Jerry in his arms and held him. He'd heard the trial date had been set but hadn't inquired more about it. He should have. Jerry would have. *I'm such a jerk.* "I'm sorry."

As Jerry melted into his embrace, Dylan ached to ease the man's pain even a tenth of the amount Jerry had for him. It was Jerry who taught Dylan how to squash the past's grasp of him. It was Jerry who helped him face the suicide of his mother. It was Jerry who gave him the strength to come to Memphis to reconnect with Evangeline, to hope for a future where an opportunity like the one he had now would come to pass.

"Yeah," Jerry whispered. "It was supposed to be a slam dunk. But their attorneys kept delaying the trial. There were talks of deals. None of it made sense. Not until I got a call late last week." He inhaled and lifted his head from Dylan's shoulder. "My opponent is bankrolling the defense. He's been doing it since the murder hit the news almost three years ago. This fight has been coming for a long time and—"

"And someone knows someone who could set the trial date so you'll be distracted before and during the fight. He knows you'll beat him unless he can get in your head."

Jerry looked up and nodded. "Yeah. I'm distracted. I had sex in a bathroom last week. I'm damn distracted."

Holy shit. "That's not like you."

"No. It's not. I don't regret it, but I also don't want it to happen again." Jerry slouched and dropped his head back onto Dylan's shoulder. "I miss my family."

The loneliness that bonded them from their first conversation in Vegas all those years ago, that solidified their friendship, weighed heavy in the air. The family filled with love each of them had counted on to be around forever had been stripped away by people and events out of their control—Jerry's by strangers and disease, and Dylan's by his mother's struggle with depression and Matteo Zanipolo's careless actions. A family of his own was all Dylan hoped for. His father had moved on and found the love he'd lost. Now, it was Dylan's turn.

Dylan stroked along Jerry's muscular back, hoping to comfort him. "When's the trial?"

"Starts on Monday."

The sadness and defeat rolling off the man who never displayed either hit Dylan in the section of his soul that had been reserved solely for the loss of his mother.

"The prosecution called me today," Jerry said. "Some evidence went missing. They're trying to find it."

You shouldn't be dealing with a trial and training for a fight. "Let me look at your contract. I'll find a way to reschedule the fight."

"There's no rescheduling. Even if there was, I

wouldn't do it. I'd get in that cage tomorrow." Jerry hugged him and separated from the hold. He inched to the right side of the couch. All his protective walls seemed to snap back in place. The calm, collected, and in total control Jerry Wynn sat beside him—although the fragility of the champion's heart hung by a strand of worn rope that had begun to unravel.

"Let me look into your opponent's part in all of this," Dylan said. *Will you let me help you?*

"I would appreciate it. I fired the law firm that represents me. One of the attorneys is related to my opponent and had access to my personal and business information. My public and private life will get ugly soon. My attorney was supposed to keep all my personal information private, not allow access to anyone else in or outside the firm. He put his trust in the wrong people and now I'm paying for it."

"Do you need representation?" *I will crush them for doing this to you.*

Jerry nodded. "Would you?"

The helplessness in his eyes undid Dylan. *I'm going to be your shield. I'm going to protect you from those fuckers.*

"I would have asked Evangeline, but she doesn't need the stress that is going to be linked to the case and the fight and... God, if she ends up pregnant with my child, she might not be prepared for the backlash."

Dylan stared at strongest man he'd ever known and saw an anxious kid with dark secrets he'd hidden all his life—the vulnerable Jerry who compelled him to kiss the fighter for the first time, making sure Jerry knew he wasn't alone. He needed Jerry to know without a shadow of a doubt that as long as they had each other, they could handle anything.

"Evangeline doesn't care what strangers may or may not say about you," Dylan said. "She loves who she loves, Jerry. And of course I'll be your attorney, friend, lover—whatever you want me to be. Tell me what is worrying you. Let me carry that burden. If it's part of a social media smear campaign, let's bring in Brice to spin it in your favor. As long as the four of us work together as a team, we can get through this. Trust me, like I will always trust you."

Jerry closed his eyes and nodded. "Thanks."

Waiting for Jerry to elaborate or to set some sort of rules they would all have to abide by, Dylan watched for any movement from the man he never stopped loving. *I should have contacted you. I should have told you years ago why I never called.* "I stayed away because I wasn't ready to let you or anyone else into my *real* life. I buried myself in work. I kept my relationships at a distance. I wanted a life I was scared to live, Jerry. I'm not scared anymore. I have you to thank for that."

Jerry looked at him. The green eyes that had cut to the heart of his fears softened as understanding flowed through them. "That was all you. I only told you that it was okay to be where you were and to take the time you needed."

"You allowed me to walk away with honesty, without making excuses, without the past resurfacing to close off the love I held and will always hold for you. I came here to face my demons and take back the woman whom I love as much as I love you. I'm not lying to myself anymore. The past doesn't control me."

"I wish I could forget the past. Move on from all of

it. This trial… The life Momma Mae and Major saved me from is about to resurface." Jerry squeezed his eyes shut as despair carried over in every word he spoke of his childhood. Truths buried deep surfaced as each slice of childhood misery released more and more secrets—secrets Dylan would take to the grave. Secrets that strengthened their connection and their level of trust.

"Who knows about the fire? About the abuse? About the adoption?"

"Besides you, Ella, her husbands, and Evangeline?" Jerry asked. He opened his eyes and gazed at Dylan. "My head trainer Danny got a letter taped to his front door today. He knows now. He knows about you and me too. There was a picture of us in Las Vegas. It wasn't anything out of the ordinary and it was one of so many to show someone is watching me, but Danny knows me and put two and two together. This will end up being a—"

"Let me worry about what will and won't happen," Dylan said. "You are to focus on winning that fight. Everything else is my responsibility. Now, where is the letter and photo?"

Jerry just nodded as he stood up, his shoulders rounded. His head hung lower than normal. He seemed like defeat had already settled into his bones.

Dylan rose from the couch. "Hey." He took Jerry's hands in his. "You are Jerry Wynn." He squeezed the fighter's strong hands. "You fought and won all those championships. You did it. No one helped you. You won on your own merit. You. Are. Jerry. Wynn."

Jerry shook his head. "What are people going to think of me?"

"Your fans are going to love you even more, and

the haters are going to hate you a lot more."

Jerry nodded. A tiny smile spread across his lips. "Momma Mae and Major used to say that."

"They were right, and so am I."

Emerald eyes met his gaze. "This is different."

"Yeah. It's a fight in my area of expertise, and I'll be victorious. You have no idea what I'm capable of, but the attorneys who dare to walk into my ring, Jerry, they do. They know that when I get involved, a reckoning is coming."

The twinkle of victory in Jerry's Irish eyes appeared.

"There's the man I know." Dylan let go of Jerry's hand. "Now, get me that evidence. I've got some work to do." *And you just gave me everything. You want a family, lovers, a life with us. I'm going to make sure you get everything you really want—me, Evangeline, and Brice.*

Chapter Thirteen
Brice

Brice rubbed the sweat from his palms on his drenched athletic shorts and tried to act normal.

"Grab some water," Jerry said. The man casually walked over to the wooden bench and picked up his jug of water and took a swig. He barely perspired. "We've got two more minutes before we start the next round."

Drowned in sweat, Brice's willpower to keep going slowly faded. *Another round? I'm going to have a heart attack.* "Yeah, okay." He lifted legs which were close to giving out and strode at a snail's pace to the bench. Every inch of him already hurt. Tomorrow would be a bitch.

"You're a beast," Jerry said. "Dylan would have quit after the first round." He smiled and tapped him on the arm. "I could make a boxer out of you."

I could have quit? Shit. Dylan is young, and I'm a dumbass. "I'm not sure I'll be able to walk tomorrow."

Jerry laughed. "You'll be fine."

"Really, I may not be able to get out of bed in the morning," Brice admitted.

Another hearty laugh came out of the gorgeous man's mouth. "Okay. Okay. Let's go grab a snack and talk. I hit my workout hard earlier."

All the blood from Brice's face drained. *I can't keep up with you.* "Yeah. Food sounds good." *I might not be able to lift a fork. Hell, moving my fingers is a struggle.* His stomach growled.

Jerry picked up both his and Brice's water jugs and led Brice from the gym to the kitchen.

Nothing had changed in the man's house since the last time Brice had been there with Cade, Ella, and the twins. The light green hues blended with neutral walls and formed a calm and soothing space in the kitchen. Shiny pots and pans hung over the island, an easy reach from the wall cabinets, counters, and range.

Brice pulled out a barstool and sat at the island counter. "Need any help?" *Please say no.*

"No, sir," Jerry said. He opened the stainless-steel fridge and took out two meal containers marked *snack* and placed them on the counter next to the water jugs. He went back to the fridge and grabbed two more containers of fruit and closed the doors. As he walked around the room, grabbing items and setting the table, he paused at the cabinet with the plates. "Do you want to make this formal or family casual?"

A snack for you looks like a casserole for ten. I am going to have to learn how to cook for you. "Casual, please."

Jerry nodded and grabbed two plates from the cabinet. He finished their settings and sat down next to Brice. "I like making everything, even snacks, seem like a family meal."

I wouldn't have thought that about you. "Me, too," Brice said. "My mom would place a tablecloth and we'd eat off fine china for most of our meals. My dad would get upset and tell her that the dishes were for *special occasions.* My mom insisted that every day when we gathered together was a *special occasion.*" He cut the turkey rollups into sections. "Mom didn't have much money or anything else growing up, but she loved the finer things in life. She would take me to yard sales to find treasures. She negotiated like a pro. After she passed away, we found boxes of china and silver that my father and I had no idea she had bought."

"I have some china," Jerry said. "We could—"

"No. That's okay. I don't do that anymore," Brice said. "Not since Mom."

"Maybe it's time to start once again," Jerry said. "These were Momma Mae's favorite plates. She said they were for family and friends who deserved to be called family." Jerry looked down. "I appreciate your help with..." He cleared his throat.

Brice gently placed his sweaty hand on Jerry's dry back. The sentiment wasn't lost on him. They'd both lost a part of themselves when the matriarchs of their families had passed away. "I'm glad I could help. What your opponent is doing is wrong. The prosecution is going to get a guilty verdict. And, best of all, you're going to kick that prick's ass and make him bleed."

"I will do that," Jerry said.

Brice patted him on the back and released contact. "Good." He looked at Jerry's back and the man's shirt had a darker mark in the shape of a hand where Brice had patted him. "Sorry. I sweated on your shirt."

"You're good." Jerry ate his turkey rollup. "We probably should have washed hands before we ate, but..."

"Yeah, but it's not like we were playing in the mud. A little dirt won't hurt."

Jerry chuckled as he picked up another turkey rollup. "So true."

Dylan doesn't know what he's talking about. You are not into me. Brice adjusted his sudden erection. "What are we going to do about Evangeline?"

Jerry nodded without saying anything.

It's not a yes or no question. "What are your thoughts about a relationship with me, Dylan, and Evangeline?"

Jerry's head bobbed up and down.

Say something.

The man nodded and continued to eat.

"Do you want a relationship with the three of us? With me?" Brice asked.

Jerry finished chewing and swallowed. He exhaled, swiveling his chair to face Brice. "I want to marry Evangeline. I want her to have the Wynn name. The only intimate guy relationship I've ever had was with Dylan. He let me run things when we were together. I'm not sure you'll be comfortable with my level of control."

I can work with this. "I've had my share of discreet male companions, but Dylan has been my one steady partner over the years. I hadn't anticipated being in a relationship like this, but it feels right to me."

"You want this with me too?" Jerry pressed his lips together and scrunched up his eyes in what seemed like disbelief.

"Yeah. I want us all to live together." *I want more, but it doesn't look like that is what you want.* "Evangeline is into the kind of kink Dylan enjoys. Are you into kink?"

"No."

"Exhibitionist?"

"No. You?"

"Yeah," Brice said. "Which is another reason this would be ideal for me."

"I like to watch Evangeline." Jerry closed his eyes and growled a sigh. "I recently found out about the sex tapes. Shit. I jerked off to one of them, more than once."

"Those are hot. I've made a few private films with Evangeline. She's amazing in everything she does," Brice said. *I don't know how to broach the subject of us. Of the us I want us to be.*

"She sure is." Jerry nodded.

"I consider you a friend. I think a relationship with all of us together would be good long-term." *This is so freaking awkward.*

Green eyes zeroed in on him. "Me, too, but you need to know that I'll be the one who has final say in decisions. I'm up for discussion, but when it comes down to a decision, I will make it."

Brice barked a laugh. "What is that supposed to mean?"

"If the four of us can't come to an agreement, my decision is the one we'll all be abiding by. This is in personal life, not business. I won't stick my nose in your businesses, and you won't stick yours in mine."

Here goes the make-or-break moment. "I can live with that if you can live with me marrying Evangeline."

"She needs to be a Wynn."

I hope Dylan is right about this. "What if she has your name and mine, but she is legally married to me?"

"What the hell?" Red spread from Jerry's neck to his face in seconds.

"She'd legally change her last name to Wynn-Loffiten."

Jerry leaned back. "Can she do that?"

"Yes."

"People will think she married me first and that it was a secret." Jerry tilted his head. "You'd be okay with that?"

"Yes and yes. I'm also okay with her having your children. Although, she's probably pregnant with my child right now."

"But she might be pregnant with mine," Jerry said.

Brice nodded. *I doubt it.* "So, are we in agreement about Evangeline marrying me, changing her name and adding yours to mine?"

Jerry nodded. "Yeah. That works."

"I like to cook. Is that going to be a problem?" *This is going too well.*

Jerry crossed his arms over his chest. His biceps bulged. "Explain."

Explain what? I like to cook. "I usually cook my meals and those for guests."

"If I gave you recipes, you'd cook them?" He rolled his eyes and shook his head.

"Yes. I would."

Jerry straightened and dropped his arms to his side. "Really?"

"Yes. I might need some help now and again, but I enjoy cooking. It's a stress reliever for me."

"That's cool. All right. I'm good with that. I'm going to keep my chef around, for some of my performance meals. Are you okay sharing a kitchen?"

"Yeah. This is going to work, Jerry." *It really is. I'm going to have a full life.*

"I don't know if I can move permanently to Texas."

"We have to move. Henry is a good kid, but he's a threat to Evangeline. I don't want to go into it, but you saw what he did to her. She won't admit it, but the broken arm she had last year was because he pushed her down the stairs. She didn't trip. She was pushed. Henry's father, Cal Westland, witnessed it. A switch flips inside Henry when he's off his meds or decides to take drugs, and he goes on a search to find her. He used to be self-destructive. But, when he moved in with Evan, his focus shifted outward—namely, on her. Cal is worried for her and Henry. If you can't move immediately after the fight, let's work on a timeframe that will work for you. Maybe you can commute? But you have to call Texas home, and Tennessee a home away from home."

"It's that serious with Henry?" Worry lined Jerry's face. "Even with me around?"

"Yes. Even with you." *Even with you and Dylan and the rest of the world barricading her door, she's not safe.*

"I thought he was fine now."

"Evangeline thinks so, but I'm not convinced, and neither is Henry's father. Let's get the trial and the fight over, then move."

"I'll look into commuting. I can't move that quickly. Not with so much happening. The publicity surrounding me is going to be—"

Brice covered Jerry's hands. "Let me handle the publicity. You plan the commute. And I can get you packed and moved in three days flat."

"I have a ranch there I could move into immediately. We all could move in. It's big enough and private enough. But I don't want to miss—"

"Ella. Her husbands. The kids," Brice said. "I know you'll miss them." *I'm working on a plan for that.* "But you'll have us. I have a ranch in the area too. We can take a quick day trip and see which of our places would be best for our family."

"I don't want to leave Ella. I don't think commuting would work."

"Figure out a short-term commuting schedule, and I'll see what I can do about Ella and her family moving." *I'm going to make sure you have what you need in Texas.*

"Okay," Jerry said, but the disbelief in his tone hurt Brice's heart.

"I'm not going to let you down. I know you don't love me, but we have trust, which is the first step in a strong relationship." *I hope you will love me one day the way I love and admire you.* He stood up and kissed Jerry on the cheek. "Thanks for the workout and lunch."

"Can Evan sleep over at my house tonight?" Jerry asked.

"No. Don't bring Evangeline into the middle of the paparazzi spotlight right now. Not with your life under a microscope and Henry watching Evangeline's every move. Not until after Evangeline is my wife. Come by the penthouse anytime, day or night. You're welcome to visit, move in, or stay over. That's up to you." He gazed into Jerry's eyes. *You're so strong. Why do Dylan, Cade, and Ella think you're fragile?*

"That's fair. My house is open to you and Evangeline. Always." He leaned forward as if he was about to return the kiss on the cheek but stopped and leaned back. "Thanks for working out with me."

"I'll see you soon." As Brice walked out of the room and through the house, he felt an overwhelming sense that, without Jerry, none of them would feel whole. Jerry was the head of the family. *That's what he meant. He's the head of the family. He's the leader. The one we can all depend on. Without him, we would argue. Without him, we wouldn't have true peace. I need to talk to Cade. Figure out a way to convince Ella to move.*

Brice grabbed his phone from the leather tray on the foyer table and walked out of Jerry's home. He climbed into his car and turned on the ignition. In seconds, he drove down the road and made the first call to start the ball in motion for the main obstruction to Jerry moving to Texas.

"Cade Jackson," Cade answered.

"Cade, it's Brice. Are you serious about moving your family to Texas?"

"The conversation with Jerry went well?" Cade asked.

"Well enough."

"Damn. He didn't commit to the move long-term. Ella won't budge as long as he's living here, and Jerry hasn't said a word about Dylan or you or Evangeline to her. I don't think he will."

"He's looking into commuting, but that's hard. Troy does it, and it's wearing on him."

"May I tell Ella about the situation? She won't say a word. You know her."

"Yes." *I'm taking a big chance on this.* "But she has to keep the part where I'm in love with Jerry to herself. I didn't say a word to him and don't plan to for a long while."

"You're making a mistake not telling him you love him. He might just surprise you with his response."

"I don't know about that, but he is open to us all living together. So—"

"You and Jerry are like Garrett and me. It took me a while to understand my feelings and accept them, but once I did... You and Jerry deserve to be as happy as I am with my relationship with Ella, Garrett, and Derek."

"I hope we will be. I might have gotten Evangeline pregnant. She's not like your fertile woman, but there is a really good probability that I'm going to be a dad in nine months."

"Then you need to get Evangeline on a plane today. Fuck everything else. Henry is dangerous. I know you're going to say he's a good kid, but having a good heart doesn't mean shit when he's not on his meds. He's unpredictable, Brice. I do not want you dealing with what I'm dealing with and have dealt with."

"We can't leave until the trial and fight are over. Jerry needs us."

"Have Dylan stay with Jerry while you and Evan get the fuck out of town. Meet him in Vegas for the fight. You know that woman who attacked Ella a couple years ago is back. She's done her time in the hospital *and* in jail again."

"Yeah. Did you see her at the grocery store? At the spa?"

"She showed up in human resources looking for a job as my administrative assistant."

"Felicity showed up at your office?" *What the fuck?* "Isn't that a violation of her probation?"

"Apparently not. If the triplets weren't due any

minute, I'd have Ella on a plane or in a car and..." Cade unloaded on him all that had happened since they last talked. "If Jerry moved to his ranch next to mine, Ella wouldn't hesitate to leave Memphis. But he's tiptoeing around her because she's on bedrest. He doesn't want to upset her about the trial. It's killing her that she can't go to court and sit with him. But we all put our foot down on that. Even Jerry told her that if she showed up, he was carrying her out of the courtroom and taking her home."

"They usually tell each other everything, don't they?"

"Yes, and they're both reassuring the other that they're fine and not saying a damn thing about what is going on in either of their lives. Jerry is going to have a fit when he finds out that Felicity got through my building security. I'm on my way to talk to him. I pulled the short stick with the guys."

"I just left his house. Maybe I should turn around."

"No. Jerry and I have some personal stuff to talk about, anyway. If the conversation doesn't go well, I'll call you."

Brice stared at the faded white lines on the road and turned around. His mind ran a thousand miles a minute. *Why would Felicity go to Cade's office? The woman has steered clear of them since she got released. Why now? There has to be a reason. Could it be Jerry? Everyone knows Jerry and Ella are tight.* "Hey, Cade?"

"Yeah?"

"This might be a stretch, but check and see if there are any ties with Felicity and Jerry's opponent in the Vegas fight. The guy has been bankrolling the defense to screw with Jerry. He might be trying to mess with

Ella to get to Jerry. There's a chance Felicity had a financial windfall."

"You think?" Cade asked. "I'll get Garrett to look into her finances." His tone dropped as though he agreed.

"The more I think about it, the more I think I might be right." *I hope I'm wrong.*

"Something is off. Whether Felicity is taking a bribe, off her meds, or actually trying to make amends, I'm ready to move to a small town far away from here to raise my kids and grow old with my family. I need Jerry on my side. He has so many ties here. I don't know that even Ella moving would get him to leave this town."

"Ella is his strongest tie here. If she moves, he will too. I'll meet you at Jerry's. See you soon." *You have to be wrong about Jerry's ties to Memphis. I need him with us.*

Chapter Fourteen
Jerry

Jerry leaned forward and pressed his palms against the kitchen counter. He stared down but couldn't focus on anything Cade said. *Not Ella. No.* "Get her out of town today."

"She won't go," Cade said.

Focus. She's fine. She's at home in bed ordering Derek around. Jerry inhaled and faced Cade and Brice. He looked Cade in the eye. "Garrett can get her out of town, right?"

"If she agreed, Garrett could make it happen. Otherwise, you know Ella. She is not going anywhere she doesn't want to go," Cade said.

"Tell Garrett to get whatever she needs to travel. Y'all need to leave as soon as possible." He shifted his focus onto Brice. "Take Evangeline to my ranch in Texas. Henry won't find her there. I can handle the trial by myself and meet y'all in Vegas next week. I don't know what I'd do if anything happened to my girls." His throat closed up. *I am not going to lose anyone else. I can't.*

"Nothing is going to happen to the girls," Cade said. "But you're going to have to talk to Ella. She won't listen to me."

Jerry nodded. *Ella is going to leave me. Evangeline will move. I'll be here fighting for my career and reputation alone.* He glanced at Brice. *You'll have Evan and Dylan.* He kept nodding as he thought through everything he'd lose in a matter of days.

"Does this mean you'll be joining us at your ranch after the fight?" Brice asked.

"Depends on the trial and what comes out in the press." *I may lose all my sponsors. I never needed to win a fight more than I do this one.*

Brice bumped Jerry's shoulder with his own. "Trust me. You're going to love what I have planned, Jerry. If that fucker does anything to you, I'm drowning him with more bad press than he can possibly imagine. He will lose all his endorsements. Best of all, you're going to come out of it smelling sweeter than honeysuckle. I hope that guy tries fucking with you in the media." Brice grinned so wide that Jerry started smiling too. "My team is as fired up about this as I am."

"I don't see how I could come out of this in a good light."

Brice put his arm around Jerry's shoulder. "You were a victim, Jerry. You're not a victim anymore. That asshole isn't going to make you a victim again. He can't harm you. You have the truth and us on your side."

"People think Momma Mae was my biologic—"

"They jumped to that conclusion. And she was your mother. She adopted you. And don't worry about the fire. It further validates the challenges you've faced in your life." Brice hugged him. "We'll keep Evangeline safe, get you through this trial and fight, and start our lives together as one big family."

"I don't know," Jerry said. *So much can go wrong.* He wanted to lean on someone, but so much uncertainty seemed to cling to him.

Cade's phone rang.

"What's up?" Cade answered. He inhaled. "He's with me and Jerry." He looked at Jerry and then Brice. "No. He's not supposed to be there... On our way." He slid the phone into his back pocket. "We've got to go. Henry tripped Evan's alarm system at her house. He cut access to the surveillance cameras I put in but didn't see the ones Garrett installed."

"She's at the spa with Troy," Brice said. "Damn it. Henry won't leave her alone."

"It's thirty minutes to the spa," Jerry said. *Shit. Troy better keep my girl safe.*

Cade moved toward the door. "I'm so fucking tired of this shit. There is something about that location that isn't safe. No matter what I do, we get crazy people thinking they can get to my girls."

Brice gripped his car keys. "If this doesn't convince Evangeline we need to move now..." Brice couldn't seem to go on. He swallowed hard several times before inhaling deeply.

Jerry's voice failed him. He pulled Brice into a hug and the words he had been scared to say came out in a whisper. "Troy will keep her safe until we get there."

Brice pressed his face against Jerry's neck. "I need you with me."

Jerry cradled the back of Brice's head, and the desire to be intimate with him surged to the surface. Electricity buzzed through his veins. *Together we are conquerors.* "I'm coming with you. We'll handle this together."

Chapter Fifteen
Evangeline

"You sure about staying here alone?" Troy Shields, Evangeline's friend and Ella's sensual product line partner, asked.

"Yes, sir," Evangeline replied. "I'll be done in a few minutes. Brice is expecting me home soon."

Troy leaned over and kissed her on the cheek, a rarity for him. He flirted, but he never, never touched. "Lock the door behind me. Text me when you leave and let me know when you get home."

She rolled her eyes. "Yes, *Dad*."

He flattened his lips and gave her the stern father look. "I'm serious. I've been trying to get Ella to close this spa and relocate for a couple of years. Cade wants to burn the place down. There's a reason for that, Evangeline. It's not safe."

"It's safe," she said. *The security is excellent. No one is coming in who shouldn't be here.* "Don't worry. I'm going to clean up a bit and—"

"I'll be in my car in the parking lot waiting for you. If you're not out in ten minutes, I'm coming back in and making you go home. Don't forget how well I know you. One minute turns into an hour." He walked over the threshold and onto the sidewalk. "Ten minutes, Zanipolo. You do not want me calling Brice."

"Yes, sir." She closed the door and locked it.

He pointed to his watch and tapped it. "Ten minutes."

The man had softened the last few years. Ever since he partnered with Ella, Troy Shields showed a gentler side to the people he cared about. Ella did that to people. She opened her heart and forced everyone around her to open theirs, Evangeline included.

A sense of loss washed over her as she walked into her massage room at Ella's Spa for the last time as a massage therapist. No more crystals wrapped in silver mesh and velvet bags on the shelves. No more free-standing gems sparkling with energetic potential resting on glass trays along the gray granite counter. No more nature sounds softly drowning out the worries of the real world outside. No more lying on white sheets over a custom-designed massage table to meditate—not that she did, but she could have, if sex and marriage and babies weren't always on her mind. No more clients. Not that she had many, but still.

She ran her hand along the smooth leather covering the most luxurious table available in the industry. *I'm going to miss this place.* She'd miss Ella. She'd miss Derek and Cade and Garrett always rotating shifts to check on her and Ella and Rory.

She gazed at the open door to the empty lobby oasis. Working at Ella's had been the escape she'd needed these past few years. *Maybe Ella will move. Maybe she'll offer the spa to Rory to manage. Maybe she'll...* The probability of Ella moving away from the business she'd built with hard work and grit was most likely slim to none.

The prospect of Jerry moving to be with her, Brice, and Dylan seemed impossible unless Ella moved her family too. Ella might not be blood, but she was as close to it as Jerry had in this world, and Evangeline respected their bond. A large part of her would miss the world Ella created for herself and those she loved. Evangeline had been honored to be invited into Ella's safe place filled with love and peace. *If only Ella would come…*

Her heart ached a little more as the determination to move to the small town in Texas where Dylan's father lived became steadfast. She'd go, even if Jerry decided not to. Living with Brice the last week and a half made it clear that the previous long-term love relationships she'd chosen to stay in had all been verbally abusive with men who lashed out with the back of a hand or a chair or…

She shook her head, realizing they had all been men like her father. She was breaking the cycle. She was done making excuses for the men in her life. Brice wasn't like her father. Dylan wasn't either. And Jerry… When Jerry was in a room, arguments came to peaceful resolutions. The man was a walking pacifier.

She sat on the edge of the massage table. *I can change my future. I've done it before. I can do it again. This time will be different. I'm not running away. I'm setting down roots and planting a garden which will sprout leaves and expand until everything around me is blooming with beautiful flowers.*

She placed her hand on her belly. *If you're in there, I'm going to protect you and give you all the love in the world. Your father will love you with all his heart and will shower you with sweet words. You'll know what it's like to be loved unconditionally, treated with respect, and protected.* She exhaled as she raised her chin up and gazed at the white ceiling. *Please, give me the desires of my heart.*

Bells jingled.

"I'm coming, Troy," she shouted. She stood and walked out of the room and quickly turned tail and slammed the door shut. *Shit. Shit. Shit.* "Henry, you should go."

"I just wanted to tell you I'm sorry," Henry said. "I'm not going to bother you. I'm back at my dad's. I'm sorry. Please come out and let me see you. See what I've done to you. I don't remember what I did to you or anyone else. I don't remember anything."

"Did you disconnect the alarm system?" *I know you did or the chime would have alerted me, not the bells on the front door.*

"Yes, but it was just to check if Cade changed this system like he did at our house," Henry said. "I checked for you there first."

He knocked on the door to her massage room. "I know you're in there. Please come out. I'm not going to hurt you. I'm on meds, and Troy is probably calling my father or Cade or God knows who, so come out. I don't want us to end like this. I don't want you to hate me. I don't want your last memories of me to be me hurting you. Please, Evangeline. Please let me apologize to you, and then I can move on. I can let you go. I can go home and tell my father that I have done something to right some of the wrongs I've done in my life. Please." The sadness inside the tone of his voice made her heart ache. The man she'd fallen in love with stood on the other side of the wooden door.

She turned the doorknob and hesitated. *I should call Brice. No. Henry is apologizing. He's fine.*

She pulled the door open a crack.

He stepped back, giving her space. "Evangeline, I'm so sorry."

She peeked out farther, then walked into the lobby.

He retreated toward the spa entrance. "Are you still hurt?" He lowered his gaze. "Did I do that to your neck?

She nodded. "You need to stay on the meds, Henry. The medication allows you to be the man you are right now. The man who is husband and father material. Please, take care of yourself."

He nodded. "I didn't... Did I..." His face paled, and he hunched over as if he wore a four-hundred-pound pack on his back. "I didn't..."

"No, you didn't sexually—"

"Thank God," he mumbled. "I..." He covered his face with the hands that had given her the most loving and the vilest of touches. "This is bad enough. What I did was so horrible. I'm so, so sorry. So sorry."

She strode to him and gently placed her hand on his shoulder. "Yeah. But you're not going to do that again. You're going to take things slow. You're going to listen to your doctors. You're going to stay away from bad people and places. You're never going to take illegal drugs again. Right?"

He nodded, but she felt like she'd been punched in the gut again.

You need to commit to being sober. "You can conquer this, Henry." She glided along his arm and pulled his hand from his face. Sad blue eyes met her gaze. Genuine guilt blanketed his face. She'd seen it before, but she wasn't going to go back to a relationship that wouldn't work, didn't work. She didn't want to be his mother, and he needed a woman who wanted that kind of role in a relationship.

He nodded. "I'm going to try."

"Stay on the schedule your father and I helped you make. When you're feeling overwhelmed, talk to your doctor and sponsor. Talk to whoever you might be in a relationship with. Be honest. I believe in you. I know you can do this because *you've done it before.* You can do it again."

"Can you give me one more chance?"

"I can't, Henry. I love you. I will always love you, but we both need something neither one of us can give to the other. And that's okay. It really is okay."

"It doesn't feel okay."

The bells rattled on the door.

"Evan?" Brice asked.

Keeping her focus on Henry, she nodded. "I'm here with Henry. Give us a minute and we'll be out."

The bells rattled again.

"He loves you," Henry said. "He thinks you're going to marry him. But you're not. He's old. You wouldn't marry *him*, would you?"

Yes. I've already accepted his proposal. "Henry, I want you to be happy. I want you to meet a woman who wants one man, and you'll be that man. You'll be the only man in her life. There won't be anyone else for either of you. I'm not that woman. Promise me you'll take care of yourself."

He nodded.

"Let's go."

He nodded as he walked, slouched over, and pushed open the door.

Standing outside next to Troy, Brice extended his

arm and opened his hand as he often did to take hers.

As soon as she stepped outside, she glimpsed Jerry out of the corner of her eye staring up where a security camera should have been but wasn't. She took Brice's hand and was pulled by an invisible force into his arms, as if he were a magnet.

Brice kissed the top of her head but addressed Henry. "How are you doing, Henry?"

"I'm okay," Henry said. "The security system needs an overhaul."

"I noticed an issue and called Cade," Troy interjected. "He and Garrett are on their way to update it." Troy stepped forward covering the right side of Brice's body and all of Evangeline, serving as another barrier to Henry getting to her. "Are you headed home?"

"Yeah," Henry said. "Are you flying back to Austin?"

"In a couple days." Troy looked over his shoulder and lightly squeezed Evangeline's forearm. "Call me when you get home, Evan." He released her and faced Henry. "I'm going to stay until Ella's husbands get here. Hey, Henry, why don't you stay too? Maybe show Cade and Garrett how you shut off their security system?"

"Sure," Henry said. "Brice should stay. I can't hack into his security system. He could call his—"

"I'm taking Evan home," Brice said. "Glad that you're feeling better. See you around."

She turned as Brice guided her to his car.

"Evangeline, I hope to see you soon," Henry said.

Brice opened the passenger-side door.

She gazed at Henry. Something was off in his

expression. Maybe he thought he still had a chance with her. Maybe he was trying to screw with Brice. Whichever the reason, she worried he was going to make a surprise visit to her again. "Take care of yourself."

"Get in the car," Brice whispered.

She sat in the passenger seat, and he shut the door.

A black SUV with tinted windows drove into the space next to her. Cade, Garrett, and Derek exited the vehicle as Brice rounded the front of his car.

Henry lifted his hand and waved at Cade.

From the outside corner of the building, Jerry strolled over as if he were stopping by because he happened to be in the neighborhood. He smiled and shook Henry's hand like nothing was out of the ordinary. The normalcy Jerry brought with him wherever he went floored her, even in this strange situation. Jerry turned his head toward her and winked.

What was that for? She smiled back at him, because that is what she always did when he showed up. *That, or sex in a bathroom. Incredible sex. I love you.*

Brice slipped into the driver's seat and closed the door.

Derek tapped the hood of Brice's car twice.

In seconds, Brice backed out of the space and hit the main strip of road leading to the interstate.

"What—"

"Henry couldn't fully disable your house's security, but he tried," Brice said. "He tripped the silent alarm, which called the police and Cade's security team. He's going to end up in jail, Evan. Neither you nor Cal can help a kid who doesn't want to be helped."

"He wants help. He needs structure and therapy and to take his pills." *Cal will be there to help him stay on the right path.* She opened her mouth to ask about Jerry, but Brice's expression turned grave.

"Yes. He needs all that. But he's got a strange obsession with you. He gets upset with someone or when something happens at work, and he searches for you. He is *always* after *you*. You're not safe. And I'm telling you now, he's not getting your new phone number or address in Texas. He's not getting access to you anymore."

"He's not going to—"

"Stop acting like your relationship with him was normal. It wasn't. He's fine when you're doing what he wants, but as soon as you veer from your daily schedule, he loses it just like your father did and continues to do. He screams at you. Damn it, Evan..." Brice's voice dropped to barely a whisper. "I want you to fly, soar like you used to. I want you to be a homemaker or to start a law firm. I want you to follow your passion, wherever that leads. I want that for you. I want you to know that I'll be there, cheering you on, loving you, supporting you however you need it. The man or men in your life are there to enhance the person you already are, not to beat you down until you stop believing in your own worth. I should have stepped in a long time ago, and I didn't. No more excuses from either of us."

"You're right," she whispered. *You're more right than you know.* "My car is at the spa."

"Jerry will drive it to your house. The realtor put the "for sale" sign on the front lawn ten minutes ago. If Henry follows Jerry, he'll know there will be no access to you there."

"Henry is not going back to my house."

"You don't know that," Brice said. "Evan, you might be a shark of an attorney, but your heart is a marshmallow once you're out of that role. You think the best of people. I love that about you, but this circumstance is different." He continued on, restating everything he'd already said a thousand times over the years, and added more. He'd known her a long time and made a bazillion valid points with which she couldn't argue.

A section of her wounded heart healed as he spoke. There were no ulterior motives with Brice. There never had been. He wanted what was best for her since the day they first met.

"We're going to your father's house and telling your parents our plans for marriage and the move to Texas."

"Okay," she said. *Dad will probably lose his shit on both of us.*

"Dylan and Jerry are planning to meet us there."

She groaned. "Great. More fodder for the family dinners I won't be attending regularly or possibly ever again." She rested her head back against the seat and closed her eyes. *This is going to be a clusterfuck like none other. Mom and Dad are going to disown me. They're going to say I went from one bed with two men to a bed with three, and they'd be right. I did. I am...if Jerry will have me too... If Dylan will ever decide I've earned his bed. I have officially lost my mind.*

The gentle yet firm touch of his hand on her thigh eased little of her anxiety. "We're adults and don't need to elaborate on our private life. He's going to give us his blessing to go forth and have a family. It's going to be okay."

She huffed. "Yeah. You keep believing that." *There will be no blessing. I'll be lucky if Dad doesn't send down a proclamation that Rick and Kaila shall never speak to me or my children as long as they shall live. They'd obey him. They don't want to upset the gravy train.*

"You'll have me, no matter what happens. Am I enough?"

She gazed at the man who would be her husband soon. Worry etched the lines on his forehead. She slid her hand over his and squeezed. "You're enough, Brice. You've always been enough. I trust your motivations, your love…" She leaned over and kissed his cheek. "I can't wait to be your wife."

He turned his head and snatched a kiss from her lips. "I love you."

With those three little words, she was ready to cling to him and begin an adventure of a lifetime with renewed faith that Brice would give her the life she'd always wanted—one with him, Dylan, and Jerry.

Chapter Sixteen
Evangeline

With Brice on one side and Jerry and Dylan on the other, Evangeline could do nothing but stare at her parents positioned directly across from her in the formal living room reserved for guests and parties. The formal living room her father announced at their arrival that Joseph's wife designed. The formal living room where Joseph had turned her life upside down and sent her quitting her father's firm and running away to massage therapy school. The formal living room Evangeline wanted to demolish with Joseph in it.

"So, what brings the four of you here?" her father asked. His gaze darted back and forth between her and Dylan.

"I've asked your daughter to marry me, and she accepted," Brice said. "We'd like your blessing."

Her father stood up and smiled.

Brice rose from the couch and offered her his hand.

She placed her hand in Brice's and stood up. *Here it comes.*

"We'd love to have you as a son-in-law. Have you set a date for the ceremony?" her father asked.

What? Where's the "she's a whore" and "don't you know she's into public sex?" comments. She waited for the phrases he'd spewed like acid whenever she was in the same room with him. But the space remained an insult-free zone.

"Three weeks from tomorrow. The time and place will be announced soon. Formal attire is required." Brice squeezed her hand. "I'm sure that will not be an issue, but if it is, we'll have a designer on duty to dress you." Brice crossed the Persian rug to her father and shook his hand. "And so it doesn't come as a surprise, Evangeline and I will be moving to a small town not too far from Austin, Texas. I hope you'll both come and visit, as we won't be able to return to Memphis except maybe once or twice a year."

Her father glanced at Dylan and back at Brice. "We'll do our best to visit." He looked at her. "Are you planning to continue massage therapy?"

"No, Dad, I'm not."

"What changed? Henry beating the crap out of you?" Her father lifted his hands. His palms faced her in surrender. "I'm asking a question."

So that's the game you're playing. Throw shit at me and then retreat like it's been stricken from the record. "I—"

Jerry stepped in front of her, and Dylan joined her on the opposite side of Brice.

"Why does it matter what changed?" Jerry said. "Brice treats your daughter with respect. He loves her."

"Not too long ago, you were the one sitting at my dinner table as her date. Now, she's marrying a man she used to work for?" her father stated.

"Yes, sir. Brice won out. They have a long history. It's not a shock to you he's here, is it?" Jerry asked.

"No, it's not. Which begs the question, why are you and Dylan here?"

"You know why," Dylan said. "You know damn

well why. Your time is up. The tru—"

"I'm not walking *her* down any aisle," her father shouted. "Rick won't either."

Nice, Dad. Way to put the knife in and twist.

"You were never on the list to do the honor," Dylan said.

"You're not using the family china," her father said.

"No need for the family china," Brice said. "We're using mine."

"Your father let Joseph and his wife borrow it for their sixth anniversary," her mother said. "If I had known, I wouldn't have—"

"Stop," Evan said. "Just stop, Mom." She stepped out from behind Jerry and hugged her mother. "I love you."

Her father's voice resounded like a shock wave in the room. "The Zanipolo family will not attend your wedding to any one of these men. I won't condone another of your sexcapades that turn into total debauchery."

Evangeline hugged her mother tighter. *He will never change.* "I'm sorry you feel that way." She released her mother and stared right at her father. *Is it me? All women?* "I hope one day you stop hating me."

"Who else is involved in your marriage? Another woman? Man?" her father shouted. "Does Brice think he can tame you?"

She opened her mouth to tell him exactly what she hoped her future marriage would look like, but Brice's voice replaced hers.

"That is none of your business," Brice said. "My sex life, your daughter's sex life, or your sex life is not an appropriate topic of conversation." Brice touched Evan's back. "Darling, let's go. I have some wonderful surprises in store for you."

Her mother embraced her and whispered, "You have my blessing. Go and be happy. I'll try to attend the wedding, but you know your father." She kissed Evan's cheek. "I might be weak, but I raised a strong girl. I'm proud of you. Hurry up and go." She lowered her head and stepped back into her role as the silent wife, but there was a smile on her lips.

With her father unusually quiet, Evangeline walked toward the front door with Brice, Dylan, and Jerry. As Brice opened the door for her, she hoped her father would stop her from leaving, would give her marriage his blessing, would tell her he loved her and was proud of her. She hesitated for a few seconds, hoping he'd bridge that gap, wishing he'd reconsider his actions and words.

Matteo Zanipolo didn't do or say anything.

She stepped over the threshold of the home she grew up in and knew in her heart that it was the very last time she'd ever step foot in her father's house.

From the seat of Brice's car, she gazed out the window at the entrance to her childhood home, hoping her father would step outside and call her back or wave or make some kind of gesture that he loved her, but he didn't.

The man who had told her as a little girl to tell the truth, to stand proud in the face of adversity, to love with all her heart. A man who had promised her that he'd stand beside her and fight with her under any circumstances had done none of those things as soon as she turned fourteen. For sixteen years, she'd upheld her side of the bargain while he drifted farther and farther away from her.

Brice drove away from the house, away from her parents, her emotional devastations, her history. The love and pride her mother expressed seemed like a forever goodbye, not a temporary one. Maria Zanipolo would never visit Texas. The woman had never visited Evan's Memphis home. Not once. The comment about being weak remained the normal excuse not to visit, not to be at the wedding, not to write, email, text, or find some way to keep in touch. Maybe her mother was proud of her, maybe saying so was her mother's idea of a wedding gift. It didn't lessen the sorrow. It did put another nail in the coffin of disappointments.

As the scenery changed, her throat constricted and her heart ached for a different outcome with her parents.

"Did you...call...Rick?" The lump in her throat made it hard to speak. She couldn't look at him. She already knew the answer.

"Yes," Brice said. "He said it was up to his father whether the family attended."

She nodded as the lump in her throat expanded and the tears she refused to let fall fought to break free. "O-kay." *They really don't want me. They didn't choose me.*

"I offered to help them financially to get out from under your father's thumb, but they declined. You were smart to pay for everything on your own, to reject his financial help when you were just starting out."

She continued to nod, but the closer they came to his hotel, the harder it was to hold off the emotional tide rising within.

As he rolled to a stop in the private section of the parking garage reserved for him, she swallowed enough to speak. "Let's get married today. Now. No fancy anything. No dress. No suit. No one but us and a judge."

He turned off the car's engine and stepped out.

She quickly exited the car and joined him on his side. "What do you say?"

"I want a small wedding with friends. Neither of us have ever been married, and this is the only time either of us will ever get married, barring any tragedies. So, you're wearing a white dress, and I'm putting on a tux. We're going to say 'I do' in front of our friends and family who will be happy for us."

"What family? You don't have any living relatives. Mine aren't showing up."

He pushed the button to the elevator. "I have a goddaughter. Troy's granddaughter is my godchild. Troy and his—"

"Troy has a child?" *I've worked with Troy for seven years. He's never mentioned a daughter or grandchild.*

"Yes. One daughter. She turned thirty-four last month. Lacey Shields. He calls her Lacey Bear. I'm surprised you haven't met her. Blonde. Blue eyes. Gorgeous."

The elevator doors opened, and he guided her inside.

"That's his daughter?" she asked. *I thought she was his girlfriend.* "She's too old to be his daughter." *No way. Safe sex Troy Shields is not a father.*

He slid his keycard through the reader and typed in a code. The elevator closed and began the ascent to the penthouse. "Troy was fifteen when she was born. He and his mom raised Lacey. She's a great girl."

"He never said anything."

"And you never asked, did you?" Brice slid his arm around her and settled his hand at her hip.

"No, I didn't. I don't assume often, but I sure did when I met her. I thought she was his girlfriend." Both she and Troy kept their conversations about business, although he knew almost everything there was to know about her private life. She knew little of his, except that he traveled back and forth from Austin to Memphis for business and preferred his ranch in Texas to any other place on earth. "Does she live on a ranch?"

"Yeah. Nicki, my goddaughter, is nineteen. Lacey was a little wild child and had Nicki when she was fifteen. Lacey is no longer wild. Nikki has never been wild, but she had one night last year. She recently gave birth to a baby girl who is the spitting image of her— blonde, blue eyes, cute as a button. Nicki doesn't know who the father is. She met a guy and one thing led to another. It was her first time. She was sober. He was drunk. She panicked afterward and left without a clue to his name, where he's from, or anything. She's pining over the guy. She doesn't even think he will remember her. We're all looking for a guy we don't know much about."

"Wow."

"Yeah. Troy wants to make everything better for her, but he doesn't have a name or a picture to find the guy. All Nikki says is that he's the most handsome man in the entire world. He's got blond hair, blue eyes, and he's tall, and smart..." He chuckled. "God help the man, if he ever shows up. Troy and Lacey won't know whether to hug him or put a gun to his head."

"Are we talking about the same Troy Shields?" *The one Rory Quinn is crazy in love with?*

He laughed. "Yes, darling, your Troy Shields. My buddy. Ella's partner."

"Troy is a *great-grandfather*? He just turned forty-nine." *I have got to tell Rory about this.*

The elevator stopped and the doors opened.

"Feeling better?" Brice asked.

You were distracting me to make me feel better. She nodded. "Is that true about Troy?"

"Every word." He led her across the hall and into the penthouse. "A surprise is coming. It's pretty big, and it comes with a lot of responsibility, but I think you're going to be happy about it. I hope you'll be..." He didn't finish whatever he was going to say but kept moving toward their bedroom.

She looked around for signs of the surprise. *Could he have?* "A puppy?" *I would love a little fur ball.*

"Sorry. No puppies. They're not allowed in the hotel."

"Oh." She tried not to be disappointed, but she suddenly realized she'd missed out on a lot chasing down acceptance from the men in her life. She bought a house and had relationships, but she hadn't lived since Dylan and his father moved away. Not that she didn't do things, but the feeling of true belonging, of unconditional love, of a family who loved her had somehow vanished when they left town.

"We can get a puppy after we move." Brice stopped at the bedroom suite opposite theirs and turned toward her. "Take a deep breath and listen first. She's scared, and she's lived with a secret that she doesn't want to live with anymore. And just so you know, Dylan vetted her. He had DNA testing done a couple weeks ago to prove without a shadow of a doubt his information is accurate. It is."

She stepped back. *This doesn't sound like a good surprise.* "What is going on? Does my mother have another daughter?"

"No," Brice said. He twisted the crystal knob. "Listen first."

"I don't think I want to go inside." *Does Rick have a love child? He could. He's ten years older than me. He and Kaila have had a lot of ups and downs.* Her heart raced and the air in the room seemed to thin. *Dad. It has to be Dad. What has he done? Am I coming face-to-face with some woman he got pregnant?*

"This is a good thing, Evangeline. At least, I think this is." He opened the door. "Evangeline, I'd like you to meet…"

Chapter Seventeen
Evangeline

A scrawny teen girl, all skin and bones with long blonde hair and blue eyes, shifted from one foot to the other and rubbed her hands together. Her lips trembled and she looked as though she was seconds away from ugly crying.

"Hey, I'm Evangeline," Evan said. She offered a big smile, hoping it was enough to settle the young girl down. "Let's—"

"My mom died six months ago. I thought my dad might step in, but he filed emancipation documents and evicted me from the house my mom and I lived in. Mom left everything to him, not me." The girl's hands trembled as she dropped them to her sides. "I had some help getting a job, but then Dylan showed up and he knew. He told me that you wouldn't be mad."

Evangeline gathered the girl in her arms and held her. *Who are you?* "Tell me your name."

"Sally Fairchild. My parents are Faegan Fairchild and Matteo Zanipolo."

The names played like an endless loop in Evangeline's mind. Faegan and Matteo. Faegan and Matteo. Beautiful Faegan Fairchild. The woman couldn't type or file or read well, but she had a heart of gold, a smile that made the grumpiest old men happy, and a fabulous wardrobe that she'd gathered through years as a runway model. She'd worked as the receptionist at the Zanipolo Law Firm when she had moved to Memphis for the love of a man. Their marriage ended with an unexpected pregnancy—a pregnancy which terminated her employment at the Zanipolo Law Firm, never to be seen there again.

"I'm so sorry about your mother." *You're my sister? You're my sister. I have a sister. I have a baby sister who needs me.* "Are you in school?"

"I was homeschooled. I don't know what to do, but Dylan is looking into it," Sally whispered.

"Where are your things? Pictures, furniture, clothes?"

"Dylan is tracking down photos." Sally sniffled. "He's getting my birth certificate and stuff like that. I didn't think my father would trash everything. I kept the secret. I never told. I. Never. Told."

"Don't worry about any of that." Evan rubbed Sally's back as all her father's actions over the years suddenly made sense. If Evan's private life came forward publicly more so than it already had, his sexual history might get investigated. A daughter locked in the shadows would walk into the light. "I'm going to take care of you. We're going to be moving in a few weeks—would you want to move to Texas with us? We'll enroll you in school there."

"You're not angry?" Sally slowly raised her head and those sad blue eyes seemed full of hope.

"About you?" *I'm furious with my father. You're a victim like me. Like everyone who opposes the man.*

Sally nodded.

Evan shook her head. "No. Not about you. I have a little sister. A beautiful, smart, and tough sister. I've always wanted a little sister."

Sally's lips trembled and big, heavy tears filled her eyes. "A little sister who likes girls?" She looked away as tears ran like rivers down her cheeks.

I can only imagine what my father said to you. What more has he done? What other children are out there? "Yep. You love who you love. There is nothing to be ashamed of. I love three men. I'm not embarrassed or ashamed of it. It's the way I roll." Evan winked at her. "I remember your mom. She had the biggest heart of anyone I'd ever met. I can tell that you not only got her beauty, but her heart too."

"Sally?" Dylan said as he walked into the room.

Sally wiped the tears from her eyes and stepped out of the embrace. The sweet girl's entire body trembled like she stood at the epicenter of an earthquake.

"You were right," Sally said. "Evangeline is wonderful."

Dylan walked over to Sally and dropped to one knee in front of her. "Hey, there is no one and nothing to fear here. You're safe. And as a bonus, Brice's fridge is always stocked. You *can eat anything you want.*" He took her hands in his and smiled. "I even picked up bananas, ice cream, and peanut butter so we can make sundaes later. Go to the kitchen and have a snack. Brice likes to cook, like you, so maybe you two can cook dinner together tonight?"

She inhaled and nodded. "Yeah. Sounds good."

"Your recipe folder is on the kitchen island. Go, and do as I say."

"Yes, sir." She stopped shaking, leaned forward, and kissed him on the cheek. "Thank you." She hurried out of the room and closed the door.

Dylan rose to standing. "She's a good kid. Smart kid. Complete submissive."

Brice walked toward her and Dylan.

Dylan whispered, "Her mother homeschooled Sally until she couldn't. Sally continued the curriculum, but all she has is the current unit she had in her purse. Matteo hired a crew to empty the house the same day Faegan died. I have no school records for Sally. I've got my father looking into the options for school testing under these unique circumstances."

"Where has she been living?" Evan asked. *How could my dad have hidden Sally from Mom? From me and Rick?*

"I found her living and working as a makeup artist at an upscale strip club. The guy who runs it is aboveboard and kept her behind the scenes or in the office once she'd finished working. He seemed relieved that she'd accepted my help." He put his arms over her and Brice's shoulders and pulled them into a huddle. "She needs a stable home. Which means we have to move and settle into a house as soon as possible. I'm still working on Jerry, but I think he's going to commit after he talks to Ella."

"He's moving with us," Brice said. "We're going to stay here, help him through the trial. He wants this as much as the rest of us. Then we're all moving together. You'll be ready by then, right?"

"What's going on?" Evan asked. "When did Jerry—"

"Brice will fill you in, but Jerry is going to need a lot of support and attention from all of us," Dylan said.

She stepped forward and the huddle turned into a hugging sandwich with her in the middle.

"I've got to go," Dylan said. "I hope to be back for a late dinner." He kissed her and then Brice. "I have a solid plan."

Before she could ask what he was referring to, Dylan was out the door and gone.

"Do you know what that was all about?" she asked.

"Nope." Brice didn't seem worried or curious.

"How are we going to make all this work? What will Jerry think when he finds out about Sally? What are we going to do? How are we going to take care of her?"

"You don't know how he'll react until you tell him. So, call. No sense in waiting and wondering."

Right. Lay it all on the table. Throw one more responsibility on him. He's going to run. Run like hell, far, far away from me. She nodded and held her stomach. *He wants a baby I may never be able to give him. He wants to be a big role in Ella's kids' lives. He would have to choose me over everything and everyone. Why would he ever do that?* "I'll call him later."

Brice held her a little tighter. "Jerry is a good man. You have to trust your instincts. You have to trust that all three of us are right about him. It might take some time, but Jerry is worth the time. He's worth the effort. And the man might just surprise you."

She nodded, but her gut screamed that the addition of Sally to the equation gave him an excuse to end a relationship that had just begun. She would ask if he would love her anyway. A solid "no" would leave his lips. And the chance at a perfect life would be lost.

Chapter Eighteen
Jerry

Jerry hit the heavy bag over and over and over to near exhaustion as Jason Winthrop jumped rope beside him. The prosecution's case had slowly fallen apart as the second week dragged on. Witnesses changed their stories on the stand. The justice Jerry had expected for Momma Mae didn't seem to be on the horizon. The trial was out of his hands. The fight in Vegas held a heavier burden, a deeper justice for him, for his Wynn name, for the family he loved who he imagined watched over him from Heaven. He couldn't beat the shit out of the criminals who took Momma Mae's life, but he could knock out the asshole who payrolled the defense and would let them walk away unpunished.

"Dude, Danny texted me to tell you to stop. He also wanted to know if you were heading to court or meeting him at the airport in the morning."

"Could you text him and let him know I'm on the stand tomorrow morning, but will fly out as soon as I'm done?" *I should be texting Danny, but I don't want to talk about the trial or Dylan or Brice or the move.*

"Sure." Jay walked to the bench and picked up his jug of water. "So, everyone is packed for the move except you."

Jerry nodded. *Been kinda busy.* "Any leads on your girl?" He shook out his arms and joined Jay by the bench.

"Nope. I'm starting to think I imagined her. But I didn't. I know I shouldn't have been drinking. It was a major error in judgement. I swear if Katie hadn't been at the same hotel that night, I wouldn't have gone out clubbing with the guys. I wouldn't have taken that first drink."

"You were bound for a mistake at some point in your life. Don't beat yourself up over it." *Ella raised you right.* "I think the girl you fell for is out there."

"She has to be, but every promising lead turns to wasted time." He took a swig of water and hung up his rope on the wall. "It will take a miracle from God for me to find her."

"You'll get your miracle. I'm a firm believer in them." *Somehow, some way, the couple who murdered my sweet Momma Mae will be punished. It might not be in court, but it will happen.*

"Mom and Kyle think I'll find her. I can tell that Cade, Garrett, and Derek think I imagined her. They keep telling me that it sounded like a dream to them."

He patted Jason on the back. "You'll find her. All the details you're missing will come back in a rush as soon as you set eyes on her."

Jason dropped his gaze and nodded. "Thanks."

"I guess I'm done in here for the night," Jerry said. *I need to get a decent night's sleep.*

"You have to move with us," Jason said as he walked out of the gym. "Dude, you're the only person keeping me sane."

Jerry blew out a huffing laugh. "Back at ya." He sat on the bench and took off his gloves.

A light flickered from the security monitoring

system Brice had set up a few days ago. The publicity surrounding him had brought stragglers too close to his home for comfort. No one had broken in, but he now had guards at the entrance to his and Ella's properties.

"He's in the gym," Jason said.

"Thanks." Dylan's smooth voice carried through the house. A minute later, he peeked into the gym. "Done?"

Jerry nodded.

"How are you holding up?"

"That's a loaded question," Jerry answered.

"May I come in?"

Jerry nodded. "Sure." *I wish you wouldn't ask. Jason and Kyle don't ask. They barge right in just like the rest of their family.*

Dylan strode in and knelt before him. "I would have come sooner, but the new office manager wanted to clarify a few procedures I set in place for this weekend."

"You did the right thing." *You've been by my side during this entire trial. You, Brice, and Evangeline dropped everything to support me, even when I told y'all not to. Even when I insisted Evangeline and Brice leave for Texas to get away from Henry.*

Dylan lifted his chin and leaned forward. His soft lips met Jerry's. "I love you."

"Love you," Jerry whispered. The words seemed harder to get out today. He'd told them he would move, that he'd commute, that he was going to try to make the alternative relationship work. But something in his gut kept him from arranging a moving company to set a date to pack the house and move the contents.

"You don't have to ask permission to come into my

gym," Jerry said. "I've given you access to my house whether I'm here or not. My house is your house."

"Okay," Dylan whispered. His hand glided along Jerry's thighs, under his shorts, and caressed his balls.

Jerry's cock jumped to attention. "Hey, if you're not going to suck it, then—" He stopped before the knee jerk of an ultimatum left his mouth. *I need you to love me.*

Dylan wet his lips and half of those brown eyes disappeared under his lids.

Jerry lifted his ass and pushed his shorts down as Dylan pulled them the rest of the way to his ankles. His cock in the air, ready to erupt, Jerry cupped the back of Dylan's head. "I want you to swallow."

"Yes," Dylan moaned.

In control, Jerry guided Dylan to his raging cock. "Use your hands too."

That mouth. That tongue. Dylan knew exactly what to do.

The plug he'd bought from Troy to see if anal sex was something he'd want with Dylan and Brice shifted inside him and pressed on his prostate. It took every ounce of willpower not to give in and come.

"Dylan," he moaned. "Don't stop." He grabbed the soft waves of short hair at the back of Dylan's head. "I'm going to come."

Dylan pumped his fist up and down Jerry's cock as he sucked and swallowed. The moans Dylan made sent Jerry over.

Jerry thrust and somehow Dylan took more of Jerry's cock down his throat.

Dylan grabbed Jerry's ass and a finger slid and tapped the handle of the plug. With new fervor, Jerry thrust. Over and over, Jerry dominated Dylan's mouth until Dylan pulled out the plug and shoved the toy back in.

"Yes," Jerry shouted. "I want you to fuck me." He shuddered so hard that he dropped his ass down on the bench. *I can't believe I said that.*

Dylan's hands shifted in a heartbeat and fisted Jerry's cock. He lifted his head and smiled, then licked over the top of Jerry's cock like a lollipop and finished taking in the last drops of cum. "Me on top or you?"

"Now?" Jerry asked. *Shit. I am not ready for that right now.*

"Your ass is lubed really good," Dylan said. "Whoever you consulted did a good job advising you on anal play."

"I'm not sure I'm ready for a real cock," Jerry said. *Ceding control to you might be a bad idea.*

Dylan licked the tip of Jerry's cock again, then gazed up. "We don't have to. Did you work out with that thing up your ass?"

Jerry laughed. "Yeah. I had a rod up my ass. I didn't really notice it until you touched it."

Dylan caressed down Jerry's shaft and over his balls. "Do you have a larger one?"

Jerry's cheeks heated. He'd bought the sizes Troy had suggested and added a straight-up dildo for experimentation. Not that he planned on using it anytime soon, but the relationships he wanted might lead to more. Training made champions, and if he decided to do it, he was damn sure going to be the best at it.

"You did. That's good," Dylan said. "It's smart." He gathered Jerry's shorts and boxer briefs and stood up. The man's cock tented his pants. "Shower time for both of us."

Jerry's cock hardened and his balls felt heavy, as if he hadn't already come. He stood up and took off his shirt.

Dylan held out his hand for Jerry's shirt. "Are you expecting anyone?"

"Cade is going to stop by sometime, but he'll announce himself once he's seen something he isn't sure he should see, unlike the rest of Ella's crew who would make whatever embarrassing situation a family affair." *They're family. They are all mixed up in every aspect of my life. Like I want you to be. Like I want Evangeline and Brice to be. I need to commit. Commit and make it work... Maybe after the fight, after I stomp that motherfucker's mouth into the mat. That man has no idea how much I hold back in my fights. No. Fucking. Clue.*

Dylan laughed. "Okay, so I don't have to worry about your privacy with them. They know about us, right?"

"Yes. Of course they know." *They're my family. I love them. We don't keep secrets from each other.*

"I don't want to do anything to ruin your relationship with them. I know how much they mean to you."

"Don't worry." He picked up his phone from the bench and looked at the screen. *Evangeline.*

—*When we're in Vegas, are we staying in the same room? Me, you, Dylan and Brice?*—

He looked at Dylan. *What will it be like to make love to Evangeline and two men? Will I like sleeping in a bed with three lovers? Will Evangeline always want three cocks vying for her body? Should I make that kind of forever commitment?*

He walked toward the exit. His cock thumped against his abs with each movement. He reached out and grabbed Dylan's hand as he took the lead. Cum trickled from the tip of his cock as he continued thinking and strolling through the house to his bedroom. *Would Brice give up control to me? Suck me like Dylan does? Like it when I fuck him? Would he want me to?*

His phone vibrated. He looked at it and answered. "Hey, Brice." *Your ears must have been burning.*

"Hey," Brice said. "Evangeline and I have been talking about tomorrow. Do you want me to stay here and be in court or go to Vegas with Evangeline and Dylan? Also, are you staying at your house there or at the hotel?"

"I have a room at the hotel, but I'm not sure if I'll stay there or at the house. I've left it open to stay at either place." He placed the phone on the vanity.

"I'm switching to video call. Evangeline wants to…"

Brice and Evangeline's faces appeared on the phone's screen. "Oh." Brice cleared his throat.

"It's fine," Jerry said. "Just don't record this." *Are you going to make an excuse to get off the phone now that you see me naked?*

"I wouldn't do that," Brice said. "Celebrating?"

The spray of water hitting tile interrupted Jerry's answer. He gazed at Dylan.

Dylan smiled and squeezed his hand. "I'm going to get undressed." He released Jerry's hand and began taking off his suit jacket.

"Okay," Jerry said. *They want a relationship like this. Here goes nothing.* "I finished my workout, so I'm hopping in the shower with Dylan."

"Have you arranged for a moving company to pack?" Brice asked. "How long do you think you'll have to commute before making the move permanent?"

"I haven't contracted with a moving company. And I'm not sure how long I'll commute. A lot depends on the outcome of the fight and my sponsors." *I won't lose all of them, but with the rumors of my relationship with the three of you, I will lose some.*

"Don't worry about your sponsors," Brice said. "Any of the ones who leave will wish they stayed. There are some new ones coming your way."

"We'll talk about sponsor issues later." Dylan kissed Jerry's cheek and whispered, "Brice doesn't know too much, but a friend of his called him to find out more about your personal life. Then he called me. Brice and I don't discuss your business without you agreeing to it."

"I trust you," Jerry whispered.

Evan disappeared from the screen and Brice's jaw slackened.

"Where did Evan go?" Jerry asked.

Brice angled his phone in time for Jerry to see Evan stroking Brice's cock. Her lips parted and her mouth slowly took in the man's cock. Heavy breathing followed.

Evan lifted her head and smiled. Beads of cum slipped from the tip of Brice's cock. "I can't wait to suck three cocks, to be fucked by the three of you, to be your wife, carry all your babies."

"Oh, fuck," Brice moaned. "Show me that pussy."

Evan turned on a dime and flipped the skirt of her dress up over her bare ass. Cum and juices glistened on the folds of her sex.

Dylan brought Jerry's hand to Dylan's erection. "We're going to take turns pumping cum into her."

Jerry's heart thundered in his chest. *You've made love to her recently.* Electricity buzzed inside him with Brice and Evangeline's sexual exposure and willingness to share. *I want us to be together. All of us.* He let go of his inhibitions at being watched, and stroked Dylan's cock.

"I want you to do that to me, Jerry," Brice moaned. "I want us to be a family."

I want that. God, I want that. "Fuck her, Brice. Take her. I want to see you dominate her."

Brice dropped the phone, but the call didn't end. The screen showed Brice and Evan as clear as the day. In and out. Brice's cock entered and exited like a pro. Her pussy stretched and begged for his rod. He pushed her dress over her head and held it at her wrists, showing off the rest of her body. Her tits bounced and her nipples looked hard and perfect for sucking.

"Yeah, Jerry," Brice moaned. "You're mine, too. You're all mine. Oh, fuck. Feels so fucking good knowing you're there. Knowing you want this. Knowing you want me as much as I want you."

"Brice," Evan cried out. "Oh, God, I'm coming. So fast. So fast." She shook and pushed back, making his cock disappear inside her.

Brice retreated from her body. His cock spurted cum on her ass and pussy and back. "Mine."

He dropped back. Part of his cock remained in view. He lifted the phone and showed Evan's messy sex. "This is ours. No one else's." He showed his cock. "This is the three of yours, no one else's."

"Hell, yeah," Jerry said. No sense of jealousy overtook him. No need to go over and protect Evan. No red flags popped up. No reasons not to take that big step and call a moving company.

Dylan curled his arm around Jerry's back and gripped his hip. "Tell them what you're feeling and anything that is holding you back from moving to Texas."

Jerry wanted it all, but something was off. Brice and Evangeline hadn't asked him to move in with them. They didn't ask him over for dinner or to visit after a long day at court. Evangeline seemed stressed as soon as they talked about getting together at the penthouse. *It's probably all in my head.*

"Mind if I stop by later?" Brice asked.

"You don't have to ask," Jerry said. "Just come over."

"Me too?" Evan asked.

"Babe, always," Jerry replied. *Is that all you needed? Permission?* "My doors may be closed to everyone else, but not to the people I love." *I do love all of you. I trust you.*

Dylan kissed Jerry's neck. "I love you."

Jerry's cock jerked and even though his body prepped for sex, inside the layers of armor around his heart vanished. No fear filled his chest and stomach. They wouldn't betray him. They wouldn't lie to him. They cherished their relationships with him as he did them. He'd waited for this feeling to develop in a relationship all his life. Only, he'd never experienced that feeling of pure emotional safety from a lover. Not until now.

Evangeline smiled and his world brightened.

Whether she was pregnant with his child or Brice's or not at all, Jerry wanted to be with her. He wanted all of them to be his lovers, partners, and family forever. "We'll all stay together in Vegas."

Chapter Nineteen
Evangeline

The threads of the flogger landed on her breast with the perfect amount of sting.

Dylan, you are a master of sex. The slight flick of his wrist lifted the ends of the leather and lightly dragged them across her swollen and red nipples.

Evangeline gasped in a lungful of oxygen as his mouth covered her tender nipple and sucked. The thick, supple leather restraints won the battle against her attempts to fight, to touch, to control him. Little by little he'd broken her down until his words and actions were the only ones that mattered.

"Good girl," he whispered. His fingers dipped into her pussy. "Who decides what goes in here?" He wiggled his fingers at one of the powerful sweet spots he'd found to make her orgasm. When he touched it, she lost the battle for control. She failed him and his command to hold out for his next order. Bliss wasn't an option until he allowed it.

She panted to relieve some of the ache as the need to orgasm counted down like a timer on a bomb. "You do, sir."

"Who decides when you orgasm?"

"You do, sir." Her voice trembled on the verge of a scream.

"That's my good, sexy kitten," he said. He kissed

her breast and crawled off the bed.

No. I need to come. You're not going to let me come, are you?

He walked to a tall dresser and opened a drawer. "I'm going to admit, I'm not happy about wearing one of these with you." He turned around with a foil square. "Knowing how well your pussy has been fucked already. Knowing you allowed two men to leave their cum inside you. Knowing you loved it. But it's necessary. I am not interested in being a father. Not this year."

She stayed silent, but her heart ached for him as his fear of having a child of his own seemed insurmountable. Dylan had always shielded his heart, but he told her his mother's suicide closed him off completely for a long time. He admitted that much to her tonight. He admitted more—his deep love for Jerry and how the fighter had been the catalyst for big changes in his life. Without his serendipitous love affair with Jerry, he would never have come for her, never have opened up enough of his heart to heal the deepest wounds from his mother's death. The man he had become in the last few years was due to the man she loved too—Jerry Wynn.

He gazed over his shoulder and the love in his eyes reminded her of the desire and love they had shared as teens. "Are you going to be a good kitten?" He held up the condom.

"Yes, sir. Absolutely, sir. Whatever my master wants, I'll give." *Are you really going to do this? No more waiting and wanting and wishing?*

"You say that, but you seem to be all about work," he said. "My kitten wants her lovers to fuck her. Wants to show off her beautiful body. Wants to make me jealous." He ripped the foil and glided the condom over his big, red, and veiny erection.

If her legs weren't already splayed wide and stretched to her limit, she would have forced them into whatever position he wanted to get his cock inside her.

The nub of her clit throbbed and begged for his touch. Her breasts swayed with each breath she took in anticipation of what he might do next. Her heart ached to please him, to love away all his past hurts.

He climbed onto the bed and stepped over her until he straddled her waist. "Are you pleased with the way I sheathed your present?"

"Yes, sir," she said. *Please fuck me.*

He placed his right knee down between her legs. He lifted his left leg over her thigh and brought his knee next to his right one.

With her eyes closed, she tried to calm her heartbeat, to slow it, to steady it so she could concentrate on holding out from disappointing him or starting over with the first lesson.

He thrust, burying the long, thick rod of muscle deep inside her.

She squeaked, "Oh." *Yes. Yes. Don't come. Don't come.*

She gritted her teeth to stop the tide of bliss from taking her into subspace. Tears pricked at her eyes. He'd denied her orgasm for what seemed like hours but couldn't have been.

He moaned as he slid from her center. "You're being such a good girl." He grunted and thrust forward, driving his cock into her, grinding her clit, and stretching her walls to provide for his wide girth.

She ground her teeth to keep from opening her mouth and releasing the tension from denying her orgasm.

In and out, he punished her with delicious striking thrusts and lazy withdrawals, keeping her on the edge, giving her the choice to control her bliss and please him or acquiesce to her wants and disappoint him again.

In and out. She fell deeper and deeper into his desire for her to obey him. The further she fell, the more powerful he became. More of their old love rose to the surface. More of the heartache from when he moved away healed. More of their original bond expanded and strengthened and unveiled the forever love she had dreamed they would have again one day.

"Yes," he grunted. "Come. Come for me. Now."

At the end of her fuse, his words ignited the explosion inside her pussy. Powerful contractions hit her with a force she hadn't expected nor experienced from another dominant man.

"Dylan," she screamed. The orgasm spread from her pussy to her clit and back again. The normally closed circuit of bliss opened and expanded through her veins and muscles, into her bones and marrow.

His cock jerked inside her. "I love you," he mumbled. "I love you. I'm sorry I stayed away so long. I'm sorry I locked myself away from you, from feeling this love. I missed so much of your life, of the life we could have had all this time."

In his confession, she found entry into subspace once again. Her body hummed and filled her thoughts with a peaceful loveliness at being with him in this honest place of acceptance, forgiveness, and pleasure. She floated on air, safe in his arms.

"Angel," he whispered. "Come back to me." The delicious pull of the leather keeping her in place released. The cock filling her slid from inside.

"No," she mumbled.

He smiled and kissed her belly. "You are mine."

"Yours," she whispered.

He left the bed and slid the condom filled with cum off his limp cock. He dropped it in the trash near the tall dresser where he kept all his wonderful toys. He opened a drawer, pulled something out, and closed it.

He turned around and held whatever he had taken from the dresser behind his back. "I have something special for you, but you have to promise to be a good girl and obey my every command."

"I promise," she said. The loss of his cock left a void inside her. The warmth and peacefulness he'd provided slowly drained the longer she lay alone. *Hold me. Touch me.*

He joined her in bed. "Close your eyes."

She lowered her lids. Something rigid and thick pressed against her sex and slid inside her. A sensual moan straight from her soul tickled her lips. Her pussy walls welcomed the gift and squeezed deliciously around it. "Thank you, sir."

A hard, slick object pushed into her dark hole. She pushed out against it and her passage stretched as the thickness tunneled into her. "Oh, sir." Juices squirted from her pussy as pleasure from being his to play with combined with the joy he possessed as he worked the large toy all the way inside.

Stuffed and happy, she rolled back into her happy place as he removed the supple leather from her arms and legs. Wet cloths and warm oil glided over her as he massaged her from her fingertips to toes.

Putty in his hands, she relished the extra pampering, something a dominant lover hadn't taken the time to do in years.

He slid the toys from her passages. "Ready to go to our bedroom?"

"Yes, sir."

The honest smile on his face seemed to validate that she'd made the right decision. "Then it's time for you to dress."

She sat up and scooted off the bed. "This looks like a regular bedroom." *A non-kinky person wouldn't know that the leather bench is for sex, or that the wood-and-metal rotating cross on the wall isn't just art.* "Is all of this getting packed for the move?" *It seems to be the only room in the house not boxed up and ready for the movers.*

"Yes. We're having our own playroom. I think Brice will join us on occasion, but Jerry won't. Not with the spanking and floggers and the other toys we enjoy."

She slipped into a black dress shirt and black slacks. "Smart."

He buttoned up his dress shirt and picked up his jacket. "Ready?"

"Yes, sir." She placed her hand in his and followed him out of the room. Each step she took reminded her that sex was a workout, not dinner. Her belly grumbled. *I hope Brice and Sally have leftovers.*

He didn't try and convince her to stay with him as he drove her to the hotel.

At the elevator outside the penthouse to go back down to the lobby, he kissed her on the forehead. "I want you to call Jerry and tell him about Sally. Don't wait until after the fight. He needs to know tonight. You've waited long enough."

"I know. I know. But he's been through so much with the trial. I don't want to lay this on him right now." *The defense is going to win. Jerry is going to be beside himself.*

"Don't be like your father."

That hurt like a punch to the gut. She pressed her hand against her belly. "I'm not like my father."

"You're hiding her from one of the people you love because you're scared. You have nothing to be scared about, and she's been hidden enough. Call and tell him or I will."

"You're threatening me." *I can't believe you're—*

"Yes. I'm making you do the right thing." He leaned forward to kiss her, but she jerked away.

"I don't do well with threats."

"Jerry doesn't do well with lies. Do not ruin your spotless reputation for honesty by waiting. He will find out, if not from me or you or Brice, from someone else. We don't want that. I'm not going to stand by and watch the life I want more than anything in this world get ruined because of your irrational fear."

The elevator doors opened, and he stepped in.

"That's not fair."

He shook his head. "Really?" He lowered his chin and pursed his lips. "My relationship with Jerry is not as extensive as yours, and I feel like I know him better. How is that?" He held his hand against the door, stopping the elevator from closing.

"I'm scared. Do you blame me? He wants a baby, not a teenager."

"He's not a kid. He's a man, and he can handle a teen better than you or me. Brice and I agree—you're telling him tonight. It has to happen tonight. Do not fuck up our lives over a great kid who we all have grown to love over the last couple of weeks. He's going to love her like we do. He's going to be a fierce protector and she needs that. Maybe Jerry will be the father Sally needs in order for her to thrive. Give the man a chance and he will not disappoint you."

"You're right. Damn it, you're right." *I have waited long enough.*

"Call him. I have a playroom to pack." He dropped his hand and the elevator doors closed.

She turned and faced the penthouse doors. *I have the worst timing. What do I say to him? 'Hey, my father had a love child and threw her out like she's trash, like he did me. I'm going to take care of her now. She's living with all of us.' Ugh. Maybe 'I met this great kid and she turned out to be my sister.' Or 'my father disowned me and the sixteen-year-old half sister I just found out about.' Sally deserves better than what I'm giving her. If he doesn't want to be with me because of her, then he isn't the man I know him to be. But so far none of the men in my life, except Brice, have been the men I thought they were. Brice and Dylan. Dylan is the man I knew him to be.*

She opened the door and entered the foyer.

"Evangeline?" Brice shouted.

"Yes, sir. I'm home." She walked through her temporary home toward the kitchen. As she rounded the corner, her stomach plummeted to the floor. *Shit.*

Jerry turned his head. No smile. No greeting, just a look that told her he knew she'd been hiding Sally from him.

Sally gazed at her from the opposite side of the table from him. The red-rimmed eyes of her teenage sister displayed the agony within the girl. Whatever conversation they'd had seemed like it was rough.

"Your sister was telling me that you and Dylan were working on finding her school records. They're under an umbrella school. I made a call and they're being sent by snail mail to my address and the high school near my house in Texas." He turned toward Sally. "I've got you seated next to Danny and Jessica on the flight to Vegas in the morning. Pick out your room in my house and make yourself comfortable. I don't have an extra ticket for you for the fight, but if you're interested—"

Sally shook her head. "No, sir. That's not my thing."

"Okay, then you and Jessica will have a girls' night. She doesn't like it either." He stood up. "It's time for me to head home." He pivoted and faced Evangeline. He kissed her cheek. "I guess you don't trust me. This is the secret you've been hiding. What did you think I'd do? Of all the kids in the world, Sally Fairchild is a gem of one. She and her mom visited Momma Mae every week until… I would do anything for that little girl."

He kissed her cheek, and the fury radiating off his face burned. "I love you."

Evangeline's lips trembled. *I've lost him. He'll never move. He's doing the right thing at the moment, but this is his excuse to bail on the move.* "I love you."

He clenched his jaw and nodded, then walked out.

Sally's mouth started moving before the words

processed with Evangeline. "He walked in and he looked at me," she said. "I started talking, and the next thing I knew, I was crying my eyes out in his lap as he held me. I know you wanted to talk to him about everything, but he gave me that look. You tell him everything no matter what it is when he looks at you that way. You do know that look, don't you?"

Evangeline couldn't do anything but nod. She knew the look. She also knew the damage she'd done by not telling him as soon as she found out.

Sally hugged her and Evangeline found herself clinging to her little sister.

"It's going to be okay," Sally whispered. "It has to be. It has to be."

"A bump in the road," Evangeline said softly. "We are made of strong stuff. We'll get through this." *I have to talk to him. Explain.* "Is Brice here?"

"He's in the other room with Cade. Henry showed up at Cade's office and at the spa and here looking for you."

I should have left when Brice begged me to. Sally and I would be safe with Ella, Derek, and Garrett. Brice and Dylan could have stayed with Jerry and worked on their intimate relationship. I should have listened to them, but no. I had to be at court for Jerry, for me. I had to prove to everyone that Henry didn't scare me, but he does scare me. Now Jerry's angry. Brice is probably as furious as Jerry, and when Dylan finds out...

"They love you so much," Sally said. "They'll protect you from Henry. Jerry said he wasn't going to let anything happen to either one of us. Not ever."

Evangeline nodded. *I hope you're right.*

Chapter Twenty
Evangeline

Gripping Dylan's and Brice's hands, she held her breath as Jerry took another blow to his handsome face. *Oh, my God. Oh, shit.* She dropped her chin down and squeezed her eyelids shut. "His nose is broken."

"He's fine," Dylan said. "He's barely fazed."

"He just grinned," Brice said. "He's fucking with him. The bell is about to ring, and Jerry is advancing. You've got to see this."

"I can't. I can't watch him lose." Evangeline peeked up with one eye open, then the other. She stood up. "Knock him out!"

"Finish him," Dylan shouted.

Evangeline could hear Brice mumbling, "Not yet. Not yet. One more round. Make him bleed. Punish him for what he's done. Torture the bastard every second, until the very last."

Yeah. She glanced at Brice with new eyes. *You want him to be punished as much as Jerry does.*

The bell rang.

Jerry walked with a conqueror's swagger to his corner.

Brice put his arm around her.

She leaned toward him. "He's hurting. Badly."

"Not nearly as badly as the other guy," Brice said. "He's putting an old-fashioned ass-whooping on that fucker. It's beautiful to watch."

Dylan squeezed the middle of her thigh. "I want him to knock the son of a bitch out. This is driving me crazy."

The bell rang again.

Jerry stood up and squared his shoulders.

"This is it," Brice said on an exhale. He rose from his seat, as did everyone in the arena.

Jerry advanced and the crowd went wild.

His opponent retreated. Fear hung in the man's dark eyes with each step backward. The world would see the young fighter's cowardice.

Millions would realize, like she did, that Jerry was toying with the man. Jerry took hits so he could continue with the match. One jab turned into two. Jab. Hook. Uppercut. Each blow Jerry landed precisely where intended. Over and over, Jerry's fists pounded on the man. Jerry's knees, legs, and feet pummeled against the man who had taken justice away from him. Combinations of hits seemingly intent on keeping the rotten man on his feet kept the time ticking away.

Jerry brought the man down and ground the bastard into the mat.

The referee ended the fight.

Jerry walked across the mat, bruised and bleeding, and stood near his trainer Danny as the other guy counted stars. A slight twitch in Jerry's cheek pulled his mouth into a crooked smile that disappeared as quickly as it arrived.

The young fighter had expected to rise to the top and unseat the undefeated champion, but he had failed like every other man before him.

Evangeline stood in awe of her man in the

spotlight. Outside the arena, he seemed like a normal guy, but inside, the man remained a god.

"And the winner by knockout"—the referee raised Jerry's hand—"Jerry Wynn."

The cheers deafened her ears. Joining the crowd, Dylan and Brice chanted Jerry's name over and over.

She couldn't speak, only stare at the man she loved. She had no idea if he would come to the house tonight or in the morning or not at all. No idea if he would ever trust her again. Most of all, she had no idea if his decision to stay at the hotel instead of his house in Vegas was because he didn't want to talk to her. He didn't seem to have a problem with Brice or Dylan. He talked to and texted with them multiple times a day but hadn't bothered to call or text her.

He turned, and their eyes met. Sadness lay underneath the joy of the win for just a second. He revealed the truth to her, a truth she mirrored back to him.

"I need you," she whispered. In the blink of an eye, she could have sworn he nodded in acknowledgement before his gaze left hers for someone else. *You're not moving with us.*

She placed a hand over her belly. She'd lost weight in the last couple of weeks. She'd been moody and had a few blemishes emerge in the last few days. Signs of her period, not a pregnancy, seemed to loom in her future. One more reason she doubted he would commit. She couldn't guarantee him a child, and he desperately wanted one. She couldn't assure any of them she would be the mother to their children. A pregnancy would be an uphill battle, but she'd try. She'd try over and over as long as there was a chance.

Brice wrapped his arms around her waist and hugged her from behind. "Jerry is magnificent. He has to be part Viking."

She laughed. "Just because you are, doesn't mean he is."

"He is." Brice kissed the top of her head. "We Vikings recognize each other." His voice lowered as his lips brushed against the shell of her ear. "Tall, strong, big dicks."

She giggled.

"You know it's true," Brice whispered. "Dylan doesn't have the Viking blood. He's a warrior, but he's no Viking."

She turned her head toward him. "He's got all the attributes of a Viking."

Brice smirked. "Should we get out a ruler and measure cocks?"

"His has a wider girth." She licked her lips.

"I don't think so," Brice said. "We're going to measure them. You need to know what you're getting for the rest of your life."

Will you really settle down and stay in one place? Will I be enough of a woman for you?

"Hey, what's wrong?" Brice asked.

She shrugged. *Everything.* "I'm worried about Jerry. Do you think he's okay? He got hit a lot."

"He's fine," Brice said. "He said he wouldn't have time to talk right after the fight, but that he'd check in later. Don't worry."

"Let's go," Dylan said. "He's going to be exhausted when he gets home. And Brice and I have some work to do."

A beautiful, tall blonde in a green "Wynn" T-shirt

231

and black business skirt joined Jerry's side. Her legs went on for days.

"Who is she?" Evangeline asked.

"Ursula Ulafson. She is amazing. Another person with Viking blood," Brice said.

Yeah, she looks amazing. Absolutely, perfectly, gorgeously amazing. She's probably the most fertile woman in the world. They'd have beautiful babies together. Lots and lots of beautiful babies. He's never going to commit to me when there are Ursula Ulafsons in this world.

Chapter Twenty-One
Jerry

The interviews. The parties. The night wore on into morning, and Jerry wanted nothing more than to go home and sleep, but with the agonizing trial finally over in Memphis and his retirement announcement, he had to work the news circuit for as much good publicity as possible. Winning the fight had felt like a small vindication for his family name and for Momma Mae. The documentation proving that Jerry's opponent funded the defense team had become a discussion point at every interview. The facts of what the bastard had done turned into a rallying point for Jerry's fans. The history Jerry had worried about ruining his career had brought him new followers, instead. The real-life vulnerabilities of a lost childhood struck a chord with the public, just like Brice had said it would. Never in a million years had he imagined that his scared and abused childhood would be something to which so many people could relate.

He'd always had positive press, but the outpouring of love and encouragement from the news, his team, his fans, and strangers from around the world shocked him. Stories from the kids he'd put through all forms of higher education flooded the news. He surmised Evan, Brice, and Dylan had something to do with it, but he wasn't sure if those he cared for during a time of need had stepped forward on their own to lift him up and return the favor.

Jerry took a sip of water and set it down on the black table next to him and waited for the young college-aged blonde interviewing him to end the session so he could finally go home.

She smiled with a tenseness that seemed to increase the amount of sparkling white teeth she had in her mouth. "You had a new group in your personal box this time. Are you and Ella Jackson fighting? There are rumors she's moved out-of-state because of a tiff with you. I find that hard to believe, but is it true? There was an interview not too long ago where you mentioned a new love in your life. Is she the reason you and Ella might be fighting?"

A girl who notices the details his true fans do. She's probably got a bigger following than her numbers show. His jaw tightened as he smiled.

"Ella and I are besties as always. She is in labor right now." He looked at his watch. *She should be popping out those kids any minute.* "As for a new love, well, it's complicated. My schedule is intense and with everything that has been going on in my life, I haven't been the most available man to date. I plan on changing that soon. She asked me if I would move to be with her, and I wasn't sure I could do that, but between you and me, I think I'm going to make that move. I want to settle down."

The woman's blue eyes widened, and a big, genuine smile filled her face. She looked at the camera and the boy, maybe her slightly older boyfriend or brother, moved in closer, giving view to a couple around Jerry's age holding hands and grinning just as wide with pride at the girl who had to be their daughter interviewing him. "Are you saying you plan to propose to this mystery woman?" she asked.

He laughed. "I'm not making any promises. I don't know when or how long it will take to figure out how we'll be able to blend our lives. True love doesn't come around often, at least not for me, and I'm going to fight like hell to make sure my girl doesn't slip through my fingers."

"You heard it here first. Jerry Wynn is going to be off the market soon." She stood up from the black bar chair across from him and shook his hand. "Thank you for taking the time to stay and allow me to interview you. Most celebrities don't."

"It's my honor. I appreciate your time and that you waited." He remained seated and took a few more minutes to make that personal connection he enjoyed. The girl had waited hours for this moment, and he wanted to make sure she felt special. "I started small, worked my way up the ranks, and was fortunate to have a family who understood the process and could guide me through it. I wouldn't be where I am today without people like you taking interest in my athletic ability. I'm blessed to have fans and professionals who take time out of their busy day to talk to me. I will stay until I meet everyone here. If they want photos, I'll make it happen. Your time is just as important as mine." He stood up and side-hugged her. "If anyone gives you shit, tell them to expect a phone call from Jerry Wynn."

She softened against him and sighed.

He let her go and handed her his business card. "It's my assistant's number, but she'll patch you through to my private number, if you need anything."

She stared at the business card, her hand trembling. "This has your cell number on it." She showed him the card.

He took it back and looked at it. "I need a new assistant." He looked at her. "That's the fifth order she's screwed up. You want to move to Texas and be my assistant? You're the only person I gave a card to who noticed. The others said they had my assistant's number and I saw them throw away the card when they left. They had no idea they had a direct line to me on that card, or I don't think they would have been so quick to toss it."

"I live in Texas, outside Austin," she said. "Are you serious about the assistant job?"

He handed her the card. "Text me your resume and six referrals. I'll check them out and call you within a month. And one more thing—I'm going to give you some advice."

She squared her shoulders. "I'm all ears, sir."

"Follow up with me when I don't call you back. Because I won't call. It's a test to see how interested you are in working for me. Send me a personalized thank-you note. Remind me where we met. Okay?"

"I'm on it," she said.

"And if you're not sure about something, call me and ask. Don't assume."

"Okay. Um, can my mom and dad and brother get a picture with you?"

"Sure," Jerry said.

She bounced in her high heels and fervently waved her family forward as if they hadn't heard the entire conversation.

"I'm Shay's dad, and this is my wife and son. It's

nice to meet you." He shook Jerry's hand.

"Nice meeting y'all. Did you come all this way from Texas?"

Shay's dad nodded. "We're big fans, and Shay has been doing this video channel since she was eight. She graduated college in December with a degree in human resources, but she wants to stay in our little town and is having trouble finding work. We're close to Austin, but far enough away that a daily commute is pretty much impossible." He leaned forward. "Please don't get her hopes up about a job if she'll have to relocate. She needs to be with us right now."

Jerry took a chance on trusting his instincts about the family. "Can you keep a secret?"

The dad whispered, "I can. And I'll tell you a secret to keep us both quiet."

"I am moving to a city near Austin. I own all the property in Night, Texas. Is that near you?"

"Holy shit," the man said on an exhale. "My ranch borders your land to the east."

"Looks like we're going to see each other at the grocery store in a couple of months," Jerry said.

"Shay has a three-month-old. She won't talk about the father or tell us who he is. She's broken up about it. She's a good girl who made a wrong choice with her heart. My sister is watching the baby until we get back to the hotel room. I'll tell you this right now." He lowered his chin and stared up at Jerry. "If you hire Shay, she'll work her ass off, and there isn't a more loyal gal in the world, but the baby comes first. You'll be second."

"Make sure she sends me her resume and referrals, and I'll see where she'll fit into my organization." *I hope she follows through.* Jerry took the phone from his jacket and gathered everyone together. "Smile." He snapped a few group selfies and then took Shay's phone and did the same.

Shay hugged him. "Thank you for this incredible opportunity."

"I hope to be talking to you soon." He strode out of the room and headed toward the new publicist Brice had referred, Ursula Ulafson.

"I wish you'd stop accepting every damn interview possible. That girl is a nobody," Ursula said.

"And you need to understand that you wouldn't have a job without people like that girl. She's real. Her family is real. They're not numbers. Every person who chooses to pay to see me fight—who watches me on a show, listens to me talk on social media, comes out to meet me—is important, whether they have a million dollars or don't have a cent to their name. The person who cleans up the venue is just as important as the person who owns it. If you ever call anyone who chooses to spend their time waiting for me a 'nobody' again, I'll fire your ass and tell the person who calls for a referral why you no longer work for me. I didn't hire you to be like the last guy in your job."

The woman held up her hands and backed away. "I know that. But you could have rescheduled it for tomorrow."

"Why? To brush her aside as unimportant? No. I don't do that, so get used to it. No matter how tired, banged up, or busy I might be, I'm going to give these people the respect they deserve. They are here to support me, and I'm sure as shit going to let each and every one of them know how much I appreciate them.

If anyone stops us for a picture, I'm going to take the time to do it." His voice rose. "If you don't want to wait, then leave. I'll pay you for your time and you can go home or wherever you plan to go when you leave."

"I'm trying to look out for you. I chose to use the wrong words tonight. I'm tired, and I worry. That's all."

Jerry nodded. "Sorry. It's been—"

"A rough week." Ursula looked him up and down and frowned. "I know you're stressed. I know you've had your world turned upside down the last few weeks. I know you're hiding something from me." She casually pointed to the door leading to the private exit and walked toward it.

"I'm not hiding anything from you." Ready to get home, he lengthened his stride, increased his pace, and hoped she'd drop whatever she wanted to discuss.

She hurried ahead of him and blocked the final exit. "Okay. You're not hiding anything, you're omitting information that might make my job more difficult. Brice doesn't ask favors for other people. I know something is up because I have been somewhat blacklisted from the A-list for a while now. You're as A-list as they come. Tell me what is happening so I can either spin it in your favor or prep for an announcement neither one of us wants you to have."

He stared at her.

"Don't give me that look, Mr. Wynn. Brice Loffiten is waiting outside this door for you. He doesn't wait on anyone. At least, not in the fifteen years I've known him. His girlfriend is the girl you're in love with. Dylan Russo, your new attorney, is known to have a very interesting sex life, and accompanied her home."

She winked. "I'm not judging, but I know people and their reputations. You're the odd one in the mix. You're squeaky clean, Jerry. They are not."

He continued to stare at her. *Do I tell you?*

"You're going to make me ask you, point blank, aren't you?" she asked.

"I'm not a hundred percent sure where you're going with this," he said with a shrug.

She inhaled and adjusted the strap of her black tote hanging on her right shoulder. "Your best friend is in a loving relationship with three men. I think you're about to step into a similar relationship, but you're on the fence about it. If I'm right, please tell me. We should get together and talk about how to handle any press that might go digging around."

She placed her hand on her belly and showed a small, barely noticeable baby bump. "I'm twelve weeks pregnant and have no clue which of my four men is the father. I recognize the relationship you're either in or considering because I'm in one myself."

Jerry smiled. "Congrats. Now I feel extra bad about raising my voice with you."

She shook her head. "No need to apologize. I shouldn't have said what I did, and you had every right to call me out." She grinned. "I'm going to be blunt. My observation is that Brice, Evangeline, and Dylan are all looking for you to hold them together, and I think you might be the only man on earth who could take on that job. I know I'm right about this. About you. About your future."

"I'm happy for you," he said. "Does this mean you're going to take some time off in a few months?"

She groaned. "Yes, but not for you. You're my

number-one guy. Actually, as of yesterday, you're my only client. My guys have convinced me to slow down, and you're the only one of my clients they all like. So, I really didn't mean anything back there about the young girl."

Dang. "You dumped all your other clients?" *But you know I'm not fighting anymore.*

Long, blonde bangs drifted over her eyes. She swept them behind her ear and nodded. "I decided I needed a change. I'm only working with people who aren't assholes. You were the only one who fit into that category."

"You can't live on what I pay you." *What are you thinking?*

"You're going to pay me more because I'm going to blow you away with the sponsors and opportunities I'm bringing to the table." The smile that broadened her face lit up the passageway with confidence. "I set you up with an interview for a high-profile job, but I need to know your relationship status and who might be involved in your intimate life." She stepped aside. "Tomorrow, we finish these obligations, and then it's you and me in close quarters until you see my way is the only way."

"Ursula," he groaned. The woman wouldn't let up. "I'm considering a relationship like you mentioned. That's it. I'm in the consideration phase of a relationship. I want kids, and that part of the relationship is a gamble."

"Jerry, you'll be a dad, if you decide to accept her and the other men. The child might not be biologically yours, but you'll raise him or her."

A lump formed in his throat. "I want a child so the

Wynn name will live on. I've had names picked out since I was a teen. I will love any child who comes into my life, but is it wrong to also want one who I can give my last name to?"

"Oh, Jerry," she whispered. She stepped forward and gently hugged him. "It's not wrong to want to father a child. It's not wrong at all. It's wonderful."

He pulled her in closer. Something about Ursula reminded him of Momma Mae. *Tough and tender. Strong and beautiful on the outside, soft and sweet on the inside. Tall and slender. Protective.*

She softened in his arms. "Talk to a fertility specialist. If you need a surrogate, we'll find you the perfect one. If you love Evangeline and the other two or think you do, don't let them slip away because of this. Take a leap into love and figure out the rest later." She tilted her head and kissed him on the cheek. "Sorry."

She licked her thumb and wiped it over a small spot on his cheek just like Momma Mae used to do. "You're so fair skinned." She *tsked* and held her palm to his cheek. "He hit your face. I'm glad you knocked him out. You don't have to retire, but I'm glad you are while you're still in your prime."

The natural way she smoothed over any previous anger calmed his raw emotions enough for him to open up more than he normally would.

"Is there jealousy between the men you're with?" he asked.

"On occasion there is jealousy. I have a feeling that I'll be pregnant for the next several years. Most of the time, I'm the one jealous of them. They work together and have all these inside jokes that I'm not a part of. But as the years pass, we grow closer." Her blue eyes seemed to soften, and vulnerability shined through. "It's not always easy, but no relationship is. Having four children with four different fathers is going to raise some eyebrows, but we will have one set of grandparents for the kids who are extremely supportive and will make up for the others who have walked out of our lives."

Her cheeks tightened, producing a sad smile. "People can be cruel, but there is nothing I would change." A twinkle appeared in her baby blues. "When the guys approached me about being in an alternative relationship, I freaked out. They were convinced I would be theirs long before I realized they were exactly what I needed to keep living. Do you want to meet them? They'll talk candidly about the day-to-day reality of living with me." She rolled her eyes. "And if they mention snoring, do not believe them. I do not snore."

He laughed. *You are so much like Momma Mae.* "I'd love to meet them. How long are they here?"

"Until tomorrow night. I'll set it up." She turned and pushed open the door. "I'll see you this evening. Get some rest and do whatever you do to look so good after a fight."

Instead of immediately walking outside, he leaned over and kissed her cheek. "Yes, Momma."

She let out a snort and laughed. "Someone has to mother you. It's nice to know you've accepted my real role in your life and forgiven me for my insensitivity tonight."

He walked outside and held the door for her. A black limousine idled a few feet from the entrance and a white van with two big guys in the front seats pulled up behind it.

Jerry stood in front of Ursula. "Are you expecting someone?"

"No," she said. "Let me see what's going on."

Brice stepped out of the back of the limo as the sliding door to the white van opened.

Two guys as tall as Jerry jumped out from inside the van. Dark hair. Beards. Tatts on their arms. Black shirts. Blue jeans. Black work boots.

Fuck. These guys are going to be tough to take down. "Ursula, you need to—"

"Hey, Jerry," the broader of the two men said. "Is Ursula with you?"

Ursula huffed and scrambled around Jerry. "Y'all are not supposed to be here. I told you it would be a late night and not to come."

"It's morning, baby," the blue-eyed one said. "We got worried when you didn't answer your phone."

Ursula crossed her arms and stared him down. "I texted you. Did you not look at your phone?"

Both guys produced phones from their front pockets and glanced down. "Guess not," blue eyes said. "Are you done?"

Jerry joined Ursula. "She's done." He shook hands with both men. "Jerry Wynn. It's nice to meet you."

"Reed Kopp. Thanks for taking care of my girl."

"Oliver Speck. I see Ursula kissed you." He frowned at Ursula. "You might want to let his girlfriend know it was you and not some chick wanting to get busy with him. She'll worry that he's doing things he shouldn't because of the "not guilty" trial verdict. Text her. Jerry doesn't need that kind of doubt running through his girlfriend's mind."

Yeah. The verdict that came in while he was

seconds away from walking into the ring. *They planned everything right down to the minute. I wouldn't be there for the verdict. I wouldn't get to stare at those fuckers who took the last of my family from me.* His hands clenched into fists. *I can't go there. God will take care of that injustice. I did what Momma Mae would have done.*

"I'll let her know," Brice said. He moved to Jerry's side and shook the guys' hands. "Brice Loffiten. Nice to meet you." He gently patted Jerry on the back, reminding Jerry he wasn't alone anymore. Brice had his back. So did Dylan. He wasn't one hundred percent sure on Evangeline.

Reed and Oliver greeted Brice, but their eyes drifted to Ursula.

"I'm heading to my house," Jerry said. He unclenched his fists. "Ursula, thanks for everything. I'll see you later tonight." He gently slid his hand to her back and nudged her forward. *Stubborn girl. You don't want to give an inch.*

"I'll pick you up at your house," Ursula said.

Reed took her purse from her shoulder.

Oliver wrapped his arm around her. "Bryan took your car back to the hotel. Zeek is running a bath for you. Let us help you..." He talked as he guided her into the back of the van and closed the door.

The van drove off as Jerry stood watching it with Brice by his side.

"Ready?" Brice asked.

Jerry nodded and climbed into the back of the limo. The leather seats cradled his battered body. The fight had gone on longer than it should have. The kid got some good knocks in, but nowhere near enough, nowhere near the type of hits Jerry had taken as a child. No one but the Wynns and Ella understood what he'd endured, and only because they saw it firsthand and witnessed the aftermath.

"You look like hell," Brice said. "How much longer are you going to do this?"

Jerry unbuttoned his suit jacket. "Thanks, man. You look bright and chipper this morning. Got a good screw in before picking me up?" *Prick.*

"I deserved that," Brice said. "I don't know how you step into a ring to fight. That kid was huge and looked like he wanted to kill you."

"I'm sure he did. I wanted to kill him." The last of the adrenaline from the fight seemed to wear off, and his body began its revolt against his willpower. "Can you get this thing moving to my house?"

Brice tapped the dark window separating the driver from them.

The vehicle rolled forward.

Brice shifted in his seat and turned toward him. "When do I wake you up?"

"I'll wake myself up. Did y'all sleep okay at my house?" *Did y'all sleep in one bed? In my bed?* Even exhaustion and soreness didn't keep his cock from rising at the thought of all of them in *his* bed having sex. He imagined they made the night memorable. He would have, if the roles were reversed.

Brice gazed at the tent in Jerry's slacks and then met Jerry's eyes. "We slept great. It would have been better had you been with us."

So they had slept together as one happy little threesome. "Yeah, uh. Good." Jerry glanced at Brice's groin. *Hard as a rock. I bet I could taste her juices on that big dick of yours. You probably fucked her before swinging by to pick me up. Maybe Dylan got on his knees and licked your cock clean.*

"Are you still upset with Evangeline or are you coming home to sleep with her? Dylan? Me?"

I'm not angry anymore. Jerry's belly fluttered and his balls clenched tightly against the base of his shaft. He needed to fuck or masturbate. He stretched out his arms and legs, and then relaxed. *Here goes nothing.* "I'm going to crash in bed with whoever decides to join me. I usually jerk off when I get home. Hoping someone will take care of that for me."

"Do your hands hurt?" Brice asked in a deeper tone than before.

"Every part of me hurts," Jerry said.

"You hide it well. If you didn't have that cut over your eye…" He seemed to stop from elaborating on how banged up Jerry looked.

"I wanted the kid to suffer, which meant I had to suffer too. Ella usually gives me a massage after the fight, but she isn't here."

"I'd suggest Evan, but sports massage really isn't her specialty," Brice said.

The car pulled up to the security gate and the back window rolled down.

The security guard looked in. "Sorry, Mr. Wynn. But you know I always check." He nodded at Brice. "Mr. Loffiten."

"Thanks for doing a good job," Jerry answered.

The guard nodded and stepped back.

Jerry rolled up the window.

The car pulled forward and followed the road to Jerry's home.

As they neared the house, Jerry's heart began to pump faster and faster. *Two men. I don't know that I should even attempt to be in bed with two men. If I have a flashback and panic, I could end up injuring or possibly killing them.*

"When I was searching for ways your opponent was involved in helping the defense attorneys, I discovered some information that I kept to myself," Brice said. "It wasn't really information but the lack of it that got me piecing your reactions—or non-reactions—together. I think we share some similar history although mine lasted for—" He looked away. "I would like this kept between us."

The limo stopped on the circular drive in front of his house.

"Okay," Jerry said. *I already know your father used to beat the crap out of you as a kid. Derek told me and then Cade and Ella confidentially told me.*

"My dad would beat the crap out of me. The neighbor down the street and his roommate would clean me up and keep me for their *exclusive use* until my father sobered up. The night of my fifteenth birthday, my abusers died from carbon monoxide poisoning. I'm pretty sure my father killed them before he took his own life. The letter he left me was filled with apologies."

Damn. "I'm sorry. That's rough."

"It's been a long time, and I have learned how to live with it. I wanted you to know you're not alone."

"Thanks. Do you ever have moments or flashes of memories of the abuse when you're with Dylan or another man?"

"I used to, but it's rare now. Dylan can be pushy

and trigger some of the emotions. I sometimes need him handled. You're the one I will go to for help when he needs handling." Brice opened the door and stepped outside.

Jerry sat inside. *Dylan does need to be handled.* "Is he trying to control everyone and everything?"

Brice bent over and looked at him inside the car. "Yes. He's acting like your house is his house. Your house is your house, not his, not mine. He's trying to tell me what to do with my business and nobody tells me what to do with my business."

Jerry stepped out of the limo and strode toward the front door. "I'll take care of Dylan's attitude." He typed in the security code. *Dylan needs to get on his knees and remember I'm the head of the household in this family.*

The right side of the double doors opened.

"Welcome home," Evan said, wearing a big smile and nothing else.

All the blood in Jerry's body ran to his cock. Evan stood like a goddess, ready and waiting for him...*for him*. Her sexy curves. Her plumped pink lips.

He slipped off his jacket and let it fall to the floor. Without thinking, he took her in his arms and kissed her.

Soft lips met his. The compelling need to dominate his surroundings took over. With a renewed spike of adrenaline, he conquered her mouth as he ripped his shirt open and unzipped his pants. He hoisted her up and guided her legs around his waist. Pivoting and thrusting, he pinned her back against the closed door as his cock found a warm, cozy home to claim.

In. In. In. He thrust.

Her tight walls hugged him, begged him to stay. Her muffled moans pleaded for him to continue. Her honey scent blanketed him in her femininity.

He needed to mark her. Make her his. Her pussy creamed as his ravenous cock tunneled into her. In and out. In and out. He thrust. In and out. In and out. He demanded that she unravel more of her control until she gave in and surrendered into the bliss he offered.

The slick friction against his length pushed him to the brink of orgasm. So close. He held onto the cusp of ecstasy.

She gripped the back of his neck and the beauty of her choice to trust him to protect her, love her, and nurture her arrived with the gentle tremors of her pussy walls milking his cock for all its worth.

He left her lips and grunted with one powerful thrust.

"I love you," she shouted. "I love you so much."

He believed her with his heart and soul. He gave into the need. His cock jerked and spurted cum inside her. "Mine. You're mine. Mine. Mine. Mine."

Her fingers loosened around his neck.

He leaned his head against the dark wood and breathed deeply. It wasn't enough. He needed more, but he needed to rest or he'd make a mess of the interviews later in the day.

"Lift up your right foot," Brice said.

Jerry lifted his foot and Brice took off the right shoe, sock, and pant leg.

"Left foot now," Brice said.

Jerry did as he was told.

Brice undressed him and guided him to the bedroom.

With Evan in his arms, Jerry climbed onto the bed.

She crawled off him as Dylan joined the bed.

"What would you like?" Dylan asked.

"Your mouth on my cock," Jerry said.

"What about mine?" Brice asked.

With the suggestion, the semi-hard-on Jerry had turned to a steel rod of need. "Yeah, take turns," Jerry mumbled. He spread his legs and closed his eyes. "Evan, you too. I want three mouths on my cock until I fall asleep."

Tongues and lips glided over his length. One mouth after another covered the top of his dick until they got into a rhythm of sucking, tonguing, and stroking.

He glanced down. Brice had pushed Evan aside and sucked the helmet of Jerry's cock.

Dylan lounged beside Jerry watching them.

Jerry met Brice's gaze. Vulnerability reigned inside the man's blue eyes.

"I'm going to come in your mouth," Jerry whispered. "If you don't want that, you need to—"

Brice moaned and sucked harder.

"Oh, God," Evan panted. "I'm coming. Oh, God. I'm coming."

Dylan rested his head on Jerry's chest and curled his arm around him. "We need you. This won't work without you. You're the one, Jerry. You've always been the one person missing in all of our lives."

Electricity sizzled in the base of Jerry's spine.

"I love you," Dylan whispered. "I need you." He slid his leg over Jerry's and scooted closer. His cock rubbed against Jerry's hip. "I need all of you, not just sex."

The electrical charge spread through Jerry's groin and buzzed into his balls.

He gazed at Brice. *You need to feel safe to set boundaries with Dylan. You need me to protect you as much as Dylan needs me to control him as much as Evangeline needs me to love her. I belong here, with all of you.*

His cock vibrated with new life. "Damn," he mumbled. "Swallow." His cock jerked and spurted.

Brice swallowed and the look of satisfaction in his eyes warmed Jerry's heart. *This can work, if we're all honest with each other.*

Brice swallowed and sucked, laved over the top and licked his lips. He seemed to want to say something but held back.

Jerry skimmed his arm up across the soft sheets. "Come here."

Brice crawled to Jerry's right side and switched places with Evan. He mirrored Dylan, resting his head on Jerry's chest while avoiding the bruised areas.

Evan stretched and laid her head on his thigh. Her warm breath kissed his cock.

Jerry tucked Brice against him so that Brice's cock pressed flush along his thigh. *I need to talk to Ursula about my three lovers and continuing my career outside the ring.* He closed his eyes and let the peace and love surrounding him sink into his bones. *I have to find a way to make this work.*

Chapter Twenty-Two
Evangeline

Evangeline snapped her thighs against the sides of Jerry's face. "I. Can't. Handle. More. It's too much." She gripped the comforter of the bed and trembled. *I'm not going to be able to move after this.*

He pried her thighs apart. "Yes, you can." His tongue slid across her over-sensitized clit.

She flew apart into a million pieces and forgot the number he'd repeated over and over and over for her to tell him after her orgasm to get him to move on and give her his cock.

The man had skills no one man should possess. He should teach lessons. There were women out there whose partners could benefit from his vast knowledge.

She felt the juices rush from her with each incredible contraction of pleasure. She thrashed as he lapped every last drop of cream from her orgasm.

I'm not going to survive any more of this. I'm going to be one of those weird statistics of people who died having sex.

"I could stay here forever," he mumbled. Wet stubble grazed over her pussy and inner thighs. Thick fingers traced her inner labia and converged at the tip of her clit. "Mmm. You might be ready for my cock."

"Whatever you think is best." She'd stopped begging for his cock after she realized he wouldn't move on when she tried to control him. It took a while for it to sink in, but once it did, she was tasked with remembering a number. In sexual situations, she was a slow learner. Dylan and Brice could attest to that fact, and that they secretly loved it.

He pinched her clit and moaned.

She opened her mouth to speak, hoping this time her guess would be correct, but he laved over the swollen bud and the number was forgotten.

He kissed above her slit and stroked her skin with the stubble on his cheeks as he moved up her body to her breasts. "Still nice and red." His tongue curled around her nipple and slid across her chest to the other side.

"Thirty?" she guessed. *You're moaning. You have to be close to giving me the rest of you.*

She held her breath as his mouth pressed kisses up to her ear and his cock pressed against her pussy.

"Yes, beautiful," he whispered. He thrust.

She gasped as her body welcomed him with an electrical blast into her pussy she hadn't expected to happen again. *Jerry Wynn, you own me.*

"Evan," he grunted. He slid his cock from her and stared at her with a fierceness that surprised her.

All she could do was force each inhale into her lungs so she wouldn't pass out.

He thrust. In. In. In. The demanding stare of his green eyes broke down another layer of guilt she'd held onto for far too long. Another thrust and his cock connected to a place that laid her bare. His eyes widened and the last shield to her soul fell.

"Never hide anything or anyone from me again," he whispered. "It would kill me, Evan. I love you too much. Too much to go through that again."

"I promise."

One thrust turned to two, then three, as her wet pussy clenched tighter and tighter to hold him in. Gentle glides morphed into rough pounding pleasures. Whispers of sweetness flew out the window and grunts and growls of absolute need soared from his lips.

Her world shattered as one orgasm led to another and another and another.

"Evan," he shouted like a victory cry.

Instantly, she found her world pieced back together as he shuddered and released inside her.

He rolled off her and onto his back. "Ursula will be here soon."

"Where is he?" Ursula shouted. "We don't have time for this shit, Brice."

"Fuck," Jerry mumbled. He bolted up and out of bed. "Ten minutes," he shouted.

"Five," Ursula screamed.

The bedroom door opened and the beautiful blonde strode in with a quick glance Evangeline's way. "Jerry's closet?"

Evangeline pointed to the door to the left.

The blonde didn't miss a beat as she headed across the room.

"This is our bedroom," Evan said.

"Yeah, and I wouldn't be seeing you with a recently fucked look and nude as a buck in the woods if you gave a shit about his career." She disappeared into the closet. "Do not go in for another round. You've screwed with my schedule, and I don't appreciate that." She stepped out of the closet holding a slim black suit, white shirt, and green tie with darker green shamrocks all over.

Evangeline pulled up the sheet and wrapped it around her. "I care about his career." *Who do you think you are?*

"Then act like it and get out of my way," the blonde said as she strode into the bathroom.

Evangeline climbed off the bed.

"I offered to call, but you said you had it under control." Ursula's irritation carried over into her tone. "You can't be late. Not to this."

"I'm sorry," Jerry said. "I'm never late. I just—"

"I know what you *just.* I put all my eggs in one basket. *You're my basket, Jerry.*"

"Sorry. I know. I'm not like this."

Evan looked into the bathroom.

Ursula buttoned his shirt up as he zipped his pants. She lifted his collar and slid the tie around his neck into a Windsor knot. She moved like a pro, as if she knew him intimately. A tuck here. A pull there.

"You look like you've had sex and a lot of it. This is a fucking interview, Jerry. Not some fluff piece with a fan."

"I know. I know. I got your text." He shook out his arms. "Do I look okay?"

"Good enough for the makeup artist." She dropped her shoulders and gently cupped the side of his face. "Are you taking the pain meds the doctor prescribed?"

"No. It doesn't hurt that bad."

Ursula inhaled and frowned. "It does, but I'm not going to argue with you." She placed her hands on his shoulder and slid them down over the front of his jacket and grabbed the lapels. "Ready?"

He grinned. "Yes, Momma."

She rolled her eyes. "Say goodbye to your girl. We've got a busy two weeks ahead of us."

"Two weeks?" Jerry said.

"Yes, sir."

"But I need to get back to my house and start training."

"You can train on the road. I've got a lot riding on the next two weeks. And your little friend Shay has emailed me and you. You've got good instincts with people. I might hire her out from under you."

"I don't think so," Jerry said. He pivoted away but glanced at her. "Whatever you offer her, I'll double it."

Ursula laughed. "She's yours. I'll use her to babysit."

"Nope," Jerry said. "I get those honors." He shook his head and walked toward the bedroom with an easy smile and a twinkle in his eyes. He wrapped Evangeline up in his arms and kissed her.

"No more of that," Ursula warned.

"Thanks for the best wake-up call I've had in a long, long time," he whispered into Evan's ear. "You probably won't hear from me today, but I'll be thinking of what I'm going to do the next time I see you." He kissed the top of her head and released her.

"Nice to meet you, Miss Zanipolo," Ursula said.

Evan stood there watching him leave with Ursula and couldn't form two words to save her life.

Brice and Dylan walked into the bedroom.

"Where is he going?" *He let her dress him. She saw him naked. They seemed like a couple.*

"I don't know," Brice said. "Ursula will take good care of him."

"Yeah, I *bet* she will." *Don't you see what she's*

doing?

"Jealousy is not pretty on you," Brice said. "And Ursula is not someone who should raise the hackles of envy."

She clenched the sheet at her chest and stormed into the bathroom. She slammed the French doors shut and locked them.

"Evangeline Zanipolo, do not throw a tantrum over Ursula," Brice said.

"I need to be left alone for a few minutes," she yelled. "Give me some room to breathe. I need some space."

"You got it," Brice said. "I'll be back in an hour."

She inhaled. "Thank you." *Jerry isn't committed to us. Not yet. And with her around, he might never choose me, choose this life of complications.*

Chapter Twenty-Three
Jerry

All he had to do was sign his name and he'd be the newest commentator on the most sought-after spot on sports news television. Between Ursula's and Dylan's negotiations on his behalf, he'd never seen a better contract in his life. He'd have to travel, but if he packed up and moved to his ranch in Texas, he could jump on a plane and be anywhere in the country quickly.

"What are you thinking?" Ursula asked.

"This is a big change." *Ella thinks I should do it. I just don't know.*

"It is." She gazed at him with gentle eyes. "You could live in Texas, visit here, travel, and stay involved in the sports you love. Did you talk about it with Brice and Evangeline?"

"Brice, not Evan." *I should have talked with her, but the conversation always turns to you.*

"I see." Ursula frowned and crossed her arms over her chest.

"You see what?" *Why can't I talk with Evan the way I can talk to you? I used to talk to her like this. I miss her. I want to be with her.*

She glanced around the restaurant and rolled her eyes. "Damn it, they are watching us. I told them I was catching the flight out in the morning."

I wish Brice, Dylan, and Evan would surprise me.

"Invite them over." He nodded toward her four men.

They nodded and looked at her.

She shook her head. "This is business. They know better."

"They miss you. It's been three weeks since either of us have been in our own beds." He gazed at the signature line. *I can change all that with this one decision. I'd have Evan, Brice, Dylan, and my best friend Ella in my life again.*

"If you aren't ready to do this, I can—"

"I want to sign. It's an opportunity of a lifetime. I need to—"

"Hi," Bryan, Ursula's lover, said. He kissed Ursula's cheek. "Sorry. I hope we're not interrupting."

Jerry shook his head. "Nope." He picked up the green pen and signed the document. He handed it to Ursula. "Thanks for everything. Enjoy your evening and I'll see you in a few days."

"I can hold onto this. You don't have to decide tonight."

"I know. I worked hard for this and so did you. I'm doing it." He went around the table and shook the guys' hands. "Thanks for being patient and trusting me with your girl."

"You're the only man we do trust with her," Bryan said. "Have a good night, Jerry."

Jerry nodded and walked across the planks of the old wooden floor of the family-owned steakhouse on a farm close to his property on the outskirts of Shelby County. He unbuttoned his suit jacket as soon as he stepped outside into the fresh country air. He loosened his tie as he strode to his minivan. He slipped out of his jacket, folded it, and placed it on the passenger seat. *I don't want to go home to an empty house.*

He sat in the driver's seat and buckled in. He started the car and his cell phone rang. He didn't recognize the number but answered it anyway.

"Hello?" he answered.

"I'm trying to reach Mr. Jerry Wynn. It's Shay Andrews."

"Oh, hey, Shay. This is Jerry. What's up?"

"Is it too late to call?"

"No, ma'am. How are you?" *I'll talk all night. I don't want to be alone.* He drove down the street, headed toward home.

"I'm good. I'm sorry I haven't sent you my updated resume yet. I have a daughter. She's been in the hospital. It's not an excuse. It's just been—"

"Is she okay?" *That's a damn good excuse for only sending thank-you notes.*

"She is now. She was fine and then she wasn't and then she was. They figured out what was wrong. She had this hole in her heart and surgery fixed it. I'm sorry. I didn't mean to—"

"Hey, I'm glad you called. I wish you had called me sooner. I could have—"

"I was beside myself. Well, that is not why I called. I was hoping your assistant job was still available. Ginger, my daughter, is healing like a champ and the doctors assured me I could leave her with my parents or aunt for a few hours a day. I'm not sure what you're actually looking for in an assistant..." She explained her background and that, if she traveled, she'd need to bring Ginger. "I need to tell you something that is private but is important. You're most likely not going to hire me because of this. I'd understand if you don't."

"What is it?" *You're an ex-addict?*

"My baby's father is Jason Winthrop. I doubt he remembers the event that led to me becoming pregnant. I doubt he remembers anything, actually. Before he totally passed out, he called me Katie and told me he still loved me. So, uh, there is that."

Jerry opened his mouth and all that came out was a strange half-grunt, half-exhale.

"I don't plan on telling him. With you being so tight with his family, I felt it necessary to tell you about my connection to them. My parents don't know he's the father. I don't like talking about it. I'm embarrassed I was so stupid to get swept up in the moment like that. But Ginger is the best little girl in the entire world. She's my heart. She's my world."

"Would you consider telling him, if I gave you his cell number?" *I'm going to give Jason his miracle.*

"No."

"What if I called him and gave him your number?"

She huffed. "It isn't like he'd remember me. I'm not interested in child support or—"

"Jason is a great guy. He will welcome his child and—"

"I highly doubt that. I've asked around about him. He's a player. He is not going to drag my daughter around introducing her to every girl he dates. She's not—"

"He's not dating anyone. Katie has been over for a long time. Give him a chance. Please, let me give him your number. He will call. I'll hire you now, full-time. I'll have my attorney send you a contract. Text me your email address. We'll get this finalized in thirty minutes." *Give me permission and Jason will be at your house in less than an hour. You'll have a husband, a father for your little girl, and a life you will cherish.*

"My personal life is separate from business. I'm not accepting a job with you so that I give you permission to—"

"Shay, I need you as my assistant. My life is about to change, and I need someone like you to keep me on track and handle the miscellaneous things that pop up. I'd like to give Jason your number. The two are separate, but I want both things to happen tonight." *I'm going to be surrounded by kids. Maybe I don't have to be a father. Maybe I'll be the favorite honorary uncle.*

"Are you offering me a job?"

"Yes," Jerry said.

"Are you sure? I only told you about Jason because...I trust you, and I want you to trust me. No secrets."

"Yes. I'm hiring you." He pulled into his driveway and hit the garage door remote. Nothing happened. He parked the car and took his phone from his jacket pocket. He checked his text messages and smiled. *You've already sent me your resume.* He copied it and sent a text to Dylan. He had a good feeling about Shay, and he'd had Dylan type up a contract for her more than a week ago.

"Check your email for a contract from Dylan Russo later tonight. If it looks good, you can electronically sign. If there is something you'd like to talk about, ask."

"Jason will ask for a paternity test. I'm not paying for one."

"He'll pay for it," Jerry said. *He'll gladly pay for it.*

"He better not call me a whore, or I will make his

life hell and my daddy *will* shoot him."

"He won't call you a whore," Jerry said. "I wouldn't stand for it and he wouldn't either." He clicked the garage door remote again.

Nothing happened. *Weird.* He opened the case and put it back together. He clicked the remote again. Nothing. All the lights were out in his house, and in Jason and Kyle's house. *Must be a power outage.*

"Okay," she said. "I'll let you know when I have received the contract. Thank you."

"What about Jason?"

She sighed. "He's not going to believe me. I can't deal with—"

"May I give him your number?" *Please let me give Jason the best news of his life.*

She seemed defeated. "*O-kay.* Okay."

"Answer your phone when he calls. We'll talk tomorrow. Have a great night."

"Thanks. Talk to you tomorrow. Sleep tight."

Jerry ended the call and dialed Jason.

"Dude, is everything okay?" Jason answered.

"I found your girl. You're a dad. She's twenty minutes from you. She's awake. I'm texting you her number now. Her name is Shay Andrews." Jerry texted him Shay's number. "Her parents' ranch is the one that borders mine to the east. She lives there."

He heard the rustling of clothes. "No shit?"

"None."

"You're sure it's her? Blonde. Blue eyes. Five-nine. Legs for miles. A smile that rivals the beauty of a perfect sunrise?"

"She's a beautiful girl." *Shay is in for the ride of her life.*

"Do you think her parents are up? I need to talk to her father."

"I don't know. Ask her."

"Jerry, I'm going to marry her. Where is that fucking ring?"

"Calm down, Jay. She's not going anywhere. Call her."

"Yeah." Jason exhaled. "Ah, here it is. Kyle, get your ass up. I need you to drive. I'm too fucking nervous to get behind the wheel."

"Good luck, Jay," Jerry said.

"Tell everyone I said to bring you home to Texas." Jay ended the call.

Bring me home to Texas? Jerry looked at the dark house again. *Are Evangeline, Brice, and Dylan inside? Are they going to surprise me?* He turned off the engine and got out of the car.

He glanced at his phone. Nothing. Dylan always texted him back quickly.

He walked to the side of the house, out of view where Garrett often parked. Sure enough, the car Evangeline left in Memphis sat in the spot that had been empty a couple hours before.

He couldn't contain the happiness buzzing inside him. *You came to see me. You came.*

He walked to the front door and opened the security panel. No power. *It isn't just my remote's battery that is dead. Maybe a transformer blew.* He turned the doorknob and grinned. *You left it open. What am I walking into? Are you naked, Evan? Miss me?*

He opened the door and flipped the light switch. Nothing happened. *Damn. I should have gotten a call about this from my security company. Brice should have called me. Maybe it just happened.*

The house seemed too quiet. *What are you planning? You don't know I'm here yet? Am I going to surprise you?* He snuck through the foyer, past the living and dining rooms, and slowed as he neared his bedroom.

"Please, Henry," Evan's soft voice cried, tinged with fear. "I need to call an ambulance. I'll go with you, if you let me make one phone call."

"No. It's too late for that. It's too late, Evangeline. It's too late."

"It's not too late, Henry. It's not too late to fix this."

Jerry retreated from the hallway and dialed 9-1-1.

"Henry Westland has broken into my house. I need paramedics and police." He quickly gave his home address and texted Garrett. He placed the phone down near the floorboard of the bedroom entrance and listened, assessing more of the situation.

Keep him talking, Evan. I need to know where he is in my room.

Candlelight illuminated the space.

"Let me call your father. He can send someone here to help. No one has to die today. No one. Not me. Not you. Not—"

"I told him he couldn't have you. You're not marrying him. You're not. I won't let you." Henry's voice seemed farther away than it had been seconds before.

Jerry exhaled and squared his shoulders. *Henry, what have you done?* He turned the handle and swung the door open.

White candles with flames rising too high were

evenly spaced around the border of the room.

Dylan and Brice were gagged and tied to the bed. Bone stuck out of Brice's leg. Four bullet holes decorated the wall behind the bed. Blood stained the white sheets where Brice lay unconscious. Dylan's brown eyes begged for help.

Evan ignored Jerry. Her singular focus remained on the man with the gun at her head. Henry put the gun to his own head and then swung it back to point at hers.

Something inside Jerry snapped. "What the fuck are you doing inside my house?" He moved with speed he didn't know he had and stood in front of Evan.

"I'm going to kill her. You." Henry jerked his head toward Dylan. "Him."

"Dude, what did I ever do to you?" Jerry inched forward, but Henry held his ground and kept the gun to his own head.

"She loves you. She doesn't love me anymore. She loves you. She's always loved you. You and Brice. You and Brice and him. You and Brice. Evan, where are you?" Henry glanced around as though they were all moving, not still.

"I'm here, Henry," Evan said softly. "I'm still here. It's going to be okay. Let's call your dad. Does he know where you are?"

"Dad. Oh, God. Dad's gone. He's gone. He's gone." Henry stared at Jerry. The blank stare of a lost man. He pushed the muzzle of the gun to his temple.

A shot rang out.

Henry seemed to fall in slow motion.

Blood. So much blood.

Jerry turned around. He hadn't noticed the ropes tied around her arms, chest, legs, and neck. He hadn't noticed the cut on her cheek and chest. He hadn't noticed the dining chair that anchored her. Not until that moment.

"Jerry, please, help Brice," Evan said.

Jerry lifted her and the chair. *You're not going to see that. You're not going to… Shit. Shit. Shit.* He faced her toward the bed and looked at Brice. "Help is on the way." He ripped the shirt from around Dylan's mouth and head.

"I think Brice is dead," Dylan said. "Oh, God. Oh, God. I think he's dead."

"No. He's not dead. He's breathing," Jerry said. He pulled the tie stuffed into Brice's mouth out. "Stay with me, Brice."

"Jerry?" Garrett called out

"Bedroom," Jerry shouted. "Hurry."

Garrett strode into the bedroom. "Get me the first-aid kit I made for you."

Jerry ran into the bathroom and retrieved the metal case he'd never opened.

Garrett opened the metal lid and got to work on Brice. He called out orders and Jerry followed immediately.

Police and paramedics showed up. Garrett continued working on Brice as Jerry's world continued to turn upside down.

Cade drove up as Garrett helped the paramedics loaded Brice into the ambulance. Dylan and Evan sobbed as they clung to Jerry.

"As soon as they arrive at the hospital, Derek is going to take care of Brice," Cade said. "He's going to be okay."

Jerry nodded. That's all he could do. His mouth

clamped shut. He processed everything, but the people, the movement, the lack of control took away his voice.

The police asked questions and he either nodded or shook his head.

"Henry's father passed away this morning," Cade whispered. "Coroner said it looked like a heart attack. Cal had a history of heart problems."

Jerry's head bobbed up and down.

"I'm going to take you to the hospital," Cade said. "Brice is strong. He's going to make it."

Up and down, Jerry's head bobbed.

Up and down.

Up and down.

Chapter Twenty-Four
Evangeline

The soft hues of greens and blues meant to calm, didn't. Nurses and doctors in green, pink, and blue scrubs calmly moving from one triage bed to the next didn't stop the scream clawing at her throat to be released from aching all the more when she held it in.

Evangeline pounded her palm on the nurses' station counter for someone, anyone to tell her where Brice and Dylan were. "I need help. I need help."

The young woman on the opposite side of the counter glanced up. "We're still waiting on information, Ms. Zanipolo. It's going to be a while, but you will get a call on your cell phone with the latest updates. Did you get a text that he's been stabilized?"

Evan nodded. "Yes, ma'am. I need more. I—"

"Oh, Evan." The familiar voice dripping with fake sympathy from the bitch who started Henry's downhill spiral broke the rising panic over Brice's and Dylan's health statuses.

A new round of adrenaline kicked in as Evan pivoted around.

Her ex-best friend Rachel and her ex-fiancé Todd stood with smirks on their faces.

"Did Brice do that to you?" Rachel asked.

The holier-than-thou attitude in Rachel's question pushed Evan to her limits. The way Todd huddled close to the pregnant blonde was too much. They fucked her over one too many times.

"You're not welcome here." Evan surprised herself with the amount of calm in her voice. "You need to leave."

A short huff left Rachel's lips. She rolled her eyes and strode to the counter next to Evan. "I got a call to come here about Henry Westland. I'm Rachel Innis. The receptionist sent me here."

"I'm sorry to have had you come all the way here, Ms. Innis. There was a mistake. We thought you were next of kin, but the matter has been taken care of." The nurse's gaze met Evan's. "I'm sorry."

"Well, where is Henry? I'd like to speak with him. He's not answering his phone." Rachel shifted and bumped her belly against Evan's side, on purpose. "Well, were the two of you in some kind of accident?"

"You are to blame for what happened. You. You bitch. You think you can…"

Rachel turned her back on Evan and walked toward Todd. She glanced over her shoulder. "Real classy, Evangeline. Calling a pregnant woman a bitch is not the way to behave, especially in public. But nothing is sacred to you, is it?"

The scream nestled tightly in Evan's throat came out like a snake's strike filled with venom. "Fuck you." She opened the robe to reveal the spot Garrett stitched up her breast where the bullet had grazed her. She pointed to her forehead and cheek. "He cut me. He shot Brice. He shot at Dylan. He shot at me. He reloaded the gun *you* bought for him. Because of your reckless *gift*... Your hands are so bloody it's going to take mountains of cleanser to wash it all off. If Brice dies, I'm going to come after you with everything I've—" She lunged at Rachel.

A brick wall of an Irishman stepped in and grabbed her. "I've got you," Jerry said. "Brice is going to make it."

"Get out of my way," Evan screamed. "She doesn't deserve to be here. She started all of this. She—"

"Stop," Jerry ordered. "She's leaving with Todd. Now."

"I'm so sorry," Rachel whispered. "I had no idea. I didn't know. I swear, I didn't know."

"You didn't bother to know," Jerry said. "You stomp on everybody in your way. You don't care about anyone but yourself. You never have. Henry was a good kid who needed help. You got him back on drugs. You gave him a gun. You didn't give a shit," Jerry said. "If you see us anywhere in the world, start walking in the other direction."

"Henry's dead and I hate you, Rachel. I hate you," Evan shouted. "I *hate* you."

Jerry tucked her against his chest.

"It's not my fault," Rachel said. "It's not my fault. His father wouldn't buy him a pistol, so I did."

Jerry cradled Evan's head as he turned his torso toward Rachel. "Did you ever ask Cal why Henry didn't own a firearm? The kid has been in rehab a dozen times, attempted suicide… Don't even act like you didn't know. He ended his life in front of us. So, I'm with Evan on this. Fuck. You."

Rachel retreated like she'd been slapped in the face. "He couldn't have… He isn't violent." She looked at Todd. "He isn't—"

"He was," Jerry said.

"Mr. Russo," a woman said. "You need to go back to triage."

"Shit," Jerry mumbled. His embrace softened as he maneuvered her behind him and faced Dylan. "Dylan, go lay down. I've got this."

The anger and fury over Rachel and Todd's presence left Evangeline as she got a look at Dylan in a hospital gown. She and Jerry seemed to move in tandem toward Dylan.

Todd curled his arm around Rachel and moved her out of their way. "I'm sorry about what happened. I'm sorry to hear about Henry. I never thought he'd ever go this far, not after…" He didn't finish, but she knew the incident he was about to refer to. Todd had moments of guilt and then seemed to push those aside and return to the selfish asshole who betrayed her over and over and over again.

"I don't know how you two live with yourselves," Evan said. The anger within her for all the wrongs Rachel and Todd had done to her and others began to rise as she gazed at Dylan. *I almost lost the men I love the most in this world.* She glared at the couple. "You took a good man and helped him spiral downward. There is a special place in Hell for both of you."

"Talk about special places in Hell, Evan," Rachel hissed. "You're the one who will be in Hell. You're the one he couldn't live without. You're the one he went after, not me, not Todd. You. You're the one whose hands are bloody. You're the one who has to live with his death. You're the bitch who deserves to rot in Hell. He's plotting your death in the afterworld, Evangeline. You're the bad influence. You're the one who will lose sleep because you did this to him. You're to blame. "

"There's the Rachel Innis I know," Jerry said. "When the truth is spoken, you try and shit all over it and blame someone else." He gently curled his arm around Dylan. "Let's go back to triage. You're bleeding."

Dylan wobbled. Blood seeped through the gauze covering his wrists and ankles.

Evan stepped to the other side of Dylan and tried to help support him, but Jerry took all Dylan's weight. "You shouldn't be out of bed. I'm sorry."

"I was worried about you," Dylan said softly, as they moved him away from the nurses' station. "The doctor left to get me some medication and I heard your voice. I'm fine, just weak. I think they gave me something to sleep."

Jerry walked forward, but all the beds were filled.

The scratch of curtain tracks moving along metal stopped all of them.

Jerry bent over and—

A nurse stepped out from behind the curtain closest to them. "There you are."

Jerry's hands glided up Dylan's thigh as he stood. "Hey."

"Dr. McGregor released you to Mr. Wynn. Also, Mr. Loffiten is stable and with Dr. McGregor and Mr. Winthrop. Hang on a second and"—she dipped her head and arm behind the curtain and pulled out a clipboard—"I've got the paperwork for you here." She handed Evan a stack of papers. "Mr. Russo and you will be checking into Dr. McGregor's private clinic within the hour. Give them these papers. Cade Jackson is waiting for you in the car outside. Follow me."

Jerry picked up Dylan and carried him like a baby

in his arms. "You okay to walk, Evan?"

Her limbs began to tremble the closer they came to the private exit for celebrities. "Yeah," she said. Fear scraped along her veins as her heartbeat accelerated. "No. I'm not okay."

The nurse pushed open the door.

Evan couldn't breathe. She was going to pass out.

"Cade," Jerry yelled. "Evan needs help." His big hand landed on her back. "Hurry."

The lights flickered. The darkness seemed to close in.

"Hey, beautiful," Cade said. He scooped her up. "No passing out on my watch. I've got you. Ready to see Brice?"

"Yeah," she whispered.

"Breathe with me, sweetie. We're getting y'all to a safe and secure place." He carried her to the car and opened the door.

Jerry helped Dylan inside and then helped her.

Cade hurried around the car and hopped into the driver's seat of the idling car. He slowly accelerated, but almost came to a complete stop as he turned out of the parking lot onto the road. "It usually takes thirty minutes to get to the clinic," Cade said. "Brice has a rough few surgeries ahead, but he's going to be okay. Derek saved his leg and stopped the internal bleeding. We'll get you three examined by Garrett's doctors once we get there."

Evan nodded. "Thank you."

"I'm fine," Jerry said. "I don't need to be examined but Evangeline does. And Dylan is bleeding. His back is wet. He needs immediate attention when we arrive."

"I'll make sure he's the first one seen, but you're

getting checked out too, Jerry," Cade said. "We've got an escort to get us to the clinic quickly. Garrett leaves nothing to chance."

Evan gazed at Dylan slumped against Jerry's chest and at the man who saved all of them. "I'm sorry."

"It's not your fault," Jerry said. "We don't know what happened. We don't know what happened to Cal. We don't know anything, except this wasn't your fault. Don't do that to yourself, or to us."

She closed her eyes as tears overwhelmed them. She nodded. *It's my fault. It's always my fault.*

Chapter Twenty-Five
Dylan

The documentation all pointed to the same thing. The pharmacy gave Henry the wrong meds. The kid had told the truth. He had taken his medicine, only the medicines in his system weren't the antipsychotic drugs he was supposed to be on. Henry probably didn't think about the slightly smaller-sized pills. An honest mistake. A mistake that took one life and had the potential to take many more. *Thank God Jerry walked in when he did.*

Dylan glanced at Brice. *You were right. The lights went out and it was Henry. The surveillance that boy had... You knew. You knew someone was not going to make it out of Jerry's alive. You stepped in front of us and—*

"Hey," Brice whispered.

Dylan put the folder on the small table next to the couch where Jerry and Evangeline slept and got up from his chair next to Brice's hospital bed. "Hey. Do you need some water?" He reached for the pitcher of ice water and the cup on the metal rolling tray on the other side of the bed.

Brice rubbed his lips and closed his eyes. "Yeah."

Dylan poured the water and held the cup as Brice sipped from the straw. "The nurse should be in with more pain meds soon. Should I call her?"

"Is Evan okay? Jerry? Did they get Henry? Is he in jail? I need to talk to Cal. I need to…" Brice seemed to run out of steam.

"Evan and Jerry are right here. They're sleeping, but we're all okay."

"Good. Good," Brice whispered. "I want coffee. I'm so damn tired. I need to go to work."

Dylan placed the cup on the tray. "Work can wait, but I can probably sneak in some coffee. Let me check with the nurse."

Brice shifted and groaned. "Shit. I hurt like hell."

Dylan pressed the button for the nurse. *You need pain meds.*

The light switched off and the nurse popped her head in. "Is he ready for pain medication?"

"Yes, ma'am. Also, Brice would like some coffee," Dylan said.

"Food. I'm hungry," Brice added.

"I'll check with Dr. McGregor before I make any promises. I'll be right back."

The door closed.

"I want to…" Brice opened his eyes and inhaled. He slid his tongue over his dry lips and exhaled. "I was shot. My leg. Is Evan okay? Jerry?"

"Yes. You're going to be okay. The bullet missed major organs." *Derek is a miracle worker. I don't know how you're still here with us.*

"My leg?" Brice exhaled.

"The second surgery went really well. You're part bionic, but that is a good thing."

Brice rubbed his face. "I need to shave."

Dylan grinned. *You must be feeling better.* "You can tackle that tomorrow."

Brice grunted as he shifted a little to the side. "I'd like to sit up. Where's my phone? I need to check my email. I need to call my assistant. I need to reschedule appointments."

"Cade called your assistant and is handling anything that pops up. He said that you two had planned for emergency situations." Dylan handed him the remote for the bed.

"Yeah. We did." Brice confirmed the agreement he'd made with Cade as the fog cleared from his head. "I remember. I remember now. How long have I been here?"

"Three days. It's not been long," Dylan said.

"How long before I can go home?" Brice asked.

"Maybe tomorrow." *I have no idea.*

Brice closed his eyes. "How are you doing? Really?"

The nightmares keep me up unless I'm next to Jerry. "I'm doing okay. Sleeping is a struggle, but it's only been a couple days. You're going to have to make a statement to the police. My dad is our attorney on this. He flew in as soon as I told him what happened. He already spoke to the police and found out Henry's history was documented by Cal in case Henry ever went after Evangeline or you. None of us are suspects. Jerry called 9-1-1, and the last minutes of Henry's life were recorded. It was..." Dylan looked away as Henry's last-minute decision to turn the gun on himself replayed in his head. "It was awful. So awful."

"I thought we were all going to die," Brice mumbled.

You almost died. "We didn't. We survived."

"How is your back?" Brice asked.

"Sore, but Garrett stitched the wound as soon as he handed you over to Derek. Mine was a minor injury in the scheme of things. The bullet grazed me." *You took the brunt of Henry's wrath. You protected us. You're brave, so brave. I love you.*

The top of the bed raised up until Brice sat almost fully upright. He grunted an exhale and clenched his jaw. "Is it weird that my leg hurts worse than my stomach?"

"I don't know," Dylan said. *I'm surprised you're sitting up.*

A gray-haired nurse wearing pink-and-blue scrubs with green frogs printed all over walked into the room with a small tray. She placed the tray on the counter to the right of Brice's bed.

"How would you rate your pain?" The sincerity in her tone eased some of the worry Dylan held onto. She twisted the back of her gray hair and clipped it up.

"A seven or eight," Brice said.

She picked up a tablet from the tray and typed in something. She scanned his wristband and asked him some questions. Within a few minutes, she'd administered meds through the IV and gave him some pills to take orally. "You're going to get sleepy again, but the confusion you're feeling is going to go away." She explained the plan for the rest of the day, and that Derek had gotten delayed with another patient.

"Thanks," Brice said.

The nurse walked over to the couch. "Miss Zanipolo, we're ready for you."

Evangeline groaned. "I'm tired."

"I know, sweetie," the nurse cooed. "You've been through a lot. We need to take care of you and those babies."

"Babies?" Jerry asked.

Evangeline nodded. "I'm barely pregnant. Derek thinks there may be two, but hasn't found a second. I've had a lot of bleeding. Pregnancy and I don't seem to be compatible. With my history, carrying one baby is a stretch, but somehow this one is hanging on."

"Jerry, go with her," Brice said. "Please?"

"Of course," Jerry said. He looked at Dylan and raised his right eyebrow.

Dylan shrugged. *I have no idea who the father is or isn't.*

Jerry maneuvered Evangeline and stood up with her in his arms. "We're ready, ma'am."

The nurse didn't seem to miss a beat about the situation. She led Jerry and Evangeline out of the room.

"Did Jerry lose the sportscaster job?" Brice asked.

"No. He's leaving tonight to film some promos for it. He saved our lives by calling Garrett and the police. He did everything right. He…he isn't talking about it or anything." Dylan reached through the bedrails and held Brice's hand. "He's been checking in on Sally, reassuring her we're all okay. He went to the police department with Garrett and made a statement. Ursula said he's going to talk about mental illness and raise awareness about the importance of medicine and medical care. He's talking to her, but not us. I don't know why."

Brice closed his eyes. "She mothers him, and he lets her. It's okay. He'll talk to us when he's ready. Is Ella here?"

"She came by yesterday and sat with him until you were out of surgery. They're so stoic about everything.

They held hands, and I swear they could read each other's minds through osmosis."

"That's normal with them. It used to drive Cade crazy. Don't worry. Is she around here somewhere?"

"She's with Garrett." *And his security team.*

Brice exhaled. "That's good. They need to be careful. Has Todd stopped by? Rachel?"

"Surprisingly, they did. They seemed to carry some regret. Not nearly enough, but some is better than none." *Selfish assholes.*

"How did Evangeline take it?" Brice mumbled.

"She told them, more like screamed at them, to leave and never grace her presence again. Jerry stepped in as Evan lunged at her. Jerry added some choice words, and the two intruders vanished under the rock they had crawled out of. Then we moved you here. This place is a fortress. No one gets in or out without clearance."

"That's my girl...good," Brice whispered. His breathing evened out and sleep took over.

Dylan glanced at his phone and then at Brice. *Jerry is leaving again. Evangeline is scared. I'm scared. Shit. I'm terrified. I thought I could handle anything, but I can't. I can't, and I don't know how to get through this without Jerry and you by my side.*

A light knock at the door pulled him from his thoughts.

His father walked in. "Ready for a visit?"

Dylan flew from his chair, and like a child, hugged his father until he was clinging to him for dear life. "What do I do?"

"You're going to put one foot in front of the other and keep moving forward," his father whispered. "Brice and Evangeline are going to need you. Sally needs a father, a stable one. She needs you. If you need medication to get through this, I'll take you to the doctor myself. I took some medicine when your mother died. I was on it for a long time."

"I just—"

"Son, I handled a lot of things wrong with you. But you turned out to be the best son in the entire world. I love you more than the sun and moon and stars. I love you more than my own life. I love you, and whatever you need, I'm here for you."

"I need Jerry," Dylan whispered. His chest ached for the man who'd saved their lives. The man who hadn't committed to moving. The man who might be here now but wouldn't be soon.

"Then you're going to have Jerry. Whether you take his name or he takes yours... Or y'all keep your names, consider him yours. He's not going to know what hit him when my wife and I get involved."

"Dad, he's—"

"No. You're not making excuses or finding obstacles to hurdle. He's yours. You're his. I'm getting another son-in-law. That's it. He's going to call me dad within a month." He patted Dylan on the back. "What you four have been through either tears you apart or bonds you forever. All of you are coming out of this with bonds as strong as strands of DNA. You four are a part of each other. You're more like one person. Trust me. Jerry is committed, and with a visit from the Russos, he'll be wearing a ring on his finger and singing Italian before you know it."

"Please, no," Dylan said. "Do not sing a duet with him."

"Oh, yeah," his father said. "I heard he's got a nice voice. Holidays at the Russo house are going to be filled with music. I might get us a gig at the local pizza parlor."

Dylan groaned. "No. I'm not—"

"You're not going to disappoint your elderly father, are you?" His father patted his back and let him go. "Are you?"

"No, sir." Dylan rolled his eyes, and some of the anxiety he held released.

"Good. Now, business is moving along. The contract you made up for Shay Andrews is signed and dated. She's now under Wynn Enterprises. Is there anything else you need me to handle for Jerry's sponsorships?"

"No, Dad."

Big, loving hands cupped Dylan's cheeks. "You're safe. I'll make an appointment for you to talk to someone. The four of you got through that nightmare for a reason. You have a lot more living to do, Dylan. I'll take care of the business until you're ready to get back." He kissed Dylan's forehead. "I love you. I'll check on you later. I've got to get to a meeting." He pulled Dylan into another hug and left.

Dylan plopped down on the chair. He rested his head in his hands and cried. *I don't think I can make it without Jerry.*

Chapter Twenty-Six
Jerry

With his eyes glued to the screen, Jerry watched the playback of his first episode as a sports celebrity. He tried not to cringe as the journalist who sat next to him patted him on the back like they were best friends…again. Something about the dude made him uncomfortable. Well, more than uncomfortable. More like he wanted to beat the shit out of the guy for breathing the same air as him.

Ursula stepped in. "Jerry, I need to speak to you."

Jerry glanced at the producer.

The producer nodded. "We'll see you next week, Jerry. Great show."

"Thanks," Jerry said. He couldn't for the life of him remember the guy's name. He couldn't remember the smarmy journalist's name, either. The other men and women seemed pretty normal. He went around and thanked the rest of the people on the set for their time and for having him on the show.

Ursula followed him around and out of the studio. "I'm going to request you sit by someone else. You looked like you were going to knock all of Mr. Touchy-Feely's teeth out of his mouth. I'm glad he didn't do that on camera."

"Really? I thought I held it together better than that."

"Your mouth clenched like it does right before you're about to land a heavy blow. If this wasn't your first show, I would have canceled it. You did well, but you could have done so much better if you had been sitting next to Reggie or Quinn. But you're the biggest guy on there, and I think they might be intimidated..." She chatted away about the group dynamics as they got in the car and drove to the airport.

"Are you even listening to me?" she asked. She glanced at him and exhaled. "You drive like a grandma. Tell me what is wrong so I can fix it."

"I am listening. And you're right about all of it. I don't think you can fix what is wrong."

"Tell me. Let me try," she said.

He turned right onto the road to the private airport. "I don't want to go back to my house. I have this flash of Brice dying on my bed, of Henry's..." A coldness slithered like a snake across his skin and he shivered. "I'm worried about Dylan and Brice and Evangeline. I need to be with them, but I need to work. I haven't packed in order to move. I want to go to them in Texas, not to my place in Tennessee." *I'm angry, and I am regretting retirement.*

"The first one is easy. Let's fly to your ranch in Texas. I'll have my guys pack up your house outside Memphis and move your things and cars. What's going on with your three lovers?"

He parked in the private lot and turned off the engine. "Dylan is scared and freaked out by what happened. His mother committed suicide similarly to Henry, and he was the one who found her. I talked to Dylan's dad, and he's worried about Dylan too. I don't want to force him to come on these trips with me, but I think he needs me the most. I don't want to talk about what happened, but he needs to talk about it—and not just with his therapist."

The softer side of Ursula opened and the gentleness of her delicate touch on his arm soothed some of his worries.

"Let me and Shay handle Dylan's arrangements as your companion. I had no idea. No idea. He must be going through hell." She exhaled long and hard. "You don't want to hear this, but you do need to talk about what happened. The 9-1-1 call is public. It's been played over and over. The anonymous donations to mental health charities and organizations are wonderful, but this is a situation where stepping out and talking about your real-life experience could change lives. It could help people. Talking about medicine and the importance of taking it, making sure that the meds match the description on the pillbox and that the name is what the doctor ordered could save a life."

"It's painful to talk about," Jerry said. "I almost lost three people I love. I don't want to think about what happened, let alone talk about it."

"Is it worth the pain to save a person's life? Is it worth the pain to have someone on the brink of a breakdown make that appointment with their doctor to get help? To call a suicide hotline? To tell a person there is no shame in taking medication to help them have a normal life, a successful life, a happy life? Think about it. Maybe Dylan would want to stand up and talk about it with you. You're two successful men who have been through a tragic and terrifying event. You're not the only ones who have dealt with this. Bring some light into the darkness, Jerry."

Listening to her made his chest ache. *I could make a difference. Talking to groups might help Dylan heal and process what happened.* "Can we change our destination?

"We were going there anyway," she said. "I'm sure they won't mind making one stop instead of two. Let's go inside and make the arrangements."

He nodded and stepped out of the car. He walked to her side and let her out.

She curled her arm around his and held on as they walked inside to the small lobby. "I've got this." With a quick squeeze of his arm, she left him to reschedule their flight.

He walked to a private room and closed the glass door. He dialed Dylan.

"Hey," Dylan answered.

"Hey," Jerry replied. "Is Brice feeling better? How is the nurse working out?"

"Brice is feeling better this morning. The nurse is great. Thank you for arranging for her to come and stay. How did the show go? When does it air?"

"Show was okay. I sat next to a guy who kept putting his arm around me. Next time will be better. Everyone seemed happy I was there. They asked me a ton of questions. The producer had an area set up to look like a boxing ring, and he had me get in it with one of the retired quarterbacks on the team. It was funny. I hope it was funny. Everyone laughed as I taught him some combinations and what not to do." *I wish I could have enjoyed it more, but all my thoughts were on you and Brice and Evan.*

"That's great. I bet it was funny. I miss you."

"I've been thinking a lot while I've been here. I

can't manage a long-distance relationship."

"Then move here. We can live at Brice's. Expand. Live at your ranch. Renovate. We can figure this out. I'm not losing you over this."

"You're not going to lose me. I'm flying to Texas and staying with you tonight."

"When will you be here?"

"I don't know. Ursula is changing our flight destination. I'll text you an ETA when I have one."

"Jerry, I lo-ve you." His voice cracked and the sound of him holding back tears nearly broke Jerry's heart again.

"I love you too. I'm coming home, Dylan. Don't worry."

The strangled noise of affirmation that came from Dylan's mouth cut Jerry to the quick. The sound, so familiar, so ingrained in his own memories that when accessed, haunted him. An icy shiver rocked his system. The words of his father, the crack of the whip, the sting of his hand, the smell of cigarettes and moonshine...the blinding smoke. Jerry lurched forward and found purchase with the wall. His father wasn't crazy. His father was evil. Worse than evil.

Ella saved him from sure death. He had to save Dylan like Ella and the Wynns had saved him. He had to help Brice pull Evangeline and Dylan out of the paralysis of fear. *Thank God for Brice. Thank God he survived. I can't do this all alone.*

The realization that he couldn't fix everything alone, that the relationship he'd been looking for his entire life was in Texas, smacked him in the face. He needed a team to love. One person wasn't enough for him, never was.

"Hang on, Dylan. I'm coming home. It's time to make our relationship permanent. I'm ready. I'm ready to join the three of you—in good and bad times—for the rest of my life. I love you. I love all of you." His body thrummed with energy. *I wish I had figured this out a long time ago.*

"Hurry home," Dylan whispered. "I need you home."

Ursula frowned and gestured for him to come over to the counter.

"I'll be home soon. Bye." He hung up and strode out of the room with a fire in his belly. *I'm going home. My family needs me.*

"Weather is preventing us from flying straight home," Ursula said.

"Then let's get as close as we can and rent a car. I'll drive the rest of the way," Jerry said.

"I figured you'd say that," Ursula said. She took his hand and guided him outside to their rental. "It's a long-ass drive, but we'll be home tonight or early tomorrow morning."

Jerry didn't ask any questions. He climbed into the car and buckled in. With Ursula typing in directions and him behind the wheel, they could make the drive. They'd done longer and far worse drives since he'd hired her. And somehow or another, with a detour or two, they always made it exactly where they were supposed to be at exactly the right time.

Chapter Twenty-Seven
Brice

Each movement seemed to bring some amount of pain, but with the medication, he continued walking with crutches as quickly as he could manage. Even with the cast on his leg, the stitches and glue in his abdomen, and the bruising everywhere, he managed to get from his bed to the bathroom in time to use it. The nurse kept telling him to slow down, but he needed some control, some way to show he could handle this on his own now.

"You're doing great, Mr. Loffiten," the nurse said. "I don't think you're going to need me in a day or two."

"I don't think I need you now." He hated to be so curt, but she brought it up. "I can take care of myself."

"You mostly can," she said. "You heal quickly. How about a compromise?" She smiled.

"How so?" he asked. *You're in for a negotiation that will end with you leaving my home.*

"I'll write your schedule down. You follow it for the rest of today. Show me you won't do too much, and I'll talk to Mr. Wynn and Dr. McGregor about cutting back my hours."

"I can do that."

"Great. Let's take a walk to the kitchen," she said.

"The kitchen?" *Are fucking crazy? I'll fall. I'll tear my stitches. I'll... Oh. Gotcha.* "I'm not quite up for

291

that yet."

She grinned from ear-to-ear. "That was the answer I was hoping to hear."

He leaned against the edge of the mattress and placed his crutches against the wall. "I do need help, but not in the bathroom anymore. Not in here. I'm good at delegating and making calls. I want my room back."

"Who wants their room back?" Jerry walked in, and Brice's world turned right-side-up.

"Is it really you?" Brice asked. *It can't be. You're supposed to be in Memphis.*

"In the flesh," he said. "Mazel, you can have the rest of the day off. We'll see you tomorrow."

"He's a tough one, Mr. Wynn, but I believe he will listen when you tell him not to do something he would prefer to do himself," she said.

Brice slid his bottom over the sheet and shifted as he lifted one leg onto the bed and then the other.

The nurse covered him with the linens and an extra blanket. "I'll see you tomorrow."

"Thank you," Brice said.

She walked out of the room with a soft, "you're welcome" before she closed the door.

"You're looking better than when I last saw you," Jerry said.

"One week makes a big difference," Brice said. "Thank you for the nurse. I didn't need her, and it was unnecessary—"

"Dylan, Evangeline, and Sally needed her validation that you were okay," Jerry said. "Besides, I needed to know you were okay too." He sat on the bed and turned toward him. His normally bright green eyes showed signs of sleeplessness.

"I'm fine. A broken leg and a couple bullets don't keep me down for long. I've always healed quickly. I'm lucky that way."

"Viking blood, my man. Viking blood," Jerry teased.

"You joke, but it's true." *Ah, there is the smile I've been waiting for.*

With Jerry's grin releasing some of the wrinkles that had formed on his forehead, Brice settled down into bed. He'd eased Jerry's worry, and that was as big a win as going to the bathroom and back without any wobbles or mishaps.

Jerry took his hand, and Brice's cock sprung to life for the first time since the incident at Jerry's house. "Are you feeling good enough for a talk?"

"Good or bad talk?" *Please don't tell me you don't want a future with us. Not now. Not after we've been through so much together.*

"Depends on how you look at it."

"Hit me with the worst," Brice said. He tried not to hold his breath but couldn't control the natural tendency.

"I'd like you, Evan, and Dylan to move to my ranch. I know you just renovated this place, but my home has my gym and plenty of room, plus two homes for guests and their families, a security barrier, barn, pool, garden. With a few minor renovations, we could add on a section for offices for the three of you."

"You want us to move into your place down the road?" *If this is the worst, the good has to be incredible.*

"Yeah. I know it's a lot to ask, but jumping from here to there and back multiple times a day doesn't make sense. This place is great, but the cost to renovate for my specific work requirements doesn't make sense when my place has basically everything all of us need. How do you feel about that?"

"Sure. I'll call my movers and get us in by the end of the week," Brice said.

"Thank God." Jerry exhaled.

Brice squeezed the man's meaty hand. "It's good. I know how you like your creature comforts, A.K.A. your personal fitness facility. Does this mean you're making Texas your home?" *Is this really happening?*

"Yeah. Which comes to us." Jerry closed his eyes. "I need you in my life. I had a lot of time to think while I've been gone." He opened his eyes and the stoic Jerry Wynn, the champion fighter, came out. "I wanted the wedding and the rings and the babies of a traditional marriage. I could have had that, but something never felt right. It wasn't right. This is right. I *need* a team around me. One woman. Two other men. What I didn't understand until this week is that each of us brings a special gift to the others. I wanted to believe that I was the only one everyone needed, but it's not true. We work best when we're all together."

"Spell this out for me. What are you saying?" *Are you proposing?*

"I'm saying that I love you and Evangeline and Dylan. I plan to commit my life to all of you. I want us all to have some kind of symbol of our commitment on us. It doesn't matter if anyone else knows or not. If I never have my own children, I don't care. It's not about DNA, it's about raising wonderful kids, giving them love, support, opportunities, and boundaries. Momma Mae and Major took me in and gave me their last name. Evangeline's children probably won't end up with my last name, but they will have everything else that goes along with it."

"Yes. That wasn't a question, but yes. I have an idea for rings."

"I've hired a wedding planner. Ursula is going to handle the publicity for us all. Do you think six weeks is too soon? I want us to have a real honeymoon and want to make sure you're up for it." Jerry glanced at the sheet tenting between Brice's legs. "Did Derek talk to you about sex?"

"I'd like to be involved in the wedding planning. And six weeks sounds perfect. I might even be out of this cast by then." Brice guided Jerry's hand under the linens to his cock. "Two days until the stitches come out. I'm not going to last six weeks without sex. I'm not sure I can handle another week without it."

Jerry swallowed, and his eyelids slid down halfway. "We'll talk to Derek about it." He rubbed along the length of Brice's hard cock, making it harder. "I'm sure there is a way to safely take care of you." He leaned over and kissed Brice's lips. "I love you. Together we'll take care of everyone."

"Tell me you love me again."

"I love you, Brice Loffiten. I love you."

A knocking on the bedroom door accompanied Ursula saying, "Knock. Knock. Ursula and Evangeline are here."

Jerry slouched. "Shit. She talked to Evan," he mumbled. He sat up and straightened his shoulders.

"Come on in," Brice shouted.

But she had already barged in.

His sexy, confident Evangeline seemed fragile next to the woman who had taken on the role of assistant, publicity guru, master negotiator, and mom to Jerry. The genuine smile he wanted to see on his woman held insecurity as she looked up at Ursula. *You have to stop the jealousy, Evan. Ursula is good for Jerry. She's not interested in him and he would never be interested in her, not as a lover.*

"We're good," Evangeline said softly. Her hands trembled as she rubbed them together.

Last week, she'd confessed to Brice, Jerry, and Dylan that her doctor had suggested she seek therapy, and if she needed to add medication to help her struggle with anxiety, they'd talk about the safest options while she was pregnant. She hadn't made an appointment with the therapist the doctor suggested. Brice had told Jerry, who he was sure had spoken with Ursula, or the tall blonde wouldn't be in the bedroom, but with her husbands at home.

Ursula pivoted and took Evangeline's hands in hers. "This is important."

"Can I come in?" Dylan inched into the room, hesitant and unsure. The usually confident man seemed to be drowning in fear and insecurity. Medication and therapy seemed to help, but he needed Jerry. Thankfully, Jerry needed them as much as they needed him.

"Come on, Dylan," Ursula said. "I'm glad you decided to join the family." She extended her arm out and to Brice's surprise, Dylan walked over and seemed to cling to her. "I'm here to help all of you."

Dylan nodded. "I know. I know."

"We're a team," Ursula said. She smiled. "Hey, Brice. So glad you're healing so well. I'll come over for a proper greeting in a minute." She let go of

Evangeline's hand and tucked his spitfire of a soon-to-be wife against her side. "I've got to make this quick, otherwise, this room will be getting smaller by four overprotective men—my husbands."

I hope they come over. Evangeline needs to see the type of men you married. Her jealousy would be a thing of the past.

"Say what you've got to say, Ursula," Jerry said. "You're gonna say it anyway."

Ursula glared at Jerry. "I'll deal with your sass later, Mr. Wynn." She inhaled, flaring her nostrils. "First, y'all are going to family therapy to talk about what happened. I don't think the incident is a 'getting over' situation, but it is more of a 'let's learn how to live again' and a 'work through the fears' situation. This is non-negotiable. No arguments. No bullshit excuses. If I have to, I'll bring in my husbands to kidnap you to make sure you're all there because they've had to deal with some serious shit in their lives and they can relate to this. Therapy helped them. Family therapy helped all of us. So, you're going. Period."

"Yes, Mom," Jerry mumbled.

"You're the worst one, Jerry Wynn. I'll grab you by the ear and make sure you're at every one of the sessions. You know I will." Those blue eyes turned to ice.

"Yes, ma'am," Jerry said.

"Good." Ursula nodded like she was once again pleased with him. "Brice, are you in agreement?"

"Yes, Ursula. I'll go as soon as I'm able," Brice said. *Could be another couple weeks, but I'll be there.*

"There's no able." Ursula tilted her chin downward

and frowned. "The therapist will be coming here until you can go to the office. Remember I said, 'no excuses', Mr. Loffiten."

"I see pregnancy has brought out the Viking blood inside you," Brice said. *You are exactly what Jerry needs on the road. Thank you for not only taking him into your life, but all of us.*

"You have no freaking clue how true that is," Ursula said. "I have to fight off four dominant men who are dying for sex every time I walk through the door at my house or hotel or restaurant or bathroom or the freaking baby section of the grocery store. Do you know what that's like for me?" She let go of Evan and Dylan and slid her hands over her baby curve, showing off the expansion in the last week. "This one makes sex in tight spaces difficult. Which brings me to the second and last item on my list for the four of you. Evangeline seems to harbor some jealousy of me. That ends now. None of y'all have moms in your life, not real ones. I'm filling that void. Well, with Evan, I will be more of an older sister to her. So, I guess there is a number three, but we'll blame my lack of organizational thought on the pregnancy fog."

She held up three fingers. *"Three.* Evangeline needs sex. Lots of it. Right now, she's emotional, she's crying for no reason and sometimes for a damn good reason, and her hormones are in the production zone that makes her horny 24/7. So you better shower her ass with love or Momma Ursula is going to morph into Hel, the Nordic goddess of death, and do some damage. Don't even fuck with me about this." She shook her finger at Jerry and Brice and then Dylan.

She turned to Evangeline and pulled her into her

arms. "I'm sorry it's taken me so long to figure this out, Evan. I'm usually more perceptive, but again, I'm blaming it on my baby hormones. Jerry does absolutely nothing for me, sexually. Nothing. Like beyond nothing. I look at him and think of a child, not a man. He's nothing like my sexy husbands."

"Hey, you can stop now," Jerry said. "I'm not into you either."

Ursula held up her hand, palm facing him, and smiled at Evan. "I have only had to wake him and push him into the shower once since I barged into the bedroom in Vegas. And Zeek was there this last time. I caught him spying on me the day before." She managed a body wobble as she rolled her eyes. "One thing led to another and he tried getting me off my schedule and almost succeeded, so I made him apologize to Jerry with a personal wake up call as I got us back on schedule. As punishment, Zeek worked security for us that week."

"Oh," Evangeline mumbled.

"Jerry loves you so much," Ursula said. "You tell me what you need from me, and I'll do it. If you need me to video conference you when I'm with Jerry in the evening, I'll do it. If you need to talk to my men, girl, I'd love for you to be a mom to them or a sis or daughter or something. I am ready for a friend who understands my struggles."

"Ursula?" Zeek called out. "Jerry? Everything okay?"

"Oh my word," Ursula hissed. She whipped her head in Jerry's direction. "You are in so much trouble. I know you called him." She released Evan from the hug and turned on her heel toward the door.

Jerry shrugged. "I didn't want you driving home by yourself. You're tired."

"Coming," Ursula shouted. "Do not—"

A man almost as big as Jerry strode into the bedroom. The tattoos Zeek often hid under long sleeves were exposed because of the short-sleeved T-shirt he wore. His jeans hung low on his hips revealing the gray letters J-e-r-r-y W-y-n-n sewn into the black band on his best-selling underwear line. A brown hunting brand baseball cap covered his dark hair. The striking blue eyes of the man who took Ursula's safety to the extreme met Brice's, then shifted to Ursula. "Hey, babe, It's time for bed."

"Zeek, it's *time* for me *to sleep*. Do you hear me? I—"

"Shh," Zeek cooed. "Everyone's in the van. We missed you. You're gonna sleep. Jerry told us you needed to rest. We've got you, baby. We've got everything you need."

Ursula melted in his arms. "Promise?"

"Yeah, babe," Zeek said softly.

"I need to talk to Sally before I leave," Ursula said.

"Babe, Oliver has been talking with her about the mandatory family therapy. She's good."

"He did that for me?" Ursula cooed.

"Yeah, baby. We love and support you. Jerry and his family are going to be just fine. Don't worry," Zeek said. "Thanks for taking care of her for us, Jerry." He led her out of the room.

"Anytime," Jerry shouted.

"She's married to him?" Evan asked.

Jerry nodded. "Yeah, all her husbands are good guys. They don't take any shit, but they're teddy bears with her. It's cute."

"I have nothing to worry about with her, do I?" Evan asked.

He stood and hugged her. "Absolutely nothing. You're my girl. I love you. I think you two will be friends in no time."

"Just don't screw with her schedule," Brice said. "She manages her time in five minute increments and has since her first job out of college."

"That's the truth," Jerry huffed.

"I missed you," Evan whispered.

"Take Jerry and Dylan to your bed," Brice said. *I'm worn out.* "I get him when you're finished."

Jerry gazed at Brice and nodded. "I'll call Derek about that thing we were discussing."

Brice rubbed his lips together. *I would give anything to have your mouth on mine, the taste of your cum on my tongue, or mine on yours.* "Sounds good. I love you, Jerry Wynn."

"I love you, Brice." Jerry's cock hardened and the bulge in his pants pushed to find an exit from the confines of the denim fabric.

Evan slid her hand down the front of his jeans and squeezed, giving Brice a full view of her exploration. "I love you."

Yes. Unzip those jeans. Let me watch. Go down on him and let me pretend I'm sucking him and fucking you, that Dylan is fucking me, that we're all coming so hard. So hard. Brice exhaled. His cock was so hard it hurt. His muscles strained to keep him seated upright in bed. *Nope. Not ready for sex. Not ready.*

Dylan pressed his front against Jerry's back and curled his arms around his waist. "I love you."

"I love all of you. I love you with all of my heart. You're my family," Jerry said.

Brice met Jerry's gaze.

"Meet me in the bedroom," Jerry said to Dylan and Evangeline. "I need to talk to Brice alone for a minute."

The two walked hand-in-hand out of the bedroom.

"I'm tired," Brice said. He shifted on the bed, attempting to get more comfortable.

Jerry slid him toward the middle of the bed. "We both need to rest. Mind if I lay next to you for a few minutes?"

"That would be nice," Brice said.

Jerry crawled into bed and rested his head on Brice's pillow. On his side, Jerry place his hand on Brice's chest over his heart. "I feel like we should all wait for sex until you can join us."

Brice closed his eyes as his soul seemed to expand with love for this wonderful man. "Jerry, you don't have to—"

"None of us have to, but I want us to. It's not enough to tell you I love you. I want to show you. It's a small sacrifice, but it's one that is significant for all of us. We're a family, Brice. We take care of each other because we are bound as one."

Brice turned his head and gazed into Jerry's eyes. "You're acting like we're already married."

"For me, we are. What about you? Do you feel married to me? Want me in your life, to love, to make love to, to raise children with, to protect and support so all of us thrive?" Jerry cradled the back of Brice's head. "Do you love me, really love me with your body, your mind, your heart, and your soul?"

"I do," Brice whispered. "I do."

Jerry inched forward and pressed his lips to Brice's. "That's what I drove all night to hear."

"I'd love for you to stay, but this bed is small and I'm exhausted," Brice said.

"I figured you'd say that," Jerry rolled over and off the bed.

"Hey, one more kiss," Brice said.

Jerry smiled the smile that carried sunshine with it. "Go to sleep. I'll kiss you when we've both had some rest."

"It's good to have you home," Brice said.

"It's good to be home." Jerry strode out of the room.

You make the house a home, Jerry. You are our center, our due north, our glue. With you here, we'll all heal and become stronger. You're our family. I love you.

Chapter Twenty-Eight
Evangeline

"Look down," Sally said. "A little eye glitter is essential for a beautiful bride."

Evangeline fidgeted with the satin belt on her white robe. "Are Jerry and Dylan here yet?" *They should have been here by now. The drive from the airport isn't that far.*

"Not yet," Ursula said. "They'll be here. My guys are escorting them. Hang in there." She walked to the door of the bridal suite. "I'm about to rip into Zeek about sticking to my schedule. But don't you worry, Jerry and Dylan will be here or my guys will not be having sex tonight, and they are desperate for me to give them some pussy." She strode out of the room and closed the door.

"She's intense," Sally said.

"Ya think?" Evangeline half-laughed. "The more I get to know her, the more I like her."

"Me too," Sally said. She smiled and lifted an eye shadow brush. "Stare at that enormous rock on your finger. Two strokes and you'll be done."

Keeping still seemed impossible, but she gazed at her ring and smiled. *They love me. They want me forever.*

A soft feather-like touch crossed the bottom edges of her brows.

"Ready for the reveal?" Sally asked.

Evangeline raised her chin and fluttered her lashes at Sally. "Does my makeup pass the Fairchild test?"

Sally swiveled the chair toward the full-length mirror. "You decide if you like what you see."

Smooth skin, big eyes, cheekbones that she didn't think she had. "You're a miracle worker." Evangeline smiled. *I look ten years younger.*

"A good foundation, fabulous contour, and the right amount of layering for pictures enhances everyone's beauty," Sally said.

Redheaded Rory Quinn, Evangeline's friend and top massage therapist at Ella's new spa, opened the door to the bridal suite. "Wow. I leave with a minimalist bride and come back to a celebrity one. Girl, get out of that seat so Sally can do her magic on me." She grabbed Evangeline's hands and pulled her up. "Jerry and Dylan had car trouble, but Ella said they're back en route. Troy isn't here yet. I heard he's bringing guests. Is he really a great-grandfather? I can't believe that." She slid into the vacated seat. "I'm ready, Sally. Make me look irresistible."

"It's true," Evangeline said. *I'm so happy you moved to work for Ella here—we're all one big happy family.* "Troy is a great-grandfather." She glanced at the simple, white silk dress on the hanger on the wall. Soon, she'd be in it and walking down the aisle...alone. "Is Kaila here?"

"Nope," Rory said. "The only and the most magnificent Zanipolo in the hotel is in this room." She winked at Sally.

Sally dug through her makeup cases and in a couple of minutes had Rory's eyes accented and cheeks blushed. Rory's lips looked kissable and seductive.

"There you go," Sally said. "The maid of honor and the bride are picture perfect."

The door opened and a young, petite platinum blonde holding an infant peeked inside. "Hey, I'm Nicki Shields, Troy's granddaughter."

"Oh, my gosh," Evangeline gasped. *You're even more gorgeous than Brice said.* "I'm Evangeline. Come in. Come in." She rushed over and welcomed her.

"Howdy," Nicki said. "I have heard so much about you over the years. I wanted to introduce myself and my little guy, Austin. He might fuss a bit, but if he gets loud, I'll take him into the hallway."

"He can fuss all he wants. It's a small wedding, and there are a couple toddlers who will probably run around the room or join me in front."

"Sounds like my kind of ceremony," Nicki said. "Do you need anything?"

"Nope. Is there anything I can do for you?"

"No, ma'am." Nicki looked at Sally and Rory. "Howdy."

Rory stood up and hugged Nicki. "Hey, I'm Rory Quinn, and the makeup guru is Sally Fairchild."

"Nice to meet you," Nicki said. "Well, I guess I'll head out there. My Pa-paw wants to introduce me to his partner Ella and her family. He's not big on pictures, so I've heard about them all being super-smart and nerdy giants, but now I'll have faces with names." She smiled and adjusted the baby who was the spitting image of his mom. "I have no idea what I'm in for, and Brice just laughs at Pa-paw's descriptions, which tells me they're pretty accurate."

"Try tall, smart, *and* gorgeous with some nerdy

moments when they start talking numbers and business," Rory said. "And the identical twins are your age. One is spoken for and the other is single. I'll introduce you after the wedding."

"Kyle and Jason are hot. Model hot," Sally added. "Their uncle looks just like them, so if you want to know what they'll grow into..." She dropped her head and her voice. "Check the older guy out. You can't miss him. In fact, I'm going out there now. If they're here, I'll introduce you."

Sally opened the door. As Nicki strode out, Sally glanced over her shoulder and mouthed, *Nicki is gorgeous. Oh, my goodness.*

"What is your name again?" Nicki asked. "We have to be around the same age..." Her voice trailed off as Sally closed the door with her new friend.

"Damn," Rory said. "I don't have a chance with Troy. I'm closer to his granddaughter's age than his daughter's. With a great-grandson already here, I doubt he wants to procreate anymore. I need one night with him to get him out of my system. One damn night to..." She shuddered. "That man turns my horny dial up to ten."

"See how it goes. It's a wedding, so anything can happen. Do you think Dylan and Jerry will get here in time?"

Rory took Evan's hand in hers. "They will be here. Those two are not standing you up. They've been waiting for this day for a very long time." She wiggled her brows up and down. "I bet Jerry has to wear undies under his kilt because his dick is *sooo* long."

"Oh, my God. You're so bad."

"You're the bad influence, Miss I'm-fucking-three-guys-at-the-same-time. My hymen is fully intact, thank you very much." Rory dropped her hand and sashayed to the wedding dress. "Time for you to make your relationship with Brice legal, or I'll ask him to make me a woman."

Evan laughed. "You and Brice are *not* compatible."

Rory glanced at her and rolled her eyes. "Apparently, I'm not compatible with anyone. They either smell bad or their toes are ugly. Or they go on and on about their latest *what-ever*. Troy doesn't ever talk about money and his toes are so freaking hot. I love feet. He wore black flip flops once last year. He's got hairless pale feet. I don't know why that turns me on so much. But *it does*. God, it does." She dropped into a moan.

"You've put him on a pedestal he can't live up to."

Rory held up the wedding dress.

Evan took off the white robe she'd worn during her hair and makeup session.

"All natural?" Rory asked.

Evan stepped into the dress. "It's tight and holds everything in place. And no nipple showage."

One by one, Rory slipped a silk button through the loop and fastened it. "This is exquisite. Where did you find it on such short notice?"

"Brice surprised me with it. He handled all the formalwear. The pearls were his mother's." She traced her fingers over the simple strand at her neck.

"Do you have something blue and borrowed?"

Evan shook her head. *I should be wearing my grandmother's sapphire necklace and borrowing my mother's earrings. But those heirlooms are no longer available to me.*

"This isn't expensive, but it covers both." Rory slipped a blue and silver toe ring from her foot and slid it onto Evan's toe. She picked up the silk sandals with strings of diamonds and pearls atop the fabric and guided Evan's foot into each one. "Blue agate and surgical steel. It looks pretty against all the expensive bling."

Evan lifted the skirt of the dress and pointed her toes as she admired the ring her friend had worn every day for years. "It's perfect, Rory. Thank you. I'll keep it safe for you." She hugged Rory. "Thank you for being here. For doing this on short notice. For not telling me I'm making a mistake or I'm stupid or that he's too old."

"Evan, you and Brice have been in love for more than a decade. We have had more conversations than I can count about Brice, Jerry, and the guy you would love until the day you died—Dylan. I don't know Dylan personally, but I do know the other two. You'd be stupid *not* to marry Brice and commit to the other two who have topped your list of dream men since forever. You *need* three men to keep up with you. This is the right decision for you. I wouldn't be here, standing up for you and true love, otherwise."

"Thank you."

"I have nothing but blessings and happiness to shout out to the world over your nuptials. I'd kiss you, but I don't want to ruin either of our makeup."

A knock startled Evan, and she huddled closer to Rory. Evan's heart raced and a flash of memories from the last moments with Henry ran through her mind.

"Evan, are you dressed?" Derek asked as the door opened.

It's Derek. Jerry and Dylan will be here soon. Brice is here. Garrett is here. Security is all over the place. "Yes." She inhaled deeply and exhaled to settle her nerves.

"Damn." He held out his hand to her.

Troy stood beside him and offered his hand to Rory. "Ladies, you look beautiful."

Rory lowered her gaze as she took Troy's hand. "Thank you. You look mighty handsome, Troy."

He gave her a crooked smile. "No one will notice me with you in the room."

Rory bit her bottom lip and swallowed. "You are all compliments today."

"My best friend is getting married to a gem of a girl. I get to flirt with the prettiest natural redhead I've ever seen. And all my favorite girls are in the same room. As I see it, compliments are easily given tonight." He led her from the room. "Come on, gorgeous. You're mine all night long."

Evan placed her hand in Derek's. "Troy is in a good mood."

"He and Brice had a couple of drinks," Derek said. "Troy is as relaxed as I've ever seen him. He's got a crush on Rory. Don't worry. He won't act on it. She'd have to make the first move and that will never happen."

"Rory is insanely in love with him. She might make a move. If she gets any alcohol in her, she's making a big move."

"*No,*" Derek huffed.

"Yes. And she's a virgin."

"Oh, shit," Derek mumbled. "I better tell him."

"Don't you dare." She yanked on his hand. "That

was confidential. Troy can handle it."

"No, he can't. No. He. Can't."

She glared at him. "Yes. He can. He will figure it out and make the appropriate adjustment. He is experienced."

Derek clenched his jaw and shook his head. "Troy is very selective. He doesn't fuck around. She might have a very intense experience if they get together." He tugged her arm and pulled her into the outer room where a quaint seating area for friends or family sat empty. *They really didn't come. Why would they? Dad makes the rules and no one but me disobeys.*

"Rory is not your problem. She's old enough to deal with him. She knows the human body and what to expect. She is as honest as they come. She will tell him, and he will either make her every dream come true or walk away. She's prepared for either."

He stomped across the room and opened the door to the hall. "Is she on birth control?"

"Nope. But he is Mr. Birth Control." She stopped at the door and pulled him back, mid-stride. "What is your problem?"

Derek glared at her. "I'm telling him."

"Then I'm telling Jerry about your tattoo."

Derek gasped. "You wouldn't."

"Oh," she nodded. "I would. Don't test me. I tell you things in confidence. You tell me things in confidence. If you break that confidence, I will too."

"That's dirty," he said.

"No. It's fair. And you won that celibacy bet. I had sex with Brice not too long after you dropped me off."

He blinked. "You did?"

She nodded. "Looks like you and I have to arrange

a photo shoot or whatever."

He smiled. "Okay. I won't tell Troy. But if it goes bad, it's your fault."

She sashayed into the hall. "Have Jerry and Dylan arrived?"

"They're with Ella in the back row. Jay and Kyle are running late, but they'll be here."

She lost all confidence. "The back row?" *They're supposed to be at the front.*

Derek placed his hand on her back and nudged her forward. "Yes."

Troy and Rory stood arm-in-arm at the double doors. From the left side entrance, Kyle and Jason sprinted inside and stopped in front of Troy and Rory, stationing themselves on either side of the doors. The identical twins wore black tuxedos and held the handles of the doors, ready to open them for the start of the ceremony.

She put one foot in front of the other and nodded. *I accepted all three of their proposals. Where is the solidarity? They don't even know about the babies.*

Kyle and Jason opened the doors and held them as a string quartet played. Troy winked at her and walked into the ballroom. Rory seemed to float on air next to him.

The doors closed, and Derek guided her into place.

"Is this what you want?" Derek whispered. "Did you tell them about the other baby inside you? Jerry's baby? Do they know you're carrying more than one child?"

She held her stomach and inhaled. "Not yet. I don't know how to explain it. How could I have ovulated like that? Three weeks apart? There has to be a mistake. I don't want to get his hopes up."

"Look at your belly. It's huge. You look like Ella did with both sets of her twins. There isn't a mistake. I'm not doing another amniocentesis on you. Tell them. Tell them soon because that new ultrasound shows a very different story than the first, and they need to start planning for a nursery for two." Derek dropped his chin and gazed down at her. "Do not do what you did with Sally. Tell them now. Today. Before the vows."

"Sure you don't want to marry me instead?" Jay asked. "I'm in my prime."

She half-heartedly laughed. *Fuck. Derek's right. Why does he have to always be right?* "Thank you, but I can't accept."

"Then off you go," Jay said. "Congratulations."

The twins opened the doors. The music changed to announce her arrival.

Brice turned and his jaw dropped.

Butterflies fluttered in her stomach and desire surged through her veins. *Brice has seen me through my worst and best moments. He loves me the way a man should love a woman. I'm his and will always be his.*

There was some shuffling of positions in the back row. Jerry and Dylan stepped into the aisle. "We'll take her from here."

Derek kissed her cheek. "Tell him. Now." He walked around Ella and stood next to her.

Jerry glided his hand over Evan's bare back and wrapped his fingers around her hip. "Hey, beautiful."

Dylan held his elbow out and she slid her hand around his arm. "Have you been a good girl since I've been gone?"

She shuddered as the cauldron of emotions mixed

inside her. Fire from the flames of lust rose from deep within. "I missed both of you." *Nothing is the same when you're gone.*

Ella clapped and then Derek joined her as Evangeline walked forward. The clapping got louder and louder until she couldn't hear the music anymore. Dylan's father, stepmother, and stepbrothers stood clapping and cheering them on.

The young boys jumped up and down and shouted "Jer-ry Wynn. Jer-ry Wynn. Jer-ry Wynn" until everybody, even Brice, joined them.

Their enthusiasm rocked the room. Laughing turned to cheering which turned into more chanting for Jerry and adding Dylan and Brice to the mantra.

By the time Evangeline got to Brice, the handful of friends and family seemed like a sold-out stadium. Jerry and Dylan formed a semi-circle with Brice and Troy.

The officiant smiled. "We all know why we're here. This is a ceremony of love, marriage, faithfulness, virtue, and determination. Brice and Evangeline are here to add a legal component to their relationship, making them legally bound to each other. But let's remember that love comes in many forms."

The officiant held out his hand and Brice, Jerry, and Dylan handed him rings. "May those who join in this ceremony become one family, one life, one love forever." He closed his hands over the rings. "Bless these rings as a symbol of love, truth, faithfulness, honor, and respect. Bless this union in good times and bad, so that their love is strengthened through the years." He handed the rings to Brice.

Brice took her left hand and slipped the engagement ring from her finger. "This ring symbolizes my love." He slid a platinum band with diamonds and sapphires onto her finger. "This ring symbolizes my faithfulness in all we do." He glided a platinum band of emeralds that wrapped around her engagement ring onto her finger. "And this ring symbolizes my life. You are my life, my love, my everything, Evangeline. You snuck into my heart and stayed. You are my home." He slid a band that matched the platinum-diamond-and-sapphire ring onto her finger. "I love you."

The officiant handed her a simple platinum wedding band.

She slid it onto Brice's ring finger. "There is another baby inside me. We're having twins. One is Brice's and one is Jerry's," she whispered. "They're three weeks apart. I don't know how that is possible, but Derek says it is and it happened. He would know because Ella had a weird situation too, only she wasn't on fertility drugs and I was. So, I love all of you, and I'm sorry I kept it from you. I just couldn't believe it was true. I still can't."

"This is great news," Brice said.

Dylan patted Jerry on the back. "I told you she had to be carrying two babies in there, but you didn't believe me. No one believed me." He laughed. "Jerry, you're going to be a father."

Jerry's face paled. "I'm going to be a father?"

"That's what Derek says," Evangeline said. "Somehow, I have two babies growing inside me. He said the DNA match in baby B was with you. The gestation period lined up for when we first made love. I don't know. I'm still—"

The strangest look came over Jerry as his head tilted to the left and back and...

Dylan lunged. Rory ran forward. Jason raced down the aisle with Derek and Kyle behind him.

Jerry's eyes closed and down, down, down he fell. The thud of impact could have been heard around the world. The gasps that followed took all the air from the room.

Evan dropped her bouquet and crouched beside Jerry as Derek checked him. "Jerry. Jerry. Wake up. Wake up."

"What happened?" Derek asked. "Did he eat today?"

"I told him about the baby," she said. "I told him he is going to be a father."

"He didn't eat much," Dylan said. "The flight was delayed, and his schedule was thrown off."

Brice chimed in, "He was upset he didn't get to change into his kilt. We had issues with rings and they all got straightened out, but he has been worked up over every little detail for weeks." Brice squatted next to Evangeline. "Jerry, wake up."

Ella walked over and stood behind Derek, who continued checking Jerry's vitals. "Jerry Wynn, get up and finish marrying Evan. Now."

Some eye movement behind Jerry's lids appeared. An incoherent mumble or two.

"Did he knock himself out?" Ella asked.

"I'm good," Jerry mumbled. "I'm good." But he didn't move to get up, and he didn't open his eyes.

"Jerry," Derek said.

"Hey, buddy," Jerry mumbled. He turned his head from side-to-side.

"You're gonna be a dad," Derek whispered. "There is a second baby. It's yours."

"That's not possible," Jerry mumbled. "She's taking Brice's last name. She's..." The green of his eyes appeared as his lids shot up. "I'm gonna be a dad. I'm having a baby." The classic grin of the fighter spread across his face as he sat up. "I'm having a baby. I'm fucking having a baby. Mine. Me. A Wynn." He sprung to his feet. "I'm having a baby." He turned around and shouted, "I'm going to be a father! Evan is having my baby too. She's having two babies. Brice and I are going to be dads together. We need multiple minivans. This is the best day of my life."

In the blink of an eye, he picked up Evan and kissed her. "You've given me the best news I've ever had. The best. I love you. I love you so much." He kissed her again in a whirlwind and placed her gently in front of Brice. "Finish the ceremony. We have some major celebrating to do."

Everyone returned to their places.

"On that note," the officiant said, "I'd like to introduce to you Mr. Brice Loffiten and Mrs. Evangeline Russo Wynn-Loffiten. May blessings follow the four of you wherever you go."

"You did it," Sally shouted. "Go, Sis."

Evan laughed. "I did do it." *I really did.*

Brice, Dylan, and Jerry stared at her like she was the most beautiful, sexy, and smart woman in the entire world. And now that all the secrets were out, she felt every bit of love they showed inside her.

Brice stepped forward, wrapped her up in his arms, and kissed her. "I love you, Mrs. Loffiten."

She gazed into his blue eyes and knew she'd made the right decision. She might be Brice's wife legally, but she was a wife of three amazing men who would stick by her through thick and thin, support her, forgive her, and love her for the rest of their lives—and she would do the same for them.

About the Author

An avid romance reader, Anna Lores started writing steamy romance novels as a by-product of insomnia. One night, with a nudge from her husband to write a book, Anna borrowed her son's laptop and set about breathing life into her very own characters. After a month, she was surprised with a new laptop of her own to pursue her dreams of writing sensual happily ever afters.

The desire to fill her world with wonderful stories she and her close friends could not just talk about but gush over keeps Anna's fingers racing to keep up with her imagination. As the rest of the house is sleeping peacefully, Anna sheds her title as Supermom of Three to write sexy love stories.

Sleeping might still be a battle Anna hasn't conquered, but armed with a B.A. in English Literature and all the hot men in her mind calling for their own story, she stays busy during those midnight hours writing her next international bestselling spicy romance.

~*~

Visit Anna at
http://www.annaloresauthor.com

Also Available
from The Wild Rose Press, Inc.
and major retailers.

Ella's Triple Pleasure
Sinfully Hers Book One
By Anna Lores

It takes three men to satisfy one woman's needs…

Single mom and massage therapist Ella Winthrop isn't looking for a relationship. She has enough problems without risking a business that barely meets her needs. Then her world is turned upside down by three men, each offering something she isn't prepared for—love so deep it hurts, sex so hot she's afraid she'll melt from the pleasure, and a future beyond her wildest dreams.

Steamy businessman Cade Jackson has it all—money, looks, a giving heart, and a dominant nature—but Ella refuses to date a client even if she's lusted after him for a year. After his brother's death, Garrett Winthrop moves back to town opening old wounds and even darker fantasies. Dr. Derek McGregor gives her balance and understanding that speaks to her soul. All three men force Ella to question the limits of a traditional relationship.

So...Hot

The Passionate Trilogy Book One

By Sloane Maxfield

Legal secretary Rachel Stewart moves to New York City to find her soul mate. Real Estate Investor Evan Rockwell, is the perfect man, but there's one problem... His girlfriend is always with him. Funny thing is, his girlfriend doesn't seem to mind Rachel's attraction to Evan and invites her to join the couple in a *ménage a trois*. Rachel has a hard decision to make. She wants Evan, but can she share? How many lines is she willing to cross for true love?

Thank you for purchasing
this publication of The Wild Rose Press, Inc.

For questions or more
information contact us at
info@thewildrosepress.com.

The Wild Rose Press, Inc.
www.thewildrosepress.com